BETWEEN TWO WORLDS

BETWEEN TWO
WORLDS

KATHERINE KIRKPATRICK

EMBER

Text copyright © 2014 by Katherine Kirkpatrick
Cover art (girl) copyright © 2014 by Sam Weber
Map illustration copyright © 2014 by Joseph LeMonnier
Photographs copyright © Kim Fairley/Silas Ayer (pp. 272 [bottom], 273, and 274) and courtesy of Library of Congress, Prints and Photographs Division (pp. 272 [top] and 275)

All rights reserved. Published in the United States by Ember, an imprint of Random House Children's Books, a division of Random House LLC, a Penguin Random House Company, New York. Originally published in hardcover in the United States by Wendy Lamb Books, an imprint of Random House Children's Books, New York, in 2014.

Ember and the E colophon are registered trademarks of Random House LLC.

Visit us on the Web! randomhouseteens.com

Educators and librarians, for a variety of teaching tools, visit us at RHTeachersLibrarians.com

The Library of Congress has cataloged the hardcover edition of this work as follows:
Kirkpatrick, Katherine.
Between two worlds / by Katherine Kirkpatrick. — First edition.
pages cm
ISBN 978-0-385-74047-0 (hc) — ISBN 978-0-375-89924-9 (ebook) 1. Inuit—Juvenile fiction.
[1. Inuit—Fiction. 2. Eskimos—Fiction. 3. Race relations—Fiction. 4. Peary, Robert E. (Robert Edwin), 1856–1920—Fiction. 5. Arctic regions—History—19th century—Fiction.] I. Title.
PZ7.K6354Bet 2014
[Fic]—dc23
2013014735

ISBN 978-0-375-87221-1 (trade pbk.)

Printed in the United States of America

10 9 8 7 6 5 4 3 2 1

First Ember Edition 2015

Random House Children's Books supports the First Amendment and celebrates the right to read.

For Wendy Lamb

CAST OF CHARACTERS

(roughly in order of appearance)

ITTA, GREENLAND

Eqariusaq (*Eh-karee-u-sak*), aka Billy Bah: sixteen-year-old girl

Angulluk (*An-gou-luk*), aka the Fat One: Billy Bah's husband

Aleqasina (*Al-e-ka-si-na*), aka Ally: mistress of Robert E. Peary

Anaukaq (*An-a-uk-ak*), aka Sammy: son of Robert E. Peary and Ally

Piugaattoq (*Pi-u-ga-tok*): Ally's husband

Qaorlutoq (*Ka-or-lu-tok*), aka Bag of Bones: orphan boy

Nuljalik (*Nul-ya-lik*): Billy Bah's older sister

Konala (*Ko-na-la*): Nuljalik's daughter, Billy Bah's niece

Uutaaq (*Ooh-tak*): Nuljalik's husband

Inunteq (*E-non-tek*): Billy Bah's older brother

Atangana (*A-tan-ga-na*): Billy Bah's mother (ghost)

Nuktaq (*Nuk-tak*): Billy Bah's father (ghost)

EXPLORERS, PEARY FAMILY, AND *WINDWARD* CREW

Marie Ahnighito (*Ah-neeg-he-toe*) Peary: daughter of Robert E. Peary and Josephine Peary

Josephine Peary, aka Mitti Peary or Jo: wife of Robert E. Peary

Lieutenant Robert E. Peary, aka Pearyaksoah (*Pe-o-ri-ak-so-a*) or Bert: explorer

Captain Sam Bartlett: captain of the *Windward*

Duncan Gaylor: a sailor on the *Windward*

Christopher Sutter, aka Grease Beard: an engineer on the *Windward*

Charles Percy, aka Old Charlie: cook/steward on the *Windward*

Matthew Henson, aka Mauripaulak (*Mau-ri-pau-lak*), "the Kind One" or Matt: African American explorer, aide to Robert E. Peary

Musk Ox Land (Ellesmere), Greenland

Navarana (*Na-va-ra-na*): grandmother of Tooth Girl and Runny Nose

Akitsinnguaq (*A-ki-tsin-gu-ak*), aka Tooth Girl: granddaughter of Navarana, child friend of Marie Peary

Magtaaq (*Mag-tahk*), aka Runny Nose: Navarana's grandson, Tooth Girl's brother

Mikihoq (*Mi-ki-hok*): Navarana's daughter, mother of Tooth Girl and Runny Nose

Qihuk (*Ki-hok*): father of Tooth Girl and Runny Nose

America

Aviaq (*A-vi-ak*): adopted daughter of Billy Bah's parents

Minik (*Mi-nik*): boy from Itta

Qisuk (*Qi-suk*): Minik's father

Uisaakassak (*U-e-sahk-a-sak*): man from southern Greenland

North Pole

Arctic Sea

Ellesmere Land
(Musk Ox Land)

Fort
Conger

Cape Sabine

Payer Harbor

Etah (Itta)

Smith Sound

Cape
York

Greenland

Greenland and
Ellesmere Land, 1900

Baffin Bay

Arctic Circle

Canada

United
States

0   120
miles

CHAPTER ONE

● ● ● ● ● ● ● ● ●

Itta, Northwest Greenland
August 1900

I climbed toward the sky, my fingers curling around the cold rocks, thousands of shrieking birds around me. Just under my feet the sheer red cliffs dropped to the water. Though it was summer, it was still cold and the wind felt fresh. I let it brush my face while my husband, Angulluk, sprang on ahead. "I don't see why we need to climb so high," I said. "We're passing the birds lower down."

"Quiet, woman. You don't know any more than the seaweed floating in the ocean."

He said this even though he knew I was smart and he often boasted of my talents, especially at making warm and beautiful garments. In our land, a good fur coat or boots can make the difference between life and death. Angulluk the Fat One and I had been married for three summers. In the white man's years, I was about sixteen and he nineteen. He was lithe and strong—"fat" was what the villagers called a lazy person.

Angulluk had taken me on a path that angled and narrowed, so we had to reach for rocks, with hardly any footing. My head felt faint when I looked down. We climbed until I needed to catch my breath.

My land was the top of the world! That was what Lieutenant Peary, the explorer, had told me. On a day like today I could believe that the world was round, the North Pole was capped with ice, and everyone but my people lived below us. Reaching an outcrop, I took a moment to look down to Itta, my beloved village. It was always home to me in summer, when the birds returned and our people stayed put. At other times, many hunters and their families journeyed to the south, where the snows melted earlier and caribou grazed. Just beyond where the beach curved, rock igloos and skin tents appeared like shell beads on a necklace. Offshore I could see rocky shoals dotted with walrus, and beyond, many small islands, odd and lovely shapes among the ice floes in the shining water.

The sky was so clear I could see across the sound to *Umimmaat Nuna,* Musk Ox Land, what the white men call Ellesmere Land. It was known for good hunting, though our people rarely crossed the dangerous sea ice to go there. Now, in summer, I could hear the cracking and groaning of giant icebergs out in the bay.

We climbed higher, where glossy black-and-white auks nested above us on every ledge and filled the air with their musical piping. Angulluk knew how to find them.

The birds eyed us as we came closer. Their calls turned angry, frightened, and they fluttered restlessly. "*Qaa, qaa,* hurry, woman!" said Angulluk.

2

With clattering, shrieks, a great whir of wings, birds filled the sky. Wings swept against my face. "Oooh!" I teetered on the edge of the path.

"Eqariusaq! Quick! Take the eggs before the birds come back."

Gathering eggs was women's work. He sat on a flat boulder under an overhanging rock to protect himself from the sun and wind.

Pale blue eggs with brown spots lay wedged among the rocks. The eggs were pointed at one end, the better to stay on a ledge without rolling off. They'd make tasty dinners. I took as many as I could reach, placing them carefully in my birdskin bag. Then, my chest tight with fear, I hugged the cliff until I came to a wider path and climbed even higher to collect more. My long hair blew out of the knot at the top of my head and whipped against my face.

I rested at a wide spot, and I looked out at the ocean. The vast blue-black sheet of water below teemed with ice floes and icebergs gleaming in the sun. A dark speck far out in the bay caught my eye. I shielded my eyes with my hand to see; the speck seemed to move. I knew what it was; I was almost sure. Could it be?

Carrying the eggs in a sack over my shoulder, I climbed down to Angulluk. "Look!" I pointed.

He frowned. Above his thin lips, a few hairs formed a sparse mustache. "What?"

I said, "Surely I would not notice something important that you cannot see."

"Be quiet!"

I knew that his sharp eyes had spotted what I saw and he'd want the honor of telling the news.

The speck in the distance grew larger. I remembered it well from other years. What gifts and excitement—and perhaps what trouble—were in store for our village?

Angulluk turned to me. "A ship with Peary's men?"

"*Ai*, who else?" I said. Only men who had something to do with Lieutenant Robert Peary came to our village from America across the ocean. And when his ships arrived to drop off supplies for him, it was always now, during the short summer season, after the solid ice broke into pieces and opened a way in. Peary and his companion, the dark-skinned explorer Matthew Henson, whom we called Mauripaulak, were not in our village now but at their second camp in Musk Ox Land.

A stone rolled past us and fell toward the water far below.

We looked up. A boulder had loosened above us. It could fall with the rocks around it! I was frozen in place.

He yanked me into the niche and shoved me down. Rumbling filled the air, louder and louder, like spirits arguing in the sky.

All went dark. Fur pressed against my face: Angulluk's coat. He was leaning hard against me. I could hardly breathe.

I waited for the boulder to smash down and kill us. I

silently called out to my mother and father in the world of the spirits: *Come to me, Anaana and Ataata!*

In the darkness, I heard dirt and rocks tumbling as the cliff beneath us rocked violently and the boulder hurtled down in a deafening roar.

Then silence. Sunlight glared in my eyes as Angulluk rose, stepped out of the niche. Brown-red dirt covered his face. Blood ran down his cheek from a gash under his eye. The bag of eggs I'd dropped was flattened under rubble. I didn't care. We were alive!

"*Ai!*" Angulluk said with a smile. He acted as if it were nothing to be trapped under an avalanche. To save my life, he'd shielded me with his body.

How could I thank him without embarrassing him? "Someone thinks quickly. Someone is brave," I said.

His eyes lit up his broad face and he smiled, looking out over the water.

I stood up and stretched my legs. "Let's go back down," I said, brushing the dirt from the long boots, the *kamiit,* I had made.

"Quiet! The birds are returning."

A flock of the auks flew near us in a rush and whir. Angulluk thrust out his net and caught five at once. He yanked the auks out of the net by their necks and twisted them, killing them swiftly, then gave me the birds.

I smiled as I accepted them. My husband could climb down the cliffs with pride, having caught food, and feathers for a shirt.

I turned to the water; now I could see the ship's two masts and white sails. "Look there," I said softly.

Angulluk nodded.

When we reached the village, we'd say that he'd seen the ship first. But later I'd be the one to talk to the *qallunaat,* the white men. I could speak the *qallunaat* language better than any of my people. For I was the only one of us to cross the ocean to America in Peary's ships and come back alive.

Carrying the auks by their necks, I walked behind Angulluk down the widening path. The ship was here! If the sailors stayed on for more than a few days, our hunters provided meat for them, traded for goods the village had come to depend upon: guns, axes, steel needles, and wood for harpoon handles and sled runners. White men could create a windstorm of activities and requests. What would the sailors want this time? Part of me couldn't wait to meet the ship, and another part wanted to stay right here above the village.

Halfway down, we heard children chattering as they gathered feathers from empty nests on the lower shelves of the cliffs. They asked how Angulluk had been injured. He told them of the avalanche, but it wasn't until we entered the village, in sight of women scraping hides, and men tossing walrus meat to their dogs, that he raised his arms and shouted: "A ship is coming!"

CHAPTER TWO

● ● ● ● ● ● ● ●

We crowded on the beach as the ship sailed toward us between the dangerous ice floes. Peary's ship was called the *Windward*. Nearly every summer it dropped off supplies for him, or picked up Peary to go back to America and return a year or two later. These past two winters, he'd remained on our side of the vast ocean.

It was a warm day, so instead of our heavier fox or bear furs, we all wore parkas and trousers of gray sealskin. Angulluk stood beside me with his arms crossed, his eyebrows knit, probably planning how to win a new rifle from the white men. My chest fluttered inside to think of seeing the crewmembers. Most would be familiar. During the past two summers, Angulluk had traded my favors to a few sailors for a gun and ammunition. Others I'd known because I'd sewn and mended their clothes.

Apart from the crowd, eager as ever to see the *qallunaat*, Ally stood waiting. Sammy, her fat baby, rode on her back, naked and warm inside the soft sealskin of his carrier. His head was covered with thick, shaggy black hair. He had the blue eyes of his father, Peary.

How lucky Ally was to have a baby, especially a son!

7

And besides, Ally was plump and round, with a bright smile and neat, square teeth, petite hands and feet, and a tiny nose: she was Itta's beauty, and would not let anyone forget it. Reluctantly, I stuck by Ally. In order to survive, our people shared all that we had: food, shelter, skills, tools, weapons. Now and then, a husband might lend his wife to another hunter for a few days, to help with his chores, or relieve his boredom during the long winter. Such trades were never made with outsiders. But Ally went to Peary so often, it almost seemed she had two husbands; the villagers always gossiped about her. The truth was, Ally needed my friendship even more than I needed hers.

The *Windward,* furling its great mainsail, eased its shiny black hull into the rocky shallows of our harbor. Crewmembers guided by Captain Bartlett, who was plump as a walrus (and just as whiskery), let down the ship's heavy anchor. From this distance, he was the only man I recognized. Then, scanning the deck, I spotted a small, yellow-haired shape in a green cloak, and standing alongside was a giant of a woman in a long dark dress and wide-brimmed hat. It was Peary's daughter, Marie, and her mother, Mitti Peary!

I waved. "I see you! There you are!" I called, even though they were too far away to hear me. I had spent a year with them in America.

"Why are you babbling, Eqariusaq?" said Angulluk. "Why are you smiling like that?"

"It's Peary's wife and daughter," I said. "They're here!"
Angulluk looked at me blankly.

"Don't you remember them? They came with Peary three summers ago. It was the summer you married me. It was the summer when Peary took the—"

"Ah. *That* summer."

I felt a catch in my throat when he said "*that* summer." The last time I'd seen Peary's wife and daughter was also the last time I'd seen my mother and father.

Now sailors lowered a dory from the ship, and the captain rowed himself to shore. When he reached the beach, our people surrounded him and talked at him in our language, which he couldn't begin to understand. I pushed through the crowd. "Captain," I said in English. "Hello. We are happy to see you." Relief sprang into his eyes.

"It's Billy Bah, is it?" he asked, running his hand over his thick beard.

"Yes. It's me." I smiled. People stopped talking and watched keenly.

"Is Lieutenant Peary here?"

I shook my head the way white people do. "Gone."

"When did you last see him?"

"Not since the winter."

He opened his hands. "Do you know where he is?"

I pointed across the dark water to the mountains of Musk Ox Land in the distance. I could tell by the deep lines on his forehead that the news was a shock. "Follow me," I said, and led Captain Bartlett to Peary's house.

On the bluff, the rock igloos of our village formed a half circle facing the water. Peary's house stood out from all the rest, a red caboose. He'd brought it by ship and then pulled it up the hill on rails after the first house he built burned down.

I said, "Look, Captain. He left this." I showed him a bag nailed to the door under the roof's shelter.

Captain Bartlett thanked me, already opening the bag. He drew out a piece of paper, read, then folded it carefully. The letter seemed to satisfy him. Out on the water, two rowboats went back and forth to bring sailors from the ship.

At last, Mitti Peary and Marie arrived. Marie had her hair in two long yellow braids tied on the ends with pink ribbons. She wore a pink dress under her green cloak. How grown up she looked—she must have been seven or eight, nearly as tall as I. I waved at her but could not get her attention. Tears streamed down her face. What could I do to help her?

"Where is my dad?" she cried. She turned and looked, knocking her boot against a patch of snow.

Mitti Peary leaned down to talk to her in a low voice. She led Marie by the hand toward our village, whispering to her. I followed them with the crowd. By the time we reached Peary's caboose, Marie had stopped crying and even smiled.

Mitti Peary helped Marie up the stairs of the caboose.

The girl stood on her toes and reached for the key that hung on a nail, put the key in the lock, and opened the door. I inched forward, hoping she would notice me.

"If Daddy keeps the door locked, then why doesn't he take the key?" Marie asked her mother.

"He only locks the caboose to keep the wind from blowing in. He knows the Eskimos would never take anything."

Eskimos—that was Mitti Peary's name for us. We call ourselves *Inuit,* the people.

I was close enough to see inside and catch a whiff of Mitti Peary's wonderful scent. She smelled like lavender—flowers that grow in her faraway home. She was so strong and handsome! Mitti Peary and Marie walked around looking at his desk, tools, and barrels for keeping his supplies. Marie rapped the fat iron stove in the middle of the floor. It made a hollow sound. She opened a barrel, took out a package of biscuits, and gnawed on one. "It's so stale!"

Mitti Peary was staring at a framed photo of herself in a plumed hat that was larger and even more elegant than the dark red one she now wore. She seemed restless as she searched through the things in Peary's desk, then slammed the desk drawer shut. "There's no letter for us, Marie. Perhaps he didn't receive word that we'd be coming on the supply boat. I'm going to talk to the captain. Do you want to stay here?"

"Yes, Mother."

"Remain here, then, and look around."

When Mitti Peary left, I climbed up the steps and stood right in the doorway. I would have entered, except for the owl that Peary kept in the caboose. It was dead, but Peary had made it appear to be alive. Its yellow eyes gleamed in the light and seemed to follow me.

"Marie!" I said. "It's me, Billy Bah!"

She looked at me curiously for a few long moments, then, at last, gave a little hint of a smile. She remembered me. "Billy Bah!"

I didn't mind that she still called me Billy Bah. When Marie was a baby, she gave me that name. All the white people still used it.

I jumped from the caboose. Marie hesitated, and I lifted her down.

Soon our people surrounded us, talking and gesturing. Those closest to Marie reached for her braids. "*Tassa!*" I told them. I'd been scared when people in America touched me this way. Marie just laughed.

Qaorlutoq, the orphan boy, jumped in front of me and cried "Marie!" I called him Bag of Bones because his arms and legs were so thin. His patchy coat of furs and skins looked dirty.

Her nose wrinkled.

Marie and Bag of Bones stood facing each other. She was taller, though he was a few winters older, about eleven. "Qaorlutoq," she said, "is that you?"

"It's me!" He grinned.

Qaorlutoq tried some English he'd learned on Peary's ships. "Marie, you tall. You plenty bad now."

"Bad?" Marie laughed.

"He means that you are plenty *big*," I said.

Three summers earlier when she'd visited our land, Marie loved that bony orphan boy as much as I loved her. We were her two closest friends.

Mitti Peary moved toward us through the crowd. You could always see her coming. She was much taller than our people, including the men; we didn't even reach her shoulders. Why hadn't she recognized me? Before I could talk to her, she took Marie by the hand and whisked her away. "Don't let anyone grab at you!"

Marie looked at me, eyes wide. I could tell she wanted to stay with us. But her mother took her down to the beach, where a sailor rowed them back to the ship. I watched as Marie, green and pink, glided away from me. Would I see her again?

Angulluk came up to me, Captain Bartlett with him.

"Please tell your people that we're leaving soon," said the captain. "We'll go across the sound, to Ellesmere Land, to find Lieutenant Peary."

I translated proudly. "Husband, the ship is going to *Umimmaat Nuna*, Musk Ox Land. They want to see Peary."

Angulluk talked excitedly to his friends. It impressed them that the white men had a way of crossing a wide body of water without waiting for it to freeze over. Our men used their kayaks only for short trips. I'd already guessed their plan of asking the captain for a ride to Musk Ox Land.

"There's good hunting on that shore," one said. "Fat musk oxen. Herds of them." All summer we'd eaten mostly birds, and we hungered for larger game. And, as always, we planned for winter. We needed meat.

Angulluk knew a few words of English. "People go ship hunting," he said to Captain Bartlett, who stared at him blankly.

"Woman! Tell the *qallunaaq* to take us with him."

"Our people want to come to Ellesmere Land with you," I said to the captain.

He stroked his curly beard again and paused before answering. "I only have room for ten."

I relayed the message to Angulluk, though I was fairly sure he'd understood. The men responded with much talking and gesturing. A few roared at each other; I stepped back in case there was a fight. Many more wanted to go than the ship could take.

"Quiet!" Captain Bartlett raised his hand. He pointed at me first. "You. Stay there." Then he began to divide us into two groups.

"Don't be so proud, woman!" said Angulluk. Our hunters always liked to show that they were the ones in charge. Even so, I could tell he was pleased. If I went on the ship, Angulluk would have to accompany me. The captain wouldn't separate couples.

I silently guessed whom the captain would choose and I was right. He singled out the young, unmarried hunters who'd worked for Peary. And Ally, the only other woman. The white men all knew her and liked her, and Piugaat-toq, her husband. He'd often hunted for them. Finally, the captain picked Qaorlutoq. Like a loyal dog, Bag of Bones nestled himself in the captain's side. The white men felt sorry for him. They didn't realize that orphan boys, left to care for themselves, often became our people's best and bravest hunters.

It took us several trips from our igloo to the beach to pack. Angulluk and I assembled everything we owned in his kayak: our tent and furs, our winter clothes, our sled, chunks of seal blubber, my cooking pot, my two large seal-oil lamps, and Angulluk's harpoon, rifle, axe, and three knives, including his snow knife. I carefully wrapped my smaller, very precious items in skins. I'd keep these with me in my carrying bag: my four needles and other sewing things, and my *ulu,* which my mother had given me when I was about six winters old. My father had fashioned its curved blade using a saw from Peary. The *ulu* was so sharp it could cut through bone. I also slipped my small wooden chest of keepsakes into my birdskin carrying bag; these treasures I always kept hidden in furs, under the sleeping platform, near my sewing things, which my husband never touched.

Angulluk harnessed our eight sled dogs in a group. "I'll meet you at the shore. There's something important I have to do," I told him.

He grew serious. "All right. Come back soon." He knew exactly where I was going.

CHAPTER THREE

● ● ● ● ● ● ● ●

I couldn't resist lingering in our empty igloo and taking my secret box from my carrying bag. I kept my chest of treasures away from prying eyes. It had been many seasons since I'd shown these treasures to anyone.

With its glossy brown wood and shiny yellow handle, the box was in itself a wonder. In our treeless land, anything made of wood was very precious. I opened the lid of the small, polished chest and lifted out a china cup with blue flowers on it. I put each item back in the box before taking out the next. Pinecones and acorns. A bloodred feather. Shiny gold buttons. Fragments of silk, lace, and velvet that I stroked and held against my cheek. A comb. A pink silk ribbon that had been Marie's. How surprising it was to see her again today! Her hair was much longer now, but she still wore the same kind of ribbon.

For every treasure, I had a memory, a piece of my story that no one else could understand. How could a cardboard box, flattened and faded, with pictures of strange animals on it, make any sense to someone in our land? Years ago the box had held biscuits shaped like animals.

I placed the flattened box on top of other treasures

and picked up a photograph of myself as a child. In it I was wearing a stiff, tight dress and an ironed pinafore. How itchy that dress had been! I'd hated the way it kept my arms bound to me. Another image, one that had been printed in a book, showed me as a baby tucked into the pouch of my mother's seal furs, safe and warm on her back. She was scowling. Was she angry at having her picture taken? Or was she simply frowning because the sunlight was hitting her eyes?

The last items, small ivory seals and an ivory *nanoq,* an ice bear, were carved by my father. Above all, these were the most precious to me.

Years earlier, I'd felt so lucky when Mitti Peary chose me to sail to America with her. Mitti was what I called her because I couldn't pronounce *Missus.* I was about ten winters old and had never traveled more than a moon's journey by dogsled away from our village. "Eqariusaq," Mitti Peary said in her language. "Wouldn't you like to travel aboard a big ship? Wouldn't you like to see my land?" She needed me to help care for her baby, she said. The ship was called the *Hope.* Her husband wouldn't be coming on this journey. She'd bring me back to my parents after one year.

"Yes, Mitti Peary!" I replied. I could understand much of what she said from hearing the Pearys talk with my parents. My family lived in a rock igloo next door to their tar-papered shack, so my parents could sew furs and hunt for them. When Mitti Peary permitted my mother to enter the house, I followed. She was always surprising us. Unlike our women, she had a rifle, and once she'd shot an attacking walrus from a rowboat.

None of our people had ever gone to America, and my parents and I didn't understand what we had agreed to. I only knew I wanted to be with Mitti Peary, a lady so important and courageous that even without her husband, she could come and go as she pleased.

That day, I climbed aboard the ship with my birdskin bag, went into the main cabin, and sat with Marie, holding her. I went onto the deck for air with Mitti Peary and looked out at a wide bay separating me from my family. Beyond the railing, the ship dropped down like the face of a cliff. There came a rumbling and the boards under my feet began to shake. Clouds of black, oily smoke filled the air; my eyes burned. Suddenly, the ocean was moving and the ship began to roll. My village became smaller and the people standing on the beach appeared tiny, like the toy figures my father carved. When I could no longer see either the rock igloos or the people, a terror filled me and tightened into a great pain in my heart. I screamed and cried.

Frantic, I tugged on Mitti Peary's coat sleeve. I pleaded with her in my language. "Take me back! I want to go home!"

"It's all right, Eqariusaq," Mitti Peary said, stroking my hands. "We'll take care of you."

The coast disappeared. I could see the far, wide horizon, blue and full of white clouds, but when I looked down, there was only dark water.

I pointed over the wide ocean and yelled, "I want my mother and father!"

Mitti Peary held my hand, took me inside her small dark room, and sat me beside her on the bunk. She held Marie. "The ship can't turn. There's no going back until next summer. Please don't cry!"

I bit my lip and held back tears. Marie gave me a huge smile. Mitti Peary passed her to me and I cradled her, pressing her soft cheek to mine.

I couldn't go home! Mitti Peary was in charge of me now and I'd have to do what she wanted. But there was something else I understood. Though I dreaded the year to come, I knew I'd have Marie, who was like a baby sister to me. Marie was *my* baby now. Mine.

I filled my days on the *Hope* with Marie, dressing her, cleaning up after her, and flushing with pride when she pulled herself upright and took her first wobbling steps. I held her tiny hands and I talked to her in my language. She repeated words back to me from my own land. She couldn't say my name; instead it came out *"Eeek-lee," "Bill-eee,"* and finally, *"Bill-ee-bah."* She had gifted me with that name. Marie recognized me, talked to me, clapped for me. Sometimes I was so happy in her presence, I almost forgot my sorrow.

My parents' burial chamber stood on a hill among the other graves near the village. My older sister and older brother and I had built this long, low mound of stones after we'd learned of our parents' deaths. It was a rock house meant for three because an orphan girl named Aviaq, a few years younger than I, had accompanied my mother and father to America and died with them there. Though the chamber did not contain any of their bodies, it would welcome their spirits. This is where my feet took me now. I needed to say good-bye to my parents, for all water crossings are dangerous, and there was always the chance I wouldn't return from Musk Ox Land.

Greetings, Anaana and Ataata, I said in my thoughts. While waiting for them to respond, I peered through spaces in the rocks into the chamber. Good, the rifle, the two *uluit,* lamps, harpoon, and other objects placed in the grave had not been disturbed by animals. Outside lay my father's kayak, which my brother had dragged to the rock house.

Aviaq's spirit no longer hovered in this place, and I missed the beautiful girl with the blue-black hair. Still, I was happy that her spirit now lived in a toddler who'd been given her name.

"*Hello,* Panik," said my father.

"*You are looking well.*" My mother smiled.

"*Thank you, Anaana.*" I sensed my parents' spirit forms seated on the ground with their backs supported by the rock house. My father's pure white ghost dog stood beside him. It held its pointy ears erect, and its tail was bushy and tightly curled.

The kayak made a good resting place for me as I told my parents of my upcoming journey. It was mostly by feeling that I knew my parents were there. My father had been short, stocky, and strong from years of hunting. Now, in shimmering form, a sense of his strength remained. He held a whittling knife and a piece of walrus tusk in his lap; in life he'd enjoyed carving. My mother, tiny but vigorous and energetic even as a spirit, kept herself busy by cleaning a ghostly sealskin. With the *ulu* my sister had left for her in the grave, she skillfully cut through the layers of fat and rolled them away without slitting the skin.

"*Angulluk the Fat One is still playing tricks,*" I said to them. "*After the qallunaat take us across the sound, he'll find a way to get himself more ammunition. If he was better with his harpoon, we wouldn't need so many bullets.*"

"*Relying on the qallunaat's weapons. That's no good,*" Ataata said, frowning.

"*Many hunters are helped by the white man's guns, but Angulluk won't even try to use a harpoon,*" I said.

"*But that Fat One is smart,*" Anaana pointed out. "*He's managed to provide well for you, hasn't he?*"

"*Not at all!*" I replied. True, Angulluk was a fine hunter

when hunger or pride or his sense of adventure moved him to it. My mother always came to Angulluk's defense. He'd charmed her from the day he'd appeared at my parents' igloo and said he wanted to trade six dogs for me. She liked his smile. "He's as buoyant as a seal," she'd said. At first, my father wouldn't agree to the marriage because Angulluk was lazy. He kept numerous caches of auks because he rarely brought in larger game. Still, Angulluk had passed his father's test of becoming a man: he'd killed a seal, a walrus, and a narwhal. His father and brothers were known as the best hunters in our community. So my parents felt that the Fat One must have potential. One day the marriage trade was made, and the Fat One, like all new husbands, yanked me off to his igloo and made me his wife.

Young couples often separate and remarry, and at first, and sometimes even now, I thought about finding a new husband who wasn't so lazy. But I discovered that the Fat One, with his easy laugh and lighthearted disposition, was good company. As rude and bossy as he was, he never hit me; I could have done worse. And I needed him more than I could ever know. That summer, Peary took my parents to America because he said he wanted to teach the *qallunaat* about the "Polar Eskimos."

Until recently, the *qallunaat* assumed that no one lived at the icy top of the world, Peary explained, and here we were, a few hundred of us, so cut off by ice and snow that we rarely saw our neighboring communities. Peary wanted to show the white people how strong and skillful the Polar Eskimos were, he said, for surviving in a treeless, frozen place where there was no sunshine for half of the year. We were strong in our land, but in America, my parents and others who'd never been sick for a day in their lives quickly caught illnesses and died.

I told my mother and father, *"Angulluk's parents and brothers have gone south to hunt for caribou. We'd have accompanied them if the Fat One could tolerate their teasing. You know how his brothers always call him a good-for-nothing!"*

My mother's spirit laughed and when she opened her mouth, I could see the place where she'd lost two of her bottom teeth.

We talked of my brother, who was about Angulluk's age, eighteen or nineteen. *"Inunteq has gone hunting for caribou,"* I said. *"He met a woman last summer whom he arranged to marry and will stay in her village."*

"He told us," my father said. *"It's good that he's found both a wife and a place where he can better support a family."*

"I think so, too, but I'll miss him."

Now I had only my sister, Nuljalik. But I was used to our villagers dispersing for moons or even a year at a time, depending on the weather and the success of their hunts; and I wished my brother well in a land bountiful with big game. Itta was known for its auks and eider ducks, which came to our red cliffs in noisy clouds, blackening the sky. But all too soon the birds departed. Wintering in Itta meant starvation if our hunters could not put large caches of meat aside.

I told my parents about seeing Mitti Peary and Marie. Then, finally, I worked up the courage to let them know what was pressing on me. *"Let me be the one to receive you into life again, Anaana and Ataata!"* I said. *"Let it be soon!"*

Like the other times when I'd made this request, their spirits and the ghost dog dissolved into the air like mist. *"Don't go!"* I shouted. *"Will you never answer me?"*

Spirits could be reborn when babies were given their names. For the orphan girl Aviaq the matter had been easy because she belonged to no one in particular and, because of her beauty, was beloved to everyone. After the villagers learned of her death, her spirit had gone into the first girl baby born to our community.

As for my parents, it was understood that either my sister or I would bear a child and take on that special responsibility. Until that time, no one must ever say the names of my parents out loud. My sister already had a child. It was my turn.

"Anaana and Ataata. Send me a sign, if you cannot tell me now," I implored. *"Come to me in my dreams."*

The wind whistled through the spaces in the rock graves and seemed to say, *It is not permitted for spirits to speak of the future.*

CHAPTER FOUR

● ● ● ● ● ● ● ● ●

Later that day, my sister Nuljalik stood with me on the beach, holding the hand of her five-year-old daughter while the confusion of people boarded the ship. Nuljalik and her husband were among the villagers who had no interest in dealing with white men and had not tried for a chance to go to Musk Ox Land. Even so, she wanted to see what the *qallunaat* would do next. We watched Ally, her husband, Piugaattoq, and son, Sammy, crowd into a rowboat full of tents, guns, harpoons, and yelping dogs.

"I wish you'd change your mind," Nuljalik said. She looked at me intently with her dark, wide-spaced eyes. "You're better off here, away from the *qallunaat*."

"You may be right. Do you think they're going to eat me?" It was an old joke of my father's. My sister and I both knew that she couldn't persuade me to stay.

"When do you suppose you'll return?" she asked.

"I hope we come back in one moon with a ship full of meat! Otherwise, we'll wait until the sound freezes."

I thought again about the deep water separating Musk Ox Land from Itta. My father and other hunters had crossed the sound in three days when it was solidly frozen. Though winter ice made sled travel possible, it was also the time of darkness and frequent snowstorms. So crossings could be made only during the full moon on clear days.

Nuljalik frowned. "The white men could return to America in their ship and leave you stranded at Musk Ox Land for a very long time. We don't know what the ice will do."

She'd guessed my worry. Crossing sea ice was very dangerous in the best of conditions. As the ice moved and shifted, gaps of water opened that could easily swallow a sled team. Perhaps the Fat One's plan for us to go to Musk Ox Land wasn't so good after all.

"Peary will arrange for Captain Bartlett's ship to take us back to Itta," I said, though I wasn't so sure.

"If you're not able to come home this winter and one of us has a baby, what will we do?" Nuljalik asked.

"Then the naming of the baby must wait until we're together."

"Good, we agree," she said.

What if we both had babies? I smiled at her.

Behind me I heard whispering and turned to see two young women who used to be my friends. They stared at me and stopped talking. Ever since Angulluk had started trading me to white men, some of the villagers seemed afraid of me. I wasn't loaned nearly as much as Ally was to Peary, but I'd gone several times, to different sailors.

I stared back. Silently, I told them, *Sooner or later, one of you will be traded to a white man. Then let's see how smug you are.*

Now sailors were throwing biscuits on the ground for villagers who had not been chosen. Our people quickly picked them up. Peary's ships had been coming to our land for as long as I could remember, so we'd grown accustomed to the white men. But most villagers didn't realize when the *qallunaat* were making fun of us.

My little niece, Konala, tried to run toward the biscuits. I yanked her back.

"Do *not* eat food like a dog." Konala broke into tears, and Nuljalik also looked like she was about to cry.

I pushed my way into the group of sailors. "*Tassa!* Stop throwing the biscuits on the ground!"

One sailor began handing the biscuits to the villagers, but another continued to throw the food.

"This is why you shouldn't go, Eqariusaq," Nuljalik said. "You're wrong to admire the *qallunaat*. They don't respect you as much as you think." The words stung. We rubbed noses before she offered me a sad smile and walked up the winding path toward the village with her daughter.

Angulluk called, "Help me push the dogs into the boat!"

By sitting in the boat and gripping the harness, I managed to keep the dogs from jumping out. A sailor rowed the dogs and me, while Angulluk paddled our kayak. I kept my box of keepsakes between my legs. One dog bit another, the rowboat rocked and nearly turned over, but I hung on.

Marie twirled about excitedly as I climbed up the ship's ladder.

Angulluk climbed up after me. Two sailors I recognized used ropes to haul the rowboat and dogs up the side; one sailor smiled at me. Already the ship smelled strongly of dog and blubber. At the center of the deck, the dogs barked and fought as Angulluk pushed our team toward the snarling group.

We stacked our belongings against the pilothouse near the front. At the rail, Angulluk and I watched as his kayak was hoisted, and Marie came skipping up to me.

Our men were unusually quiet; they feared the ship, so large and brimming with strange objects. With its heavy wood and iron and tall sail masts, it seemed too massive to float or be steered. Most of our hunters had never traveled on a ship before. Even I could imagine it sinking in the middle of the deep sound, far from either shore.

I jumped as the *Windward* began to rumble and shake. "*Ua!*" I'd forgotten the sounds and vibrations of a ship.

Marie giggled, and I gave her a smile. A bracing wind made my face tingle, and Marie's cheeks were already red.

Just a few days before, I'd never have thought that I'd be seeing Marie again, and going on a journey with her. Should I take her hand the way I used to do? Three summers had passed since her last voyage to Itta, and she was shy with me. Mitti Peary came strolling up. I waited for her to greet me, but she just stared.

"Mother," Marie cried. "It's Billy Bah!"

Mitti Peary held me by the arms and looked me in the eyes. "Billy Bah! I *didn't* recognize you. How you've grown up!"

I returned her smile. How good it was to see her again.

Smoke poured out of the *Windward*'s two smokestacks. The captain sounded the horn, and the ship began to move, steaming out through the floes of ice. Angulluk and I couldn't return to shore now, even if we wanted to. We were on our way, our lives moving in unforeseen directions.

CHAPTER FIVE

● ● ● ● ● ● ● ●

Captain Bartlett said our journey on the *Windward* to Musk Ox Land would only take a day and a night, but we'd hardly traveled any distance at all and three days had gone by. Gigantic ice floes towered over the ship and crowded the sound, and our perilous path between them was winding and slow. Marie and I watched the sailors climb high into the rigging and chop off points of blue ice that hung over the deck. She collected the fallen chunks that clinked together with the tiny songs ice can make. Qaorlutoq, that Bag of Bones, built play igloos with the slabs of ice.

"I build igloo, give Marie," Qaorlutoq said. Marie crawled into it.

Marie smiled at me through a space in the flat roof. "Come on in, Billy Bah!"

"No. You play." I was too old for children's games.

I remembered the tar-papered house with the flat roof where Marie's parents had lived when she was born. I'd hide behind rocks along with the other children in our village and watch Mitti Peary, big with child, walk in and out. She was the only white woman we'd ever known. We wanted to see what kind of a baby would come out of her.

The morning after Marie was born, a big crowd of villagers gathered around the house with gifts of furs and carved ivory animals. Everyone loved this tiny, fair-haired child. I called her the snow baby. My mother used to sing nonsense songs for her, like *"Ah-nee-gee-ta-ta-ee."* Everyone started calling her Ah-neeg-he-toe.

I visited Marie every day, and watched Mitti Peary give her a bath. Mitti Peary would lay her to dry on the soft caribou skins. Once, Peary wrapped her in the red, white, and blue material he called the stars and stripes and took her outside to photograph her. In the spring, my mother made Marie her first outdoor clothes: caribou skin trousers with little fur boots attached to them, and a fox skin *kapatak*.

Now, on the ship, Marie often kept me company in the forward saloon, a large room at the front where our people slept on furs on the floor. Or Marie sat with us outside on deck where we ate seal meat, and Angulluk entertained her with his string games. Mitti Peary offered me kind smiles and thanked me for watching over Marie. Oddly, though, she never invited me to their cabin.

But on the fourth day of our voyage, Marie crawled out of the ice house and said, "Let me show you where I live, Billy Bah." She tugged my hand.

"Don't pull me." But I could hardly keep from grinning.

We crept through a narrow hallway past glossy wooden doors with bright metal doorknobs. The rooms behind the doors, Marie said, belonged to the captain and his officers. She took me into the place where they ate their meals, and I ran my hands across the smooth wood of the table. Wood—so foreign, such a luxury! It was hard to believe that the whole ship was made of it. Marie guided me to a tiny room where she lifted up a board. "This is where Mother and I go to the toilet," she said, "and here is toilet paper." She paused. "I've seen the Eskimos squatting over buckets. Why don't you use the sailors' toilet?"

"I don't know." I remembered the bathroom at Mitti Peary's home.

"Come on." Marie took my hand again, yanking me into the officers' saloon. It was brightly lit with small lanterns and warmed by a stove. Men sat in chairs, smoking, talking, and reading. One wrote at a desk. As soon as they saw us, they stopped talking. One frowned and seemed about to say something, but Marie pulled me out of the room.

Marie opened another door. The room, all in wood, was as dimly lit as an igloo and nearly as large. It had two chairs, a table, a trunk, and two beds, one on top of the other along a wall.

Marie climbed a ladder beside the beds and sat near a small window. "Come on up to my bunk." I joined her, ducking my head to keep from hitting the ceiling. I looked through the glass of the window to see ice masses glistening in the sunlight. Marie pulled back her blankets, and for a moment my heart stopped. I'd forgotten how realistic the white people's dolls could be. In America, I'd been so startled by the sight of one that I'd burst into tears—I'd thought it was a tiny child.

Now Marie gently handed me the beautiful doll, so realistic, so rosy, it seemed like it had just taken a breath. "Her name's Clara."

I stroked Clara's hair. It was bright yellow, like Marie's. I felt the smooth silk of her dress and marveled at its deep pink color, like a sunset, and opened Clara's blue eyes, remembering how I'd opened and closed that other doll's eyes, long ago.

Marie asked, "She's pretty, isn't she?"

"Yes, she is pretty." But the word didn't feel strong enough. The doll was almost alive.

I listened to Marie talk about how her mother would not let her bring her other dolls on the voyage. "Are you still collecting things?" she asked.

"Yes," I said, "the box your mother gave me is nearly full now."

Marie cradled her doll as I remembered the happy night when Mitti Peary gave me the wooden chest. She wrapped it to surprise me and she put it under a tree that glowed with many tiny candles. I spent hours admiring and rearranging my special keepsakes and taking them in and out of their glossy container. Each tiny thing, soft feather, fragrant leaf, had power, and each told a story about a faraway land.

My box of treasures was my reward for completing my year in America: for the pain of missing my family, getting used to a new language, the sweltering heat of their summer, a winter that was too mild, and a way of life that was so different from my own. People were always looking at me and touching me. They asked me questions and my face would grow warm when I couldn't answer. Marie's grandmother, "Grossy" or "Grossmutter," who was from a land called Germany, spoke with an accent; I couldn't understand a word she said. Still, I'd enjoyed many afternoons with these strange women, sewing dolls' dresses and real dresses with shiny buttons and soft, glittering materials.

"We still have the dresses you made me," Marie said, "and that little fox fur coat. Mother says someday we may give it to a museum."

Museum. My whole body stiffened. I could never hear that word without thinking about my parents and Aviaq. But then Mitti Peary swept in and frowned when she saw me.

"Marie," she said, "please go somewhere else with Billy Bah." I looked at her, stunned.

"Why?"

"You know why. We talked about this."

"Billy Bah did *not* put her head on my pillow. I'm *not* going to get lice," Marie said.

I gulped. In another minute, the tears came.

I climbed down from the bunk to run out the door, but Mitti Peary said, "Billy Bah! I'm sorry." She held me gently by the arm. "Why don't you let me bathe you? You'll soon feel better."

"Yes, Mitti Peary," I said slowly. As always, I wanted to make her happy. I wiped my tears. In America, every morning after Mitti Peary had bathed me and dressed me in a dark green dress with a pinafore, she'd present me to her family; how they smiled at me! Harsher memories came back. She had pulled my hair when she combed it. Forced a prickly brush into my mouth against my teeth. My new clothes kept me from lifting my arms. I'd yearned for my own soft furs and sealskin, hungered for seal and narwhal meat, to pick up food with my hands without being scolded. In winter, I missed the cozy days of darkness that my family shared in our igloo. In summer, I wanted to roam free on the windy hills and clifftops with my brother and sister.

Most of all, I'd yearned for my own mother.

Now Mitti Peary led me down into the lower level of the ship to the boiler room. There she ran warm water into a shiny copper tub and bathed me behind a red and white curtain. White people are so silly, using precious fuel to heat water, and washing away the oil that keeps our skin from becoming dry and chapped. Even so, I enjoyed the warm water. I liked the smell of the soap, made from lavender flowers. And when she was finished, my skin glowed. I was cold after stepping out of the tub, but I almost didn't want to put on my sealskin. It felt so good to be naked, just as we are—warmly—inside our igloos.

Mitti Peary combed out the tangles in my hair. "Stop!" I ordered. "Please." I took the comb to finish.

Mitti Peary held up a mirror. "Look at yourself, Billy Bah. You've grown into a lovely young woman."

I held the mirror, seeing not only myself, washed of grease, but Marie beside me, beaming.

Marie stroked my hair. Then she took a dark pink ribbon from one of her braids and gathered my hair behind me. She tied it. "Mother, see how beautiful she looks."

"I'm glad to see you smiling again, Billy Bah," said Mitti Peary.

Angulluk would have laughed to see me with my skin rubbed so bare. Possibly it would mean trouble, or even danger, for me—I'd likely attract attention among the sailors. It's not always safe to act like a *qallunaaq*.

But at that moment, I could only think about being praised, and finding my place among Marie's family again. My heart felt full.

CHAPTER SIX

● ● ● ● ● ● ● ●

A few hours after my bath, I found Angulluk on deck shaping the fitting for the point on a harpoon with a new knife. He carved it from a large piece of dark wood.

"*Hainang.*" He greeted me with unusual courtesy. He had traded well to have the new knife and the even more valuable wood. It didn't break, as bone did, so we liked to make our tools, weapons, and sled runners out of it. He looked me over. "You should wear that silly *qallunaat* trifle in your hair more often. Can you believe it, Eqariusaq? I had three different offers for you tonight."

"Who did you choose?" I felt my heart rush, but I looked at him boldly.

"Duncan."

"Good," I said. "I could use some time away from you." I remembered the young smiling sailor with a head of curly red hair, and the nervous fluttering in my stomach eased. Duncan Gaylor was tall and thin, with large protruding ears. He seemed harmless. At least, I hoped so.

"It's almost *too easy* to trade with those sailors," Angulluk said. "They have no women to keep them company."

"You're as heartless as a stone," I said. "Let me see your knife."

I took the block of wood. It smelled fresh and sweet as I practiced shaving off a curl with the sharp blade. *Generous gifts.* It was because of me he had such good things.

* * *

Late that evening, I joined Duncan in the sailors' quarters, where the men slept behind musty-smelling brown curtains. Loud snores came from several bunks; the men would not wake, because they'd collapsed into sleep after drinking.

He drew the curtain closed behind us and hung his small lantern on a hook at one corner. I removed my *kapatak* and spread it across the bed. At least I'd have the familiar feel and scent of my own furs, some comfort. I folded my *kamiit* in a corner and lay on my back, watchful; Duncan might pounce on me like a bear as other sailors had. Instead, he leaned against the wall, his head nearly touching the bunk above us.

"Billy Bah, tell me about yourself."

Was this some joke? Only Marie would say such a thing.

I sat up. "There is nothing to say."

"Of course there is!" he said. "You speak English so well. I've never met an Eskimo who could do that. And you went to America. What was that like for you?"

Shy, I pulled my comforting *kapatak* up around me. "America is very crowded. The food has no flavor! Winters are not nearly so cold. Your pee never freezes in midair! Ha!"

I'd added this last detail because it was the sort of tidbit that my father, a wonderful storyteller, would have included.

Duncan laughed. How was it that I could be myself around this white stranger, who'd soon take his pleasure from me?

"Tell me," I said. "What do *you* think of *my* land?"

He grinned. "The glaciers are beautiful. The stars . . . and yes, it's strange! In this cold, like you say, pee freezes! The hair on my face stops growing."

"Why did you come here?"

He leaned toward me, eyes shining, as if he'd just returned from a hunt. "An Arctic voyage—ah. I love danger. I feel sharp and alive when I risk my life every single day."

"But living here is *not* dangerous."

His eyebrows lifted. "No?"

I said what my father had once told me, "It's mostly fools or the young who die in accidents. We know how to gauge the snow, and to wait until the right time to travel. Things happen very slowly here. In fact, not much happens at all."

Duncan was disappointed. I'd taken something from him. "But the Arctic ice can rip apart ships," Duncan said.

"Ships vanish. Great leaders prove themselves, or make mistakes, on a grand scale. Then a lot of people die."

"If your leaders were really great, they'd know when it's best to stay home." I eyed him. *"Never* speak of tragedy. If you forecast terrible events, say them out loud, they might happen."

Duncan pressed his back further against the wall. "So what do you think of Peary?" he asked. "He's a great leader?"

"He might be, if he didn't take so many risks. Peary likes danger. Like you."

"Yes," Duncan said, "but we're different. Peary craves fame."

"What is that?"

He tried to explain how Peary wanted to claim new territory, go farther north than any man. To show he'd been somewhere, he was always building triangular piles of stones and planting flags.

These markings were a silly reason to undertake long, dangerous journeys, but I nodded. "Ally says that when Peary sets out, he wears his flag under his clothes, so he never loses it."

"Ally would know." Duncan looked away. "Why are *you* going to Ellesmere Land right now?"

"For food," I said. "Food is the only reason to make a journey. In Itta we have seals and narwhal. But we don't have musk oxen. Their meat has the best flavor of any meat."

"I still think your people like to travel just to travel, same as us. The lure of the unknown."

"Ha! Nonsense." Because he'd been honest with me, I asked, "Why did you trade for me and not Ally?"

He averted his eyes. "Ally is Peary's girl. I would never trade for her." Then hesitantly, "I wanted you, Billy Bah."

"But Ally is prettier," I said. "Her teeth are perfect. She has a small nose."

"Stop talking about Ally. You can speak better English. You're smart. When I saw you with your hair combed out—you're lovely!"

Hair! Why did white men value it? Long hair was a nuisance, something to get out of the way. But I smiled and moved closer.

"I don't want you to be afraid of me," Duncan said. "I would never hurt you." Then he pressed his lips against mine. I drew back.

"No! Kiss me on the nose, never on the lips."

"Why?"

"Our people don't do that," I said. "We don't like it."

From the shy way he looked at me, it seemed he'd never seen a woman before. This thought made me laugh out loud.

He was a quick learner. He was older than me by a few seasons but seemed so much younger. When I touched him in return, he looked away, embarrassed by his desire. Later, he rolled over onto his back and closed his eyes, peaceful, as if taking in sunlight. "This is the best day of my life."

We left the bunk early the next morning, while the men still snored. He invited me to drink tea with him in the galley. Instead, I twisted my hair into a topknot and returned to the forward saloon, where the hunters soon woke to tend the dogs on deck and, because the *Windward* traveled so slowly, to hunt seals on the ice floes. My husband and I did not speak of the trade.

But something important had happened. I felt changed, happy even. According to custom, I was not free to go to a man unless I was traded by my husband. At the same time, if I showed Duncan which supplies to offer Angulluk, the trade was as good as done. A plan began to take shape in my mind.

CHAPTER SEVEN

• • • • • • • •

And so Duncan arranged to have me for the remainder of the voyage. Our passage on the icy sound lasted eight days. It was the time of year when the sun never sets, so every day felt wonderfully, endlessly long and gave us the light we missed in other seasons.

Each night, Duncan asked questions. One was "Do you miss America?"

"Sometimes. I wish I could see trees again."

And as for him, a few weeks after arriving in Ellesmere Land, the *Windward* would set sail for America, and all the while, he said, he'd be thinking of the Arctic, and of me. "We have something in common. We're not completely happy in our own land or with our own people. We're restless because we know there's something more."

Maybe he was right. I was *pivviit akornganni*, between two places, and didn't know where I belonged. Duncan's stories helped me to recall America's bright colors, loud sounds, and endless variety of things to hear, to taste, touch, and smell. But each morning, I'd shift back into my own landscape.

On the ice floes with Ally, we skinned and cleaned the

seals our husbands caught. We slit the seal through the length of its belly, first one side, then the other, and then cut away the skin and fat in one large piece. The blubber and tasty, solid meat we'd keep for ourselves. "Here, Eqariusaq, you can have the tongue," Angulluk would say, because he knew I liked it best. His favorite part was the tender flipper. Ally and I scooped out the steaming, warm entrails, and back on deck, we tossed them to the barking dogs. Even though we were on the rolling ocean, and I was lying with a white man, this part of my life hadn't changed.

Marie often helped Ally and me as we scraped, stretched, and folded the skins for later use. We had seal pelts with us that had already been cured and dried, and these we cut into strips to sew mittens for ourselves and the hunters.

While we worked, Marie asked questions like "Aren't you too young to be married?"

"Here we must grow up faster," I said. "Boys need to hunt, or else we don't have enough food. And our people don't seem to live as long as yours. Or grow as tall." I kept waiting for her to ask about Duncan, but she didn't. I also wondered whether she'd realized that Sammy was her brother. I'd never tell; it wasn't my place.

Was Duncan right, that I was restless around my own people? The more he talked of America, the more I remembered about it. Sometimes I even wished to see America again, despite all the pain it had caused me.

On the eighth morning, the *Windward* sailed through a narrow, high-walled passage of ice. The cold wind roared through the channel as those who had to be on deck held on for their lives. Low dark cliffs loomed ahead and the sky shone misty gray, as if it might snow. The ship pushed past small ice floes and swerved around a shoal of jagged black rocks. The sailors were tense handling the ship, and we waited with nervous excitement, until the sea opened at last to a pebbly coastline protected by dozens of tiny islands. We'd arrived in Musk Ox Land, at the cove the *qallunaat* called Payer Harbor.

Everyone came on deck. Marie and I took turns looking through her mother's field glasses. To the east, tents and igloos sat on the lee of a small cliff above the beach. Though most hunters visited Musk Ox Land for short periods only, some of our people had long ago stayed on and formed their own community. Their tiny village blended with the gray-black shore and brown snow-covered hills. Misty clouds moved and parted, revealing jagged, snow-covered peaks that rose behind the hills.

"Goodness," Mitti Peary said to me and Marie. "I thought we'd never arrive." Dark circles surrounded her eyes.

I spotted some figures in light-colored furs. "Marie! See the people?"

"Do you think Daddy will be wearing a white fur coat?"

"Probably gray," I answered. "His summer sealskin."

"White," Marie said. "He has a polar bear coat!"

"Yes." Ally had made Peary's fine *kapatak*.

"Let me have the glasses." Mitti Peary's mouth was thin. None of the people on the beach was tall enough to be Peary or one of his men.

Marie did a little dance. "Today is the day I see Dad!"

I hoped so.

With the engines off, we glided toward the rocky shoals and land. Captain Bartlett lowered the ship's anchor. Everyone started talking, and the dogs began to bark.

Mitti Peary motioned to the captain and straightened her feathered hat. "I want to be the first on shore. Why don't you and I go together, Captain? Then we can come back and report to the others."

"I'm not sure that's a good idea, Mrs. Peary. I'd rather you waited."

"I want to go!" Marie begged. "Take me!"

Mitti Peary held her finger over her mouth. "Shush, Marie."

The captain and Mitti Peary were worried. Did they wonder if Peary was alive?

"Let me come to shore, Captain," I said. "I can translate for you."

"Ah," he said. "Thank you, Billy Bah."

Mitti Peary sighed wearily, but said, "I appreciate your help, Billy Bah."

As the sailors readied the rowboat, snow flurries

swirled. Too late I realized that I didn't have my mittens, and there wasn't time to look for them. The wind rocked the rowboat the sailors lowered, but I refused to be afraid. Soon enough we reached the water.

Snow blew on my face as I put on my hood. It was the dry snow that sticks on the ground; winter would be coming early this year, and it might be cold living in our tents until we could build our igloos. But the Musk Ox people would help us if we needed anything. Smoke spiraled out of their roof openings, a welcome sight.

The rowboat scraped up on the shore. Villagers rushed toward me as I climbed out of the boat, and I recognized a few people from their hunting trips to Itta. Hunters from all over came for our birds, as we from Itta sought large game elsewhere.

A man wearing a shaggy musk ox coat came up to me. Since he was older, I spoke formally. "Our people from across the water have arrived."

"You are welcome here."

"The snow blows from the north," I said. "It looks as if it will be cold, with more wind."

"Well, I see! It may turn into a blizzard."

We talked for a long time, observing the weather and giving our greetings and news of our villages. I pulled my numb hands up into my sleeves.

After a while, Captain Bartlett interrupted. "Ask them if they've seen Peary."

Turning, I put up my hand. "When it is time."

I explained to the elder how it was that our people came by ship. Then I asked, "Have you seen Peary?"

The man peered out from his hood. "He's gone."

Something in me sank. Peary was dead?

He said, "He left here a short time ago."

I blew out a cloud of misted air in relief. I learned that Peary camped inland with several men in a huge building that the *qallunaat* had built years earlier. The previous winter there, Peary had his frostbitten toes amputated, and he recovered; now he managed to travel quite well. I translated for Captain Bartlett.

"Fort Conger." Captain Bartlett brushed snow out of his beard. "I believe that's a great distance from here."

The elder invited the captain and me to come into his family's igloo and warm ourselves. But we wanted to get back to the ship; the sky was darkening and the snow was turning to heavier flakes. My hands were numb. Most of all, I wanted to talk with Angulluk. He would know what our people should do next. Was it best to get off the *Windward* now and set up camp? Where would we place our tents?

The wind picked up strongly as Captain Bartlett struggled to row against the current. The cold wind stung my face. The captain grasped the ropes to attach the dory, and sailors above pulled us toward the deck, rocking in the fierce wind. Angulluk waited at the rail. I grabbed his hands and he lifted me on board. We rubbed noses. My hands were frozen, and his face felt cold against mine.

Marie called: "Billy Bah! Did you see Dad?"

I squeezed her warm hand tenderly as the captain spoke rapidly to Mitti Peary. I moved close and heard him say, "Your husband has gone inland to Greely's old fort. My maps don't show any details of the Ellesmere interior. Some of the Eskimos know where the fort is, but it would take days for them to get there with any messages. And now the harbor is crowding with ice. We will leave Lieutenant Peary his supplies—that is what we came to do. Then we depart tomorrow. Otherwise we could lose the ship."

Marie pushed in. "Mother, we can't!" She stamped her boot.

"Hush, Marie." Mitti Peary's voice was low and heavy. "We face a very serious situation. Right now, everyone has important work to do."

Once more, Captain Bartlett called on me to translate. "The Eskimos are welcome to stay on board an additional night because of the snow. Or if you wish to leave now, my crew will help you."

Angulluk held a council with the other young men, and then said to the captain in English, "We want to leave the ship now."

"Good!" I said. When we'd left Itta, the ship had felt immense; now I was tired of being trapped on board, and of going back and forth to the sailors' quarters, as enjoyable as my time with Duncan had been.

Soon, rowboats loaded with people and possessions

rocked on hooks toward the water. Dogs snarled and barked as the snow continued to fall.

For a while, I forgot about the Pearys as I helped Angulluk. With only four rowboats, it would take several trips to transport ten people, the dogs, and all our belongings. Ally and Piugaattoq went first because of their baby. Angulluk and I sat with others in the forward saloon.

My hands had almost no feeling. I rubbed them together.

"Look how red your hands are, silly woman." Angulluk took them and rubbed them hard.

"That hurts!" My hands stung as sensations came back, but soon they felt better. I found my mittens in my bag. How good it was to slip my fingers into the soft, warming fur. From the nearby galley, I smelled canned meat frying for the *qallunaat*. I was hungry but pushed the thought of food out of my mind and settled into Angulluk's arms.

As I was nearly asleep, the door swung open and Marie ran toward me.

Traces of tears streaked her cheeks. Breathless, she said, "The captain says we'll be sailing tomorrow. If we don't leave now, the ship may be caught in the ice." She started crying. "We would leave without even seeing Dad. And I want to visit with you longer. Billy Bah, tell Captain Bartlett that we can't go."

"I'm sorry you cannot see your father." Still, right now all I could think of was getting into our tent with our warm lamps, and falling asleep after a meal of juicy seal meat. I didn't even worry about how I'd eventually return to Itta.

"Will you talk to the captain, Billy Bah? Will you see if we can stay longer?"

I sighed. "Marie. Go and find your mother." Silently, I added, *Be grateful your father may still be alive.*

The door blew open again and a snowy figure came in, cap pulled down. "Billy Bah and Angulluk," Duncan said. "A dory's ready to take you. But are you sure you want to go now? It's snowing pretty hard."

"We will go," Angulluk said in English.

"All right, I'll row you," Duncan said. "Come quickly."

I wished another sailor had offered. But he'd sought me out. Seeing Duncan and the Fat One together felt so strange, and I couldn't talk to Duncan. Would I see him again before he returned to America? Right now, leaving quickly to find shelter from the storm was all that mattered.

Marie hugged me. "Good-bye." We rubbed noses, then I slung my bag over my shoulders and picked up my chest of keepsakes.

Laden down with our packs, Angulluk and I heaved ourselves out on the deck.

A howling wind whirled gusts of snow against us. We pulled our hoods tight. Had our dogs been rowed to shore yet? I would let Angulluk worry about them.

Angulluk climbed down into the dory, then turned toward me. "Get in, woman!"

"I can't see where we're going." I could barely make out the shape of the dory. One wrong step, and I'd fall over the side and into the icy water.

"Go on!"

I took a breath and jumped down toward the boat. Angulluk grasped my hand and guided me to the bench. Duncan handed down our gear. The boat, overcrowded with people and belongings, lurched as Duncan climbed in. The ship's pulleys screeched against the chains until finally the boat hit the water with a thud and a splash.

The wind screamed around us as Duncan heaved into the slow rowing. Snow clung to my eyebrows and eyelashes until I thought my eyes would freeze shut.

All was cold, blinding whiteness.

CHAPTER EIGHT

● ● ● ● ● ● ● ●

The shock of arriving in Musk Ox Land during the snow-storm was nothing compared to the shock I'd experienced when my first sea voyage ended, six summers earlier in the city of New York. Huge beams and stout ropes lifted crates off the ship to the dock, where I stood with Mitti Peary and Marie in a great crowd. I looked about in wonder. So *many* people! Giants talked all at once, pushed, walked with quick movements. What bright, pretty colors they wore! Beyond the dock, buildings rose, larger than I could have imagined, even blocking the sky.

I did not know that the world was so big.

And the overwhelming heat! The air was hot though no fires burned.

Somewhere in the crowd Mitti Peary found a dark-skinned boy to carry her suitcase. Inside it was my own birdskin bag, which held my *ulu,* a sharpening stone, some small ivory figures my father had made, and my fur clothes that Mitti Peary had taken from me.

I grabbed her sleeve and followed her through the crowd to a wide street where strange creatures, like sleek musk oxen, pulled carriages. Mitti Peary had told me about horses and carriages, but seeing them was a wonderment. Unlike our sleds, they rolled on large wheels, and the animals were far stronger than our dogs, tossing their huge heads and long tails, stamping their iron feet. Mitti Peary called out to a carriage driver and told me to climb in.

Mitti Peary said, "The carriage will take us to the train station." We were in a great city called New York and we were going to another grand place called Washington, DC, where she lived. With a snap of the straps in the driver's hands, the horses trotted off and we rode high above the street at a steady, fast clip—such a strange way to travel. The smell of the animals was sickening. I covered my ears from the loud sounds.

After we'd passed endless rows of buildings, Mitti Peary took Marie and me into the darkness of the train station, which was so large I drew in my breath. We waited on the edge of a chasm, like the long cracks that can be found near cliffs or on sea ice. Mitti Peary had told me about trains. But when one came into the station with terrifying noise and belching smoke, it looked like a huge monster, its eye shining, racing toward us with terrifying speed and wailing like Lieutenant Peary's whistle, only much louder. My chest pounded, and as the train screeched to a halt, I screamed and buried my head in Mitti Peary's dress. "It's all right, Billy Bah," she said tenderly, and pulled me close. I felt better when the monster stopped bellowing and puffing.

Trembling, I let her push me into the train. Mitti Peary guided me to a seat and put Marie in my arms. I looked out the window at the people standing outside. The monstrous train began to shake. In a few minutes, all was darkness. The people outside the window disappeared, and then a sunlit and fast-moving landscape emerged. Buildings and green shapes streamed by; we were going faster than I imagined anything could move. It made me dizzy to watch. I held on to Marie and to the seat.

Everything in this new life seemed impossible, but there were more surprises to come.

Mitti Peary's house had lots of rooms, all hot and stuffy. There was a kitchen with a coal stove so enormous that for weeks I felt certain it would swallow me if I got too close. The bathroom faucets let out either cold water or hot water, and if I turned the handles too far, the spouts drenched me. I slept alone for the first time in my life, missing my family and our snug igloo, in which we all shared one platform.

I clung to the things I knew: the comfort of holding Marie and playing simple games with her; the taste of meat (though it was not seal); the feel of furs. I loved to stroke Mitti Peary's sealskin coat that hung in a wardrobe in one of the rooms. And sometimes I'd lie on the great white, shaggy bearskin rug in her parlor, though I avoided looking at the beast's angry, gaping, fang-filled mouth and its black glassy eyes. The white people saved the heads of animals, which scared me. Even so, I was glad for the company of the bear.

Ours was a household of females: Mitti Peary (who was also called Jo); her mother, Mitti Diebitsch, a short woman with a wrinkled, kind face; Mitti Peary's sister, Mayde, who wore her yellow hair in long braids gathered at the back of her head; two older girls who cooked and cleaned; and Marie and myself. The old woman, Mitti Diebitsch, sometimes talked to her daughters in German. Usually, they spoke English. Out of shyness, I didn't join in their conversations, but I began to understand what they were saying.

One day, entertaining Marie with her dolls on the bearskin, I heard Mayde say to Mitti Diebitsch: "Once again, Jo has gone out and left us with the Eskimo girl."

"She's no trouble."

"But, Mother. She's slow-witted. She doesn't seem to understand anything I try to teach her. What are we supposed to *do* with her all day?"

"What we always do, Mayde. Sew, embroider, bake. She can watch us. Play the piano for her; she likes that."

Mayde was calling me *slow*? I felt ashamed.

A short time later, while Mayde played the piano, which I *had* come to like if the sounds felt cheerful, Mitti Diebitsch brought out a piece of thin cloth, blue as the summer sky. She spread it on the dining table. With a pencil she drew designs, then cut the shapes with scissors.

It wasn't long before she was stitching two pieces together, making a tiny dress.

I stood beside her. "I can ... sew. Give ... give me needle!"

The old woman gazed at me intently as I threaded a needle. Making my finest, smallest stitches, I joined two of the pieces of fabric. What joy! It seemed forever since I'd helped my mother make clothes.

"Why, Billy Bah!" Mitti Diebitsch said. "You sew beautifully." Her smile felt like the sun.

By the time Mitti Peary joined us, we'd finished the dress and slipped it on Marie's doll. Marie babbled happily.

"Not only can the girl speak English, she can sew better than I," the old woman told her daughters. I felt a flood of pride as they examined my stitches.

"She's full of pure enthusiasm for her work," Mitti Diebitsch went on. "I believe she could make a lady's gown in a single day."

Mitti Peary looked at me. "Billy Bah, would you like to do more sewing?"

I beamed. "Yes."

My morning grew even happier. Mitti Peary took me upstairs to her room and opened a chest. Inside, in boxes with pictures on them, were needles, thread, buttons, laces, ribbons, and materials of every color. She smiled and put a gold button in my hand.

The shiny, patterned button and scraps of the blue material I gathered from the table became the start of my collection of treasures. One day, I'd describe the white man's world to my family. With my treasures, my proof, I'd show them the beauty and the strangeness of the place. Without these things, no one would truly believe I had seen such wonders.

* * *

Now, in Musk Ox Land, snug and warm between layers of thick seal furs, I awoke to sounds of children all talking at once. Then a woman said: "They don't think they can save the ship." *Save the ship?* What was happening? I sat up and rubbed my eyes. A small boy and girl crouched around a cooking pot, taking turns sipping soup from it. As the previous night came back to me, I recognized the shapeless woman with long white hair sitting next to them.

After Duncan put us ashore, Angulluk and I had struggled against the wind to set up our tent. As we fought the snowstorm to find a temporary shelter, we were lucky, and came across the old woman's igloo. She and her son and daughter-in-law had welcomed us and given us warm musk ox broth. We'd feasted on musk ox meat and fallen asleep.

Now my eyes met hers. The white-haired woman said, "You look better today. My name is Navarana. Tell me yours again."

"Eqariusaq." Then I added, "The *qallunaat* call me Billy Bah."

"What does it matter what the *qallunaat* say?" She

scowled. "Eqariusaq is a good name. I don't like this other one—Bill-eee baah."

"I like it."

She eyed the ribbon in my hair as I studied the deep, wavy lines on her forehead. Her teeth were ground down to tiny stubs from chewing hides. I had rarely seen a person so old. She must have been more than sixty winters; most of our people died by the time they'd seen forty.

She looked at me with sympathy. Her shrewd eyes told me that she already knew and understood everything about me. "You were exhausted. You must have slept well."

"*Ii,*" I said. "Very well, Aana." Grandmother, our greeting for an elder woman. I stretched out my cramped legs. The fierce storm had forced snow inside the fur cuffs of my *kapatak,* leaving me wet and stiff all the way to my bones.

"The wind was very strong most of the night. You slept through all that howling."

"It was the best rest I've had in many nights," I said. "I'm grateful to you for taking care of my husband and me. Is he looking for our tent?"

She nodded kindly. "Tending to that and to your dogs. My son and his wife are down on the beach. Come, have some broth."

What did she mean about saving the ship? I was keen to know. But it would be rude to ask too many questions before we'd been properly acquainted. I joined Navarana and the children at the center of the igloo. A pretty girl about Marie's age handed me the cooking pot. She had laughing eyes and a space between her two large front teeth. I silently named her Tooth Girl.

The delicious broth warmed me.

After the meal, I ventured, "Did I hear you say something about the ship?"

"That big ship is lying on its side over the rocks."

A shipwreck! Duncan—hurt, or dead? Marie? Mitti Peary? I stood up.

"Let the men do their work. Now you should rest."

"Aana." I spoke more sharply than I intended. "I must see what is happening."

"As you like."

I pulled on my *kamiit* and furs, crawled out the entranceway, and started into the freezing air. Tooth Girl followed me out and dashed off toward the shore.

Though the blizzard was over, flakes of snow swirled around me. I relieved my bladder in a hole some distance from the igloo—how good it was not to have to use a bucket. From the top of the gentle rise where the people of this village had built their igloos, I looked at the harbor.

The light revealed an eerie scene: in the distance, the *Windward* was stuck in shallow waters, tilted away toward a shoal of rocks that thrust up like a whale's jagged teeth. I could make out Captain Bartlett and others, some in the blue uniforms of officers, wading in waist-high water. They gripped ropes tied to the ship's masts. On a second reef, closer to the shore, several more crewmembers struggled to secure the lines around massive boulders, trying to keep the ship from toppling over.

The fate of the ship did not look good. But the passengers had managed to get off. As many as thirty men, our men in addition to the crew, crowded a small, snow-covered spit of land. Some of them unloaded cargo from rowboats and stacked it into large piles at the water's rocky edge. Others rolled barrels and dragged crates up the beach past the irregular line of seaweed that marked the tide.

I saw Bag of Bones stacking boxes, but no Angulluk. I'd find him later.

I spotted Marie, a small figure in a green cloak alongside Mitti Peary. They were heaving and rolling a big barrel up from the shoreline.

I made my way along the beach as fast as I could go over the rocks and huge drifts of snow. I waved. "Marie! Mitti Peary!"

Marie ran toward me, stumbled on a rock, and picked herself up. She threw her arms around me. "Oh, Billy Bah!" Her eyes were bright. "We've had such adventures!"

"What happened? The ship has almost tipped over!"

"I nearly fell out of my bunk, but my blankets held me in. We could hardly walk when the ship was turned on its side! Mother made me put on all three of my dresses and my cloak."

I laughed. She *did* look plump. I was so grateful that she was alive that I hadn't noticed.

Her breath puffed into the frosty air. "Mother and I slid down the deck on our bottoms. Right into the rowboat!"

"You're a brave girl, Marie." I looked over at Mitti Peary struggling with the barrel. Her long skirts were soaked at the bottom. "Let's help your mother."

Mitti Peary's eyes offered me half a smile. She was too out of breath to say much.

While Marie skipped around us, her mother and I heaved the barrel above the tide line. We went back and pushed another; then we dragged a crate. Marie carried tackles and ropes. The growing piles on the upper beach, shielded by snow-covered tarpaulins, looked like sleeping walrus.

Mitti Peary sat down on the crate with a weary sigh, shivering. I sat beside her on a barrel and we faced the water and the tilted ship. Mitti Peary turned to Marie, who was climbing up the pile. "Marie! This is not a place to play. Go run on the beach."

"Come with me, Billy Bah." Marie grabbed my mittened hand.

"Not now," I said. "Maybe we'll have time later."

"Don't go far!" Mitti Peary called to Marie.

Already dashing away, she ran through the snow, heading toward the upper beach. Beyond it rose snow-covered hills and icy mountain peaks.

"Heaven knows how she can keep going like that," Mitti Peary said. The feathers on her hat were soggy and crumpled. Her long brown hair hung damp about her shoulders.

The tide had gone out farther, and the ship, tied to boulders by two long ropes, leaned at an even sharper angle than before. The ropes seemed strained to a breaking point.

Mitti Peary sighed again. "I don't know what we'll do if the *Windward* is lost."

"The ship could right itself if there's water under it," I said, making sure to pronounce every word correctly. "The tide will start coming in."

Mitti Peary nodded. "We can only hope and pray for a miracle."

"How did the ship end up against the rocks?"

"During the night, the sailor on watch wasn't doing his job. He must have wrapped himself heavily against the wind and fallen asleep. The gale blew the *Windward* from its mooring, and it drifted against the shoal. Before the crew could move it, the tide had pulled out, and the ship was stranded."

"Did anyone freeze? Or drown?"

"Everybody made it to shore. For a few hours last night, Marie and I took shelter in an igloo. The Eskimos here welcomed us."

"The people did the same for my husband and me."

She sprang to her feet. "Good Lord, I think that's my trunk!"

We hurried down to the shore. Duncan, his red hair frozen in points that stuck out from beneath his blue wool cap, came wading through the water, protected by high slick boots.

Kiihal. I stopped in my tracks and breathed a sigh of relief. He pulled a rowboat loaded with goods. With some effort, he wrapped his gloves around Mitti Peary's trunk and heaved it onto the beach.

He gave a weary smile, his face raw and red, and I guessed he'd been out in the storm all night. "Hello, Billy Bah." His voice was hoarse. "I was looking for you. Glad to see you made it through."

I greeted him with my eyes, and copied his words. "I'm glad you're safe."

Mitti Peary and I each took a handle of the trunk and dragged it up the beach, often stopping to rest. At last we reached the tide line. She sat and caught her breath. "Thank you for your help."

"You're welcome," I remembered to say.

Pleased and proud, I turned toward the village. Marie appeared in the distance, running alongside a child about her size. "Marie's found a friend."

"So I see."

They reached the top of the hill and disappeared from sight.

"Marie is very naughty. I warned her to stay close by," said Mitti Peary. "What if she gets lost?"

"I'll fetch her."

"Billy Bah, *thank you* again. I couldn't manage without you!"

I trudged up the beach, following Marie's footprints: Her boots had heels. Next to hers were the softer oval prints made by a child of our people.

The prints followed tracks that were round and spiked by claw marks. They'd spotted a fox. I followed the tracks beyond the hill and into a little valley where the fox tracks met with the hopping trail of rabbit feet at a frozen pond.

Marie should know better than to stray, I thought.

I followed the tracks up the valley. Here the children's voices must have chased the wary fox away from the trail. I could see only the rabbit's tracks continuing around a big boulder. There they were!

"Marie!"

"Shhh," whispered the other child. Her hood was round, the shape of a girl's *kapatak*.

Just beyond the boulder, an enormous rabbit as white as the snow sniffed the air. Marie crept toward it, and it vanished behind rocks.

Marie brushed snow off her coat, forlorn. "I wanted him for a pet."

"Keeping animals in cages is foolish," I said. "And you can't catch rabbits without traps." I added, "You shouldn't have wandered off. I spent a lot of time looking for you."

"Sorry." Marie looked down at her boots.

The other girl looked up, eyes smiling. It was Tooth Girl. "I'm Akitsinnguaq. I know you. You're Eqariusaq."

"That's right," I said, still cross. "Let's go. We need to go see about the ship, and find my husband."

The girls bounded ahead like sled dogs let out of a harness. I hadn't seen Marie run off on her own like this—so foolish, in this land she did not know.

"Don't run on the icy patches."

Marie fell, but jumped to her feet again.

The sun, now partway down to the horizon, told me that it was mid-afternoon. Time to find Angulluk, see what kind of a camp he'd made, and if he'd caught us anything for dinner. Even more than that, I wanted to know if the *Windward* had escaped the icy waters and sharp rocks.

The girls raced over the last hill that separated us from the beach. I followed, breathing fast. As I neared the top, I heard shouting.

Marie called, "Billy Bah! Look!"

CHAPTER NINE

● ● ● ● ● ● ● ●

The *Windward*, still tilted on its side, slowly moved out from the shoal in the blue-black water. It rocked one way, then the other, then stood upright. The water had risen on the rocks and was climbing the sloping beach toward the tidemark.

I half slid down the bluff and ran as fast as I could toward the crowd on the beach. The *Windward*'s crew were making a storm of their own by their yelling. "Hip, hip, hooray!"

Their happiness made me shout for joy.

Angulluk came toward me. "There you are, woman!" His bushy eyebrows knit together. "Where did you go? I wanted you to help me raise the tent."

"I didn't know where you were, either. I was busy unloading the ship."

Though Angulluk still frowned, I rubbed noses with him. The familiar smell of his damp furs mingled with the cold, salty wind.

"Lucky for the *qallunaat*," I said. "They won't be stranded here."

"I suppose not." The righting of the ship didn't mean

much to Angulluk if it wasn't going to return us to Itta. He didn't seem to care if we were stranded here; a village that didn't know his reputation for laziness was an opportunity to prove himself.

All the *qallunaat* possessions lay stacked on the sand. The ship couldn't be leaving for America right away. Could it?

Angulluk said firmly, "Let's tend to our tent."

Dogs barked as we climbed toward the village. Our dogs were tied together with many others on the bluff, though a few slept curled outside the entranceways of their masters' igloos. Our small tent stood between two igloos, shielded from the wind. Soon I had my two seal-oil lamps filled and lit; our home was cozy enough as we ate the seal meat Angulluk had hunted during our journey. With our fur covers, our cooking pot, my chest of keepsakes, and all our other tools, hunting gear, and belongings around us, life was almost the same as in Itta. No, not quite. Angulluk untied my pink ribbon, which wasn't so clean now, and ran his hands over my hair. "No trades. Tonight you are mine."

I was glad to be with him, too. Perhaps I'd forget all about the *qallunaat* in a few days. But during that night, when I awoke to the howling of the wind, I wondered what had happened to Duncan and the ship.

* * *

The next day, a bright sun shone without giving much heat. As we sat outside our tent, making a meat rack from bones and sinew, blasts of sound rumbled over the ridge. "That's not like any gunshots I ever heard," Angulluk said.

"Dynamite." I'd seen Peary's sailors use it to break apart ice floes.

"For once, woman, you must be right."

"A man is admitting his ignorance?" I let my work fall and leapt up. "Let's go look." Others came out of their tents and rock igloos as we neared the water.

During the night, the wind had shoved great masses of ice into the harbor. The ship was visible in the middle of the channel, high walls of ice on either side. In its path loomed a blue iceberg several times the height of the ship. The mountain of ice leaned over the ship like a monstrous wave about to break, blocking the *Windward*'s passage to the ocean.

A deep roar cut across the sparkling sound, followed by an even louder rumble as a piece of ice fell from the iceberg. The ship might be smashed, with Duncan, Marie, and Mitti Peary on it. My legs grew weak.

"They're trying to blow up the whole iceberg," Angulluk said. "Impossible!"

I nodded. Another explosion echoed. The ship swayed and seemed to move forward as a thin curl of smoke climbed the face of the ice.

I pictured Duncan and the sailors clinging to the rigging, hacking at the mountain, sections of ice crashing and shattering. Was Marie below deck, holding tight to her mother? Or did she think it was another jolly adventure?

A tremendous boom! The *Windward* rocked violently. Black smoke surrounded the ship and then parted into two clouds.

The iceberg stood, immovable.

All was silent, except for the whistling of the wind.

"That iceberg won't be going anywhere until next summer," Angulluk said. "Why such a mournful face? Do you really care what happens to them?"

I felt a lump in my throat.

"Even if the ship sinks, the *qallunaat* can get to land by rowboat," Angulluk said. "It's only a matter of time, anyway, until the ice freezes over. Then they can walk here."

Winter is coming on fast. Walking to the ship would make visits so much easier. Perhaps I'll see Duncan in passing soon. Now that Angulluk and I were off the *Windward,* it was unlikely that he'd trade me to a sailor.

As we left for the village, the clouds drifted from the ship and hovered like flocks of gray birds over the icy harbor.

* * *

I went down to the beach every day to check on the ship. More floes had drifted together. Five days after the attempt to blow apart the iceberg, the harbor froze over into a hilly mass. I ventured onto the ice a short way, and it began to splinter with a cracking sound; I'd have to wait to see Duncan.

Meanwhile, our group from Itta were busy among the people of this shore. Angulluk and several other men left to hunt musk oxen, taking Bag of Bones.

Most days, Ally and I took our work to grandmother Navarana's igloo while the men were away. As we chewed hides and stitched, she made delicious soups out of bones, scraps, and salty seaweed and used a walrus rib to pull out the tasty morsels. She was good company, smarter than an old fox who'd survived many seasons of hunting. She scolded us, but also praised my sewing. There was room in her igloo for us all: Ally and Sammy and me; Navarana's daughter, Mikihoq, a small, quiet woman with thinning hair and big eyes; and Mikihoq's two children, Tooth Girl (Akitsinnguaq), and her brother, Magtaaq, who was about two winters old. His red nose always seemed to be dripping, so I named him Runny Nose. Mikihoq seldom spoke to me and I knew she didn't like me, but her children were friendly.

Everyone loved Sammy, Navarana especially. No doubt she'd never seen blue eyes like his on a baby of our people; and she liked his mischievous grin. One day as we chewed seal hides to soften them for sewing, Sammy pulled himself up on the frame of the sleeping platform and stood. He'd done this before, but now Sammy discovered if he held on to the platform with his two chubby hands, he could take a step.

"Look! He's nearly walking!" the old woman said.

"He learns fast," Ally boasted.

Tooth Girl, playing with her ivory animals, looked up and clapped her hands. Her mother, who was breast-feeding Runny Nose, also smiled.

I went on chewing my pelt. As if reading my thoughts, the old woman said, "Eqariusaq, you never know what will come. Perhaps soon you will have a baby of your own."

"No, Aana," I said.

"Why not?"

"I don't know. After many seasons—I am blessed with nothing."

"Wait and see. You are young and healthy. You have many seasons for children to come to you."

"Maybe."

I wondered if my sister, Nuljalik, had become pregnant. How I wished I could talk to her. How was life for her now that winter was here? Was she getting enough to eat? Perhaps our seasons without much food were why my people did not often conceive. And I suspected the cold had something to do with it. Like most women, I rarely had a time of bleeding. Luckily, Angulluk was so lazy, he was glad that he didn't have children to feed.

That day, Sammy waddled back and forth, delighted with himself. Soon he held on to the platform with only one little hand.

"Your baby has blue eyes," the old woman said to Ally. "You and Eqariusaq spend time with the *qallunaat*, don't you? That is why Mikihoq is afraid to become friendly with you. Do the women of your own village avoid you, too?"

A sad expression passed over Ally's radiant face.

I answered for her. "That's not true, Aana," I said sharply. "Ally and I have many women friends on the other shore."

"If you say so."

We all knew I'd lied. Navarana was like Mitti Peary's looking glass. She made me see myself: a young woman ignored and often disliked by other women.

Ally picked up Sammy, rubbed noses with him, and put him to her breast. Gazing into his blue eyes, she was all smiles again. She picked lice off his head as he drank her milk. Nothing could take away her joy in having a baby: not Peary's absence, nor the early winter, nor the ship locked in ice. How lucky she was that Piugaattoq treated Sammy as his own.

"Now I have something to tell you," Navarana announced. "My father was a *qallunaaq!*" She laughed gruffly.

Ally and I looked at her, astounded. Though an occasional whaling ship passed by Itta, the only ship that had ever stopped was Peary's.

"Are you related to those people who built the fort?" Ally asked.

"No, Daughter, another ship came before that. Men who hunted whales. They didn't stay long, but long enough to give my mother a baby!" To my astonishment, she retrieved a steel axe with a wooden handle from a bag that she kept in her entrance tunnel. "My father left it behind so I'd have it when I was old enough to use it."

"A rare and excellent gift," I said.

Ally and her husband, too, had an axe. We used them for chopping frozen meat. All three of us had great wealth from white men.

"Perhaps my mother spared my life because of this one very useful tool," Navarana said. "In my day, many girl babies had to be killed."

Ally and I looked at each other, frowning. During very lean winters in Itta, mothers smothered their infant daughters. They allowed their sons to live because they'd grow up to provide for the community.

"Do others in the village have axes? Rifles?" I asked.

Navarana shook her head. "But I'm sure you've noticed that we have harpoons and sled runners made of wood. There have been several shipwrecks on this shore. Whalers."

As Sammy slept, the women and I stitched skins together. Before long, I heard people talking outside. I went into the entranceway and started to put on my furs.

The flap of the igloo opened and cold air rushed in. "Billy Bah," a small voice piped. "Are you here?"

CHAPTER TEN

● ● ● ● ● ● ● ●

Marie's bright face peered at me through the entranceway flap. She wore a baggy sailor's cap pulled over her ears. "Billy Bah!"

Mitti Peary, crouching behind Marie, gave me a tired smile. "Hello there. Thank the Lord we've found you."

I was just as happy to see them. "Are you all right? Was the ship saved?"

"The ship is fine," Marie said. "Mother and I walked over the ice. The Eskimos on the beach told me where you were."

"You spoke to them in my language?"

"*Ii.*" Marie was smart.

"Come in!" I said eagerly. Marie slipped inside, and Mitti Peary crawled after her.

"Why, Billy Bah!" Marie said. "No clothes. Only fur panties!" Marie never seemed to understand our ways.

"The igloo is very warm. Inside our homes we never wear clothes."

I rolled up Marie's and her mother's cloaks. They followed me through the tunnel into the round room. Marie joined us on the platform of furs while her mother, even after removing her hat, needed to sit on the floor so she wouldn't bump her head.

Tooth Girl and her mother and grandmother began talking at once, Tooth Girl rubbing noses with Marie. Sammy and Runny Nose both woke. Marie picked up Sammy and kissed him.

Mitti Peary said, "I'm glad to see you all."

"I'm very glad to see *you*," I said in English, careful to say the words clearly.

Marie spoke in a rush. "So much has happened, Billy Bah. When the ship lay on its side, water came in and flooded our bunks. Mother and I have been sleeping in the forward saloon until everything dries out. Our cabin smells nasty! It's so cold my oatmeal freezes in my bowl! Captain Bartlett says we'll be trapped in the ice for eleven months. I'm *happy* that the ship can't move—"

Mitti Peary said, "The ship locked in ice is not something to be happy about."

"But, Mother, now I can see Billy Bah and Akitsinnguaq and Qaorlutoq. At home, I'd be at school."

Mitti Peary's chest rose and fell in an enormous sigh. Tooth Girl and her mother and grandmother all asked me what Marie said. I did my best to translate, though soon my throat felt dry from talking so much.

"Don't bother repeating every little story of Marie's," Mitti Peary said. "I have something important to say." I could feel her thinking and planning. "Marie and I need good, winter fur clothes like yours. We have needles and

77

other supplies we can give you and your friends. Can you help us, Billy Bah?"

What joy! Mitti Peary wanted *me* to sew for her! I caught my breath and began to translate, but Ally beat me to it. She knew some English, of course. I let her talk.

One by one, all the women said they would help.

Ally beamed her lovely smile at Mitti Peary. "Yes, we can all sew clothes for you."

I translated for the old woman, Navarana. She told Mitti Peary, "To survive the winter, you and your daughter will need *kapatait,* mittens, leggings, fox skin trousers, and women's boots: *kamiit.*"

Marie clapped her hands in delight.

Our women talked noisily. Making clothing required a great number of animal pelts and furs. To obtain them, our men would spend one or two moons hunting and trapping. Mitti Peary said she'd provide guns and ammunition as rewards.

"Our men will be glad we have work." I smiled. For the first time in my life, I'd negotiated an exchange. Angulluk would be happy and the sewing would mean an opportunity to see Duncan.

Tooth Girl dumped a pile of tiny ivory animals on the musk ox fur bedding. She and Marie hopped and flew them around and gave the animals voices like peeping chicks.

As she held Sammy, Ally looked at me smugly. She, too, had translated for Mitti Peary. Or perhaps she was showing off her baby. I looked away.

Her voice low, she said to me in our language, "I'll be the one to make Marie's *kapatak*."

"Certainly not," I said firmly. "Marie is my special friend. I'll make her *kapatak*."

The *kapatak* is the most beautiful and important garment of our people. A hooded fur coat shows the skill and artistry of its maker. "You can sew Marie's mittens," she said.

"I will not!" I snapped. "Don't insult me."

Ally smiled sweetly. "You can sew better than any of us—that's true! But that doesn't give you the right to make Marie's *kapatak*. Other matters count more."

"I know, and I *do* have the right." My voice rose. "It's not just that I can sew better than you. Marie and I are like sisters. I cared for her in America."

"Hold your tongue!" old Navarana hissed to Ally.

Ally pouted with her full lips. Mitti Peary frowned. How much did she understand?

Ally craftily switched to English. She looked straight at Mitti Peary. "I will make Marie's coat! Don't forget, Marie is Sammy's sister: *Sammy is Pearyaksoah's son.*"

Mitti Peary looked like she'd been snapped with a dog whip. Her eyes popped open and her jaw dropped. She spoke low. *"Sammy is Lieutenant Peary's son?"*

"Yes." Ally looked especially self-satisfied. "The Great Peary is my baby's father."

I could hardly believe that Ally would be so foolish as to boast of her relationship with Peary to his wife. I'd thought Ally understood the *qallunaat* better, that they do not trade their wives or have more than one. I'd assumed Peary had never told Mitti Peary about Ally—and I was right. I looked over at Marie, who was busy with Tooth Girl.

Mitti Peary straightened her back and brushed hairs off her dress. "I see." She puckered her lips, thinking, then said, "Ally, you and Billy Bah each have your own special relationship with our family. You shall make Marie's *kapa-tak*. Billy Bah shall make mine."

Ally beamed.

"All right," I said crossly. Mitti Peary was giving in to Ally? She wasn't angry with her? But she gave me a look of misery and I knew she was holding back tears.

An uneasy silence followed. Sammy began crawling to the children and reaching for toy animals from their pile. Mitti Peary grabbed Sammy, brought him back to her corner of the platform, bounced him on her lap, and looked into his blue eyes.

Navarana began cutting chunks of pink seal meat.

Mitti Peary looked at our good meat as if it were rotten waste. *Qallunaat* never eat raw meat, but I also sensed she wanted to leave us. She rose, and handed Sammy back to his mother. Her voice broke. "Marie, it's time we return to the ship."

Marie looked up from her play. "Please, let's stay a little longer, Mother."

"No, we must go right away. Our supper will be ready

on the ship." She turned to us. "Thank you, Billy Bah. Thank you, everyone. We'll visit again."

Marie held Sammy and kissed him. Had she heard Ally say he was her brother? I didn't think so, but she loved him like a brother just the same.

Tooth Girl gave Marie a little walrus she'd made. In the entranceway, Mitti Peary and Marie put on their outside clothes, and Marie carefully tucked the little figure inside one of her thin wool mittens.

"I'll see you soon!" she said, then crawled outside.

Inside the igloo, Ally gave me a smile. "Perhaps you can help me sew Marie's *kapatak*."

"All right."

Tooth Girl and her brother grabbed hunks of seal meat out of the pot. The igloo filled with sounds of talking and eating, but I just sat and watched everyone while brooding. Ally was my only friend, so I had to pretend our arguments meant nothing.

It was only seven nights since the ship had become locked in the ice. I hadn't known if I'd ever see Marie again, and now here she was, her cheerful self. We'd be together all winter and the following spring. Angulluk would hunt for the *qallunaat*, and I'd make clothing for them with the skins and furs he provided.

Mitti Peary relies on me. Marie needs me. I have a place in their world, and I'll show them how talented I am with the needle.

Navarana spoke to everyone, but I felt as if she were talking to me. "Well! The *qallunaat* need clothing. It is right to give them clothes and help them survive the winter. But I want you all to be very careful."

She looked from face to face until her eyes rested on mine. "Remember, Eqariusaq. They come to our land, take what they want, and leave. My mother was very upset when my father left. She often spoke of it. You need to remain apart."

What does the old woman know about the qallunaat? *She hasn't lived in America.* But out of respect, I said, "I agree, Aana."

"Panik, I don't think you're listening to me."

"But I *am* careful." I pushed away a sudden memory of watching my parents leave for America on Peary's ship.

Navarana handed me a chunk of meat. The wrinkles on her forehead joined as she knit her brow. "You shouldn't be so eager to please the *qallunaat*. It's not that they are all bad-tempered and greedy. Some may be good. But if they want something, they will use any excuse to have it, and they will forget you when it's convenient. It's your husband you should be thinking about, sewing for *him*, caring for *him*. And when the time comes, for your children."

Why did the old woman keep talking about my having a baby?

"Aana," I said. "I don't need to be afraid of the *qallunaat*. I have lived with Mitti Peary in her home across the ocean. She and her family have been kind to me. It's my husband who is the greedy one. He wants the *qallunaat's* guns and other things, so he trades me. We have everything we need, and still he seeks more."

"A taste for the *qallunaat*'s riches? A greed that is never satisfied? That's no good." The old woman's eyes grew deep in thought. "Greed makes us confused, makes our minds like blizzards. Worse, greed separates us from each other. We are happiest when we give to others. All our people know this; you and Angulluk need to stay in the village so you can remember our ways."

"But our lives are already bound up with the *qallunaat*. Some are friends. It's not so simple—"

"It *is* simple! We have our lives and they have theirs!" She sucked in her wrinkled cheeks.

I wished I'd held my tongue. "You speak many truths, Aana." Still, could one who spent her days staring at the same landscape completely understand my life?

I waited for her advice. But she was silent.

CHAPTER ELEVEN

● ● ● ● ● ● ● ●

One moon passed without a visit from anyone on the *Windward*. Though I missed Duncan, I was busy. Even Angulluk knew there was no time for games. We needed to hunt and store away furs for Mitti Peary and Marie, and Angulluk and I needed new leggings, boots, and mittens. We hunted seals on the coast, and took trips to the nearby hills and valley to build traps for foxes and rabbits, and search for a herd of musk oxen. When at last Angulluk killed two seals, six rabbits, and a fox, I stayed in the village to cure their pelts and to soften them with my teeth. Two days later, I gave my aching jaws a rest and rejoined the hunt.

One of our dogs had six puppies: five black-and-brown and a runt that was all reddish brown. It was a happy time. I even began to daydream that I was pregnant. *I'll return to Itta with a baby in my arms. Won't my sister and all the villagers be surprised?* I would show them I had not only a child but also a skillful husband who did his share of work.

One morning a chilly wind blew through the sides of

our tent and we knew that winter had truly begun. "Go gather rocks, Eqariusaq," Angulluk said. "We need to make our igloo."

Hours later, on the land near our tent, he laid rocks on top of one another in a circle, and soon the walls of the igloo rose to my waist. My lazy man was doing a very good job. Inside the wall we used more stones to build a circular platform. The house was sunk a little into the earth so the platform would be level with the ground outside. *I can't wait to put down our furs and try out our new bed. Maybe it will be a lucky bed for us.*

Angulluk grinned. He knew I was pleased. We rubbed noses. He playfully tugged a fistful of my hair. We were getting along like *nanoq* cubs in a den.

When I was crouching to loosen a stone frozen to the ground, I felt a tap on my shoulder. "Boo!"

"Marie!"

She giggled. She looked silly in her layers of dresses, sweaters, and cloak. "My mother is talking to some of the men in the village. I wanted to come along."

What does Mitti Peary want from the hunters? I wondered. Navarana said the *qallunaat* were greedy. But if Mitti Peary ever asked anything of my people, she always gave generous gifts in return.

"Can I help you build your igloo?" Marie asked.

I showed her how to scrape moss from boulders with one of Angulluk's knives and where to add these stones to a pile. When Marie staggered forward with a rock, Angulluk quickly stepped over to lift it from her. "*Qujanaq,*" she thanked him. She could now speak our language without much effort.

Angulluk laughed. "You're welcome," he said in English. We'd all changed from our time on the ship, and one of the most surprising changes was that Angulluk seemed to like Marie.

He turned to me. "Why don't you show Marie the puppies?"

"Puppies!" Marie said.

I explained that the mother dog and puppies were in the ruins of an abandoned igloo, in the area where most villagers kept their dogs.

Marie begged, "Take me to see them!"

At the igloo with the puppies, the mother dog turned with a growl.

"Marie!" I pulled her away. "Don't touch. There is no such thing as a pet in our land."

"I'm going to help you name them."

"We don't name our dogs."

"The spotted is Patches. The little one is Cinnamon."

"The runt doesn't always survive."

"Oh, Cinnamon will live." Marie was sure, just like Peary. "May I keep her?"

"No, sled dogs aren't pets."

She pouted. We returned to find Mitti Peary sitting on a pile of stones, talking to Angulluk. He continued to build the walls of our igloo, which now rose as high as my hood top; he'd even started the entrance tunnel.

"Woman, find me a stone for our roof," he said. Was he trying to send me away from their conversation?

"I've already looked. There aren't any." The large, flat stones near the village had long since been taken for that purpose.

The Fat One bristled. "I'll have to do it myself, then, you stupid seal."

He stomped off and I fixed my eyes on Mitti Peary. She looked away, as if she could hear my thoughts. *I care about you and Marie. I'll gladly make your clothes. But don't ask for too much. If it's meat you want, you'll need to find it elsewhere.*

When Angulluk could not find a stone for the roof, we used a heavy walrus hide, weighing the skin down with rocks so fierce winds wouldn't blow it away. Tooth Girl and Runny Nose slipped in and out of the new igloo with Marie until the sky faded into a blue twilight. Though it was early afternoon, the air grew colder and our breath formed clouds.

Mitti Peary nodded kindly at me. "Good-bye, Billy Bah." Then to Angulluk, "We'll talk again soon," she said as she walked away.

I tugged Angulluk's arm. "What did you promise her?"

In the second before he turned, refusing to look at me, I detected a pained look in his eyes. What was it? Shame. Somehow, Mitti Peary had gotten the upper hand.

* * *

Just as Angulluk and I spread our skins on our sleeping platform, Bag of Bones arrived.

Even before he poked his head into the entranceway, I could smell his dirty, wet furs. *"Hainang,"* he said cheerfully.

"We're busy," I snapped. Was he looking for handouts? All villagers were welcome to take from anyone's meat rack. But no able hunter took without good reason.

As it happened, he wanted Angulluk to give him a few of our puppies, as a start to his first dog team.

"I'll think it over," Angulluk replied.

Bag of Bones beamed.

Bag of Bones is working his way into our lives, I thought as he scampered off. Perhaps it was a good thing. Giving him dogs meant that he would be obligated to do some hunting for us.

"We should have offered Qaorlutoq a place to sleep," Angulluk said.

"He knows how to take care of himself," I replied. "He's used to the cold and he can feed himself. I remember when he ate nothing but birds' eggs. Now he traps rabbits and foxes."

"And he's learning to hunt seals," Angulluk said. "He's more skillful than most boys." He paused. "I'm going to get him a rifle and teach him to shoot."

"Oh? Is that what you were talking about with Mitti Peary?"

88

"Partly. She asked me to find Peary. I said I'd try, and for company I'd take Qaorlutoq. He'd go, if he had his own rifle."

"But no one can get to the fort," I said. Massive snowbanks kept us from going north, where Peary made his home in a fort abandoned by white men who had starved to death.

"I tried to explain. She still doesn't understand. She thinks we could trek on the sea ice, then go inland. I suppose it's possible."

I playfully poked him in the ribs, but he didn't poke me back, a bad sign. "You and I have done enough for Mitti Peary. Stay here and let some of the others go look for her husband."

"Mitti Peary can't find anyone willing to go. Aside from the dangers of the ice, the hunters fear spirits of the white men who died. They think Peary and his men might also be dead."

"Do you think Peary's dead?"

"I don't know."

"You're only thinking of going because you're greedy," I said with disgust. "You have no sense at all."

He let out an exasperated sigh. "Woman, I need bullets."

I'd heard that one before! He should learn to hunt without using so many bullets.

"You stupid man. Peary is a long way away. The snow beyond the shore could be very deep. And you'll never get anywhere unless there's a full moon and clear skies."

"Exactly." He looked smug. "We won't get very far."

"I don't understand."

"Mitti Peary said she'd pay me to *search* for her husband. She didn't say I had to *find* him."

"What! You're even greedier than I thought. I just may tell Mitti Peary that you're fooling her. You're no good. I'm ashamed of you." I drew back. "Someday I'll leave you." In the past I'd often threatened to divorce him, but I hadn't suggested it lately; I was as surprised by my words as he was.

"Oh? Who will replace me?" he asked.

Maybe a white man. "I haven't decided yet."

Angulluk managed a feeble smile, as if I'd been joking.

An idea popped into my head and I dared to say it out loud. I'd find out how good I was at persuading the Fat One, or at least how much he valued me. "Mitti Peary wants me to come to the *Windward* when I sew her clothes." I paused. "Since I'll already be working on the ship, it makes sense for me to spend my nights there, too. Until you return, why not trade me to Duncan? You could get another block of wood that way."

He frowned. Then, "I don't like trading you to the *qallunaat*."

"You may only be gone a short time."

"If I trade you, it will be for bullets, nothing less. And Duncan may not be the one who gets you."

I took a long breath and tried to calm myself. Maybe this wasn't such a good idea. Taking a different approach,

I repeated what Duncan had told me. "The only guns and ammunition on board belong to Peary. And only Peary's wife and the captain have access to them. If you are convinced that you need more bullets, maybe there's another way. Use your wits, if you have any."

"Quiet, Eqariusaq!"

"You are a hundred times greedier than any *qallunaaq*, and uglier, too."

Did he plan to trade me or not? A sense of foreboding filled me.

CHAPTER TWELVE

● ● ● ● ● ● ● ●

Winter's darkness came to Musk Ox Land. As always, the change of seasons reminded me of Peary and something that happened when I was a child in Itta. When I pictured him, I saw a tall man, handsome, with reddish hair, marching up and down hills of snow and shouting orders.

"Peary is never still," my mother once said. "He makes me dizzy." Like all of us, she liked him best in small amounts.

I was six winters old on that moonless, frigid day when my family and I watched Peary and his men circling in a well-trampled loop around their camp. Leading four men, pounding his feet into the snow, Peary was bellowing, "One two three four five six seven eight!"

"Perhaps they need to stimulate their bowels," my mother suggested. "Ha! Too much white man's food gives them digestion problems."

"No, woman," said my father. "Peary marches his men around because they are terrified of the dark winter."

My parents laughed. Then my father said the men marched in a circle because they needed exercise. Living here was hard for them; during the winter's dark, they drank liquor, argued, senselessly hit one another, and, like fools, broke into fits of weeping.

Each time the men stomped by, panting, hands gripping the handles of their glowing lanterns, I braced myself in case one staggered off his path and hit us.

"Don't be afraid of these men. Don't be scared of anything." My father held me close. He knew my fear of the shadowy season we'd just entered. "Eqariusaq, look at the sky and tell me what color it is."

"Purple," I said, taking in the gently glowing sweep of the friendly Ancestors. Called the Northern Lights by the *qallunaat,* the Ancestors shone radiantly against a background of endless stars.

"Exactly so. And at midday, if you look to the horizon, you will see a flush of pink. Remember that if you hear the white men say, 'The winter sky is as black as a grave, as black as death.' They don't know what we know."

"Yes, Ataata."

His cheerful voice eased my fears, though I still couldn't embrace the darkness of winter like an old friend as he did.

Peary's men kept marching in a circle, as if to break through the darkness of their imaginations. I bit my lip, held my father's hand, and watched. Only years later, after I'd returned from the white man's land, did I fully appreciate the calm and softness, the peace and joy, of our starry season. By then I'd learned about real terrors.

* * *

The village moved into our cycle of starlit days. In a different time, I'd have welcomed the full moon, now shining bright, and looked forward to being in Duncan's arms again. But this time the trade came with a cost: Angulluk could lose his life. He'd left early that morning with Bag of Bones and Ally's husband, Piugaattoq, to search for Peary. I couldn't stop the Fat One, and now I regretted our arguments over it. What if an avalanche swallowed him or if he froze to death after falling into a break in the ice?

At least I had a distraction. A pile of rabbit, seal, and fox pelts, already cured, waited on the *Windward*. It was time to make clothes for the Pearys. Sewing new clothes was always a celebration.

With my birdskin bag slung over my shoulder, containing my wooden chest of treasures as well as my sewing things, I trekked out onto the ice toward the *Windward*. Tooth Girl and her mother walked beside me, and Ally, carrying Sammy on her back, followed close behind. Cin, a skinny, long-legged puppy now, nipped at my heels. Cin would live on the ship; Angulluk was giving her to Marie. The runt would never grow large enough to be a sled dog, he supposed.

Old Navarana shuffled out of her warm igloo to walk with our group part of the way; but I knew it was because she had stern words for me. "You shouldn't sleep on the ship again."

"Angulluk traded me to a sailor. I must go, Aana."

"That's not why you're leaving us," she said. "I hear you arguing with your husband. You *want* to go. You want to be with this white man."

Ua! As usual, her words hit their mark. I clenched my hand inside my fur mitten.

"I'll be back in a few days." Would I? If Angulluk and the others made a real effort to reach the fort, it would take them at least five days out and five to return.

Navarana turned back. The four of us walked a curving path on the sound where the snow had blown away. A cold wind howled, and I faced the land to shield myself. Everything looked beautiful: the waves of shining white ice, the purple-gray sky in the moonlight, the snowy cliffs above the cluster of igloos and tents.

Crewmembers were piling up a snow wall around the ship and had stretched canvas over the ship's deck. A row of lanterns dangling in this shelter glowed like small suns, bringing the shadowed figures into focus.

Duncan stood near the rail. He waved to us as Marie called, "Hello!"

We heard the tops of the masts rattling. The wind had stripped the clumps of snow from the icy rigging. Ally with Sammy, Mikihoq, Tooth Girl, and I passed through the opening in the snow wall and climbed on steps made of crates. Cin reached the deck first, and Marie hugged her.

Duncan came forward; even in the moonlight I could see his wide smile. I wished I could see the color of his hair. "Billy Bah! I'm glad you're here."

Shyly, I smiled with my eyes.

Marie found an old boot and offered it to Cin, who came after it, growling.

Captain Bartlett and other crewmembers arrived to play with the puppy. Cin sank her teeth into the captain's leather glove and ran off with it. He shook his hand. "Her teeth are like razors."

Duncan wrestled the glove away from Cin as Captain Bartlett arranged a pen for the puppy against the wall of the pilothouse, under the shelter of the tarpaulin, and lined it with old blankets. "I can't have this rascal coming inside the ship."

Duncan said, "I'll make Cin a leash and collar." He moved close to me and took my hand. We stood, our faces nearly touching, until Mitti Peary appeared. She ushered my people into the forward saloon, with Duncan and me close behind. There we were met by a faint rotten smell, which came from a sea-drenched carpet rolled up on one side of the room. The space seemed emptier, larger, colder. I wished we could work in the cozy officers' sitting room.

But the seal pelts, thick and black and luxuriant, heaped in a great furry pile near a coal-burning stove, made a welcome sight. Rabbit and fox pelts, skins, and bushy foxtails rose in mounds on the far side of the saloon. Duncan and Mikihoq joined me in laying out the pelts. I stroked every one briefly.

In the center of the room, where there were no tables or chairs fastened to the floor, we took off our own outer furs and sat upon them. Duncan took a seat beside me and put his arm around me. I leaned into him.

Mitti Peary eyed Duncan. "Mr. Gaylor—that's your name?" Her lips tightened. "Surely you must have tasks to do. In a few minutes, the women will start sewing. We'll need our privacy."

"Certainly." Duncan smiled at me and left.

I measured Mitti Peary with my hands, trying to forget how she treated Duncan. Usually, I could look at someone and almost guess how many pelts would be needed, how that person moved, and how the fur would give and wear over time. But I'd never sewn a coat for a giant.

"Mitti Peary, stand up. Stretch out your arms," I said. She was so tall that I could not reach her armpits, so I stood on a chair.

She allowed me and Mikihoq to stretch her arms in all different directions, and she squatted, and bent over, as she was told. Mikihoq gasped as she measured Mitti Peary's long legs for *kamiit*.

Marie giggled and laughed as Ally and Tooth Girl positioned her in birdlike poses.

Ally had taken all five of the fox pelts. "Give some to me," I said.

"I'll need them for Marie." She was curt. "It will make her *kapatak* look pretty to have white sections as well as black."

"It's not fair that you should take the best furs," I grumbled, though there were plenty of good ones left.

I chose glossy black seal pelts for Mitti Peary. I rubbed a fur against my cheek: I loved its softness and its oily, rich smell.

Now I had to be very careful. One mistake could ruin the fine fur. I took a breath and cut the largest seal pelt with my *ulu*. I sliced in a straight line, trimming off the sections where the animal's legs had been. I paused to look. My mother would have been pleased by my work.

After cutting strips for the back, sleeves, and hood of the coat, I gave a sigh of relief. The hard part of shaping the pelts was done and I could relax while I trimmed off jagged pieces. Mikihoq had also finished the challenging work of slicing long, rectangular strips for Mitti Peary's *kamiit*.

When the edges of the pelts were even, we could begin to stitch the strips of fur together with sinew. Pushing the needle through the thick pelts was hard work, and the sewing would take many days.

While Mitti Peary sat on a chair, sipping tea, Marie scooped Sammy up off the floor. She held his chubby hands and walked him. Then they played peekaboo until Ally took him to nurse.

Marie wanted Tooth Girl to play hide-and-seek, but Tooth Girl's mother made her keep to her sewing. I put Marie to the task of stitching together scraps for her doll's coat. "I wrote a letter to my father," Marie said to me. "I gave it to Angulluk when he and the other Eskimos brought the furs. Do you think Dad will read my letter today?"

"Not today. The men have only just left."

Ally put down the fox pelts she was sewing and said gently, "Marie, it's a very long way from here to the fort. The snow is deep and there are many hills to cross. Even if our men do reach your father, you must not expect him to return to the ship. He can't walk as far as he used to."

Marie moaned softly.

Mitti Peary had been gazing blankly, hardly noticing us. But hearing this, she eyed Ally like a hawk. The captain must have told her that her husband had suffered from frostbite, but she wasn't aware that Ally often accompanied Peary to his camps on both sides of the sound; she'd made the difficult ice crossing with him several times, though she remained in Itta during his longer journeys. "Tell me, Ally. Is he walking? Or isn't he?"

"Pearyaksoah, the Great Peary, walks . . ." Ally hesitated. "Like a little child."

"You've seen him, then? Since the surgery?"

"Yes. He only has two toes. The little toes on each foot."

Mitti Peary gave a slight nod. Last winter, Peary had suffered frostbite during a long trek by dogsled. The *qallunaat* sawed off his dead, blackened toes.

"I washed his feet for him many times," Ally added. "I changed the bandages."

Mitti Peary stared at her and Sammy, who slept on his mother's lap. She held back tears. Didn't Ally realize she'd said too much?

Tooth Girl and her mother looked on, confused, not understanding our English. Mitti Peary knew this.

I filled in the silence. "Peary can walk and travel by sled, but it's hard to go very far in winter."

"But you know Pearyaksoah, the Great Peary, often accomplishes what other men cannot," Ally said. "Perhaps he will surprise us."

Mitti Peary turned toward a porthole and looked out. "Pearyaksoah, the *Great* Peary," she muttered. Something in her seemed about to break.

Quickly in our language, I said to Ally, "You've upset Mitti Peary. You shouldn't be flaunting your relationship with her husband. How could you be so stupid? Are you upsetting her on purpose?"

"No. Not on purpose," she replied, round eyes all innocence.

"I was glad for your company on this ship," I said. "Now I'm not so sure."

Her beautiful lips pursed together. I immediately regretted my words. But she honestly didn't seem to realize how her behavior posed a danger for all of us. Still, I shouldn't anger her; she might talk recklessly for spite.

"We've done enough sewing for today," I announced. Looking first at Ally, then Mitti Peary, I said, "Ally and the others will need to return to shore while there's still moonlight. I'll be staying."

Marie clapped her hands in happiness. But I noticed Mitti Peary's jaw tighten. She asked, "You'll be staying on the ship, Billy Bah? Are you sure this is what you want?"

"Yes." Noticing her frown, I said, "My husband arranged it."

Tooth Girl looked at me curiously. "But why?"

"Don't worry," I said. "We'll see each other tomorrow. You're coming back here with you mother and Ally to sew."

I turned to Mitti Peary. "I want to take a bath tonight. And from now on, may I use the toilet?"

"Yes, Billy Bah. Of course. I should have told you earlier," Mitti Peary replied. "But wouldn't it be best if you slept in the village? Would you like me to speak to the captain about it?"

"I'm staying." I felt a small triumph. But though she liked me, and had come to rely on me, her concern seemed mixed with contempt. I'd been traded to Duncan, and she disapproved.

As for Mitti Peary's attitude toward Ally, beneath her displays of generosity and goodwill, I sensed jealousy and even hate. Ally must have noticed, but she didn't let on. She packed up her sewing things, humming to herself.

Marie smiled at her baby brother.

CHAPTER THIRTEEN

• • • • • • • •

In my dream, my father and my mother stood on a lone ice floe. A channel of black water separated us. Across the water, firmly grasping his harpoon, Ataata bent over the edge of the ice and waited for a seal to surface. He brushed snow off his small mustache and beard. My tiny *anaana* bickered with him, as usual. "Choose another place to hunt."

"*Quiet, woman,*" he said.

"*I'm here!*" I called to them. "*Stop arguing. Can't you see me?*" At last, my father turned and his dark eyes met mine.

"*I've missed you these past winters and summers,*" I said.

His wrinkled brown face lit up. "*Panik, my daughter, I've missed you, too.*"

"*Are you ready to return among the living?*" I asked. "*Who would like to come first? May I be the one to receive you?*"

The spirits of my parents became hazy and disappeared. "Come back!" I called. I sat bolt upright and opened my eyes.

A crack of light slanted through the small porthole near Duncan's bunk. He woke. "What's the matter?"

"I had a dream."

"A bad one?"

"No." I reached for my birdskin shirt on the floor.

Much to my relief, he just kissed me on the forehead, then held me. His voice was low and gentle. "It's good to have you here again. I missed you."

"I missed you, too."

* * *

It came to me how much my dream resembled the last time I'd seen my parents. I'd watched on shore as Peary's ship the *Hope* sailed away. Mitti Peary and four-year-old Marie were on the ship, too, as well as three others from our village, and an enormous black stone that Peary was taking from our land. The stone had come from the sky, Peary said, and the museum in New York wanted it, so my father and others had helped him to dig it out of its resting place on an icy island far to the south of Itta.

My father looked at me from the deck, saying a silent good-bye, while my mother talked at him, waving her arms.

It wasn't Peary who made my parents want to visit the world of the *qallunaat*. No, it was the stories I'd told them of trees with yellow and orange leaves dancing in the wind. They'd never seen a tree, or brilliantly colored birds. I'd collected fragrant pinecones and the beautiful red feather to show them. I'd never have boasted or shared my treasures if I'd known what would happen.

All that year I waited to see my parents come through the harbor toward me. Then, the following summer, the *Windward* entered the shallows. It was the rare warm day when no one wore furs. Many purple flowers had recently bloomed, as if to welcome my parents home. As sailors rowed boats to shore, I stood on the beach, eager, happy.

But as I watched the ship empty, my parents didn't appear. Then I saw Peary.

I was fingering the soft auk feathers on the chest of my birdskin shirt as he strode up the beach toward me. Buttons on his white uniform gleamed in the sun. He wasn't smiling. He fixed his blue-gray eyes on mine.

"Billy Bah." He reached for my hands. "I am so sorry, so deeply sorry." He paused. "Your parents have died. Two of the others in their group also. One was Aviaq, the girl your parents adopted."

"Never say the names of the dead out loud!" I cried. It might confuse the spirits who were waiting to be reborn.

I covered my face, but I didn't weep. In the igloo afterward, when I told Angulluk and his parents, I writhed and choked. But at that moment, I dropped my hands, held my face steady, and kept my bare feet firmly in the sand.

Over and over, Peary said, "I'm so sorry. My wife and I, we are so sorry." I was relieved to see Mauripaulak, Matthew Henson, walking toward us. I'd known Mauripaulak as long as I'd known Peary. He always accompanied the lieutenant.

Mauripaulak swept me up into his arms as Peary left us standing on the shore.

"I'm so sad for you, Billy Bah." Mauripaulak gently put me down. "I will also miss your parents. They were good folks." My father had taught Mauripaulak how to harpoon seals and walrus. My mother had sewn for him.

Of all Peary's men, only Mauripaulak could speak our language. It was a comfort that I could ask him questions. Because of his dark skin, I felt he must be a distant relation. And Mauripaulak, it turned out, was living in New York during the time that my parents were there, while Peary was in distant Washington, DC.

Without saying the names of the dead aloud, we talked of the people who'd traveled to New York with my parents. There was Aviaq; Qisuk, a hunter who'd worked for Peary; and Qisuk's son, Minik, who was about eight. When the sailors made a stop to trade along their route, a hunter from South Greenland, Uisaakassak, joined the group. He'd met Aviaq, Mauripaulak explained. "He hoped to marry her. That's why he wanted to go to America."

"My parents had several offers for her, but she was still too young to marry," I said. How sad that this beautiful child with the blue-black hair had died.

"Soon after we came to New York, your mother, father, the other hunter, and the girl became ill," Mauripaulak said. "All of them were taken, except for Uisaakassak and the young boy."

So bad spirits had entered their bodies.

"How long ago?" I asked.

"At different times. In the winter and spring."

Qisuk had been the first in the group to die, in February, when there was snow on the street. My mother was next, in March. By then, Mauripaulak said, the trees had grown leaves. My father died in May. Ten days later Aviaq followed.

Just after the last big snowfall here, my parents visited me in a dream. I might have known then that they'd died. Yet I'd convinced myself otherwise.

Though dazed, I asked, "Where's Minik?" Qisuk's little son was a shaggy-haired troublemaker, Qaorlutoq's friend.

"Minik was adopted by the family of a man named William Wallace who worked at the museum. They took him to a new home far away from the city." Brushing his foot over the sand and squinting as if in pain, Mauripaulak told how my parents' group lived in a dark underground room in an enormous building where there were many beautiful rocks, carvings, and other things on display. The group had coughs, sore throats, and chills. They were taken to a hospital. Qisuk died there. The others were moved outside the city. The place where Aviaq and my parents passed away was a farm: a small white house, among other buildings, surrounded by fields and trees.

Aviaq had enjoyed the animals there. My father had seen green leaves and colorful birds.

"Have you come to give me their bones?" I asked.

Mauripaulak hung his head. "No. I wanted to bring them back to you, but the folks at the museum buried your people outside the museum, in a spot with flowers and other plants."

"Was my mother's *ulu* with her? Did my father have his gun?"

Mauripaulak's voice was low. "I think so, but I don't know."

He told me how Uisaakassak recovered from his illness. Lieutenant Peary had brought him home just days earlier, on the way to Itta.

I'll never see my parents again, I thought, and choked back tears. I thanked Mauripaulak for talking to me. Just over my shoulder, at the moment Mauripaulak walked away, I felt my father's spirit. I spun around. In shadowy form, his presence appeared, then slipped away before I'd had a chance to get a good look at him or be frightened. He'd said: *"Build a grave for me, your mother, and Aviaq."*

"I will do as you ask, Ataata."

That night, Angulluk, my sister, my brother, and I prepared the things that would go into the burial house near the other villagers' graves: the rifle, the two women's knives, lamps, harpoon, carving tools, furs, and other objects. These were mostly substitutes for the treasured belongings they'd left in America. Still, I felt that the goods would give them comfort. My sister came up with an *ulu* that she'd planned to give to her own daughter. My brother found a hunting rifle that didn't shoot straight, but it had once belonged to my father.

The next morning, as I gathered rocks for the burial house, and the four walls of the grave went up, I sensed that my parents and Aviaq had returned. I caught glimpses of them watching me. My father looked the same as he always did: like a powerful hunter. My tiny mother seemed tired; she'd lost weight. Aviaq wore a stiff blue dress with a starched white pinafore over it. Her hair was gathered behind her with a ribbon. She looked the way I did in America.

When we'd nearly completed the grave, my brother made a trip to the village to bring back my father's large, pure-white lead sled dog. He had been one of the dogs my husband had traded to make me his wife. I turned away when my brother killed him, though I would always re-member that gunshot. We laid the dog in the grave.

After we'd put the last boulder in place, we etched three horizontal lines into it with a knife. "Spirits of our loved ones," my brother said, "these marks are to remind you not to roam beyond your grave. Stay here until the times when your names will be called. Then you will go into the bodies of newborns, and forget the lives you have lived."

"Let me be the one to receive you, Anaana and Ataata!" I whispered. "One of you, come to me in pregnancy before the Ancestors swing low in the sky and the stars of winter blaze."

Several moons passed and the darkness came, along with its colorful companions, the Ancestors, and the bright stars. A young woman in the village had her first child, a girl, and named her Aviaq. The next child to be reborn was Qisuk, Minik's father. Villagers who'd known him, and had placed tools and weapons for him in his late wife's grave, had spoken his name.

Another winter came and went. My sister and I did not conceive.

CHAPTER FOURTEEN

● ● ● ● ● ● ● ●

Days later, Angulluk had not come back. Taking advantage of Mitti Peary's absence from sewing one afternoon, Duncan slipped away from his chores and sat beside me. He stroked my hair in full view of Ally, Mikihoq, Tooth Girl, and even Marie.

"I'm looking forward to this evening," Duncan whispered.

"Me too," I said, using an expression he liked. I felt embarrassed by his affection, though I enjoyed it. Everyone on the ship must have known of our relations. If Mikihoq or anyone else disagreed with it, they did not tell me.

From a small sack, Duncan brought out a game called checkers that he'd made from slices of corncobs and began teaching it to me. I set aside my sewing for a rest, and just as I was settling into a rare, tranquil moment, a crewmember named Officer Sutter stomped in with a pot of something white and gooey.

I shuddered whenever I saw this gray-haired man about the ship, because Duncan had told me that this officer had wanted to trade for me; and though the man seemed friendly enough and I liked his clean blue uniform with shining buttons and cap, I couldn't imagine myself with someone old enough to be my father. He now wore a brown shirt, trousers, and shoes all caked with a dried white powder. Even his slick, pointy beard was speckled with the foul-smelling stuff. He crossed the saloon and stood over Duncan and me.

Grease Beard, as I named him, looked around at all of us, then gave me a forceful glance. "Greetings, all," he said. "I'd like to borrow Billy Bah for a special and important task."

"What?" I drew back.

"I'm going to put wet plaster on your face, just for a little while. I'd like to make a sculpture of you."

"No." I wasn't exactly sure what a "sculpture" was, but I wanted no part of it.

He touched my face. I squirmed. Duncan protectively put his arm around me. Ally, who was nursing Sammy, gave Grease Beard a sharp look.

Grease Beard sat down on a bench, folded his arms, and looked thoughtful. "I made some casts of Eskimo faces a few years ago when I visited Greenland. They turned out so well, the museum has asked me for more."

Museum? The museum in New York where my parents died? I couldn't breathe.

"Officer Sutter," Duncan said, glaring at Grease Beard. "Billy Bah doesn't want to help you. Kindly leave us alone."

Duncan was taking a risk by speaking against Grease Beard, an officer. Clearly, he was jealous of the man's interest in me. I pressed Duncan's hand to my chest.

"Would anyone else like to volunteer?" Grease Beard asked. "Ally?"

Ally shook her head. She moved Sammy from one breast to another and lovingly stroked his shaggy hair. So Grease Beard knew Ally's name as well as mine. Perhaps the crewmembers talked about us.

Marie sat on the bench, playing checkers with Tooth Girl. She looked up. "Officer Sutter! Are you going to make bronze busts? For the American Museum of Natural History?"

He nodded and smiled.

"That museum is wonderful! I've been there, Billy Bah," she said. "You must let Officer Sutter make the bust. So many people will see your face. You'll be famous!"

I shook my head. "No, Marie. I don't want my face in that museum."

"Well then," Grease Beard said, "I'll make a cast of your face, Marie. And I can cast Akitsinnguaq, too."

"Oh, yes!" Marie clapped her hands and touched their faces. Tooth Girl and her mother caught Marie's enthusiasm and agreed to what they thought was a game.

Grease Beard went out to fetch more supplies. Duncan whispered, "Let's get away and go for a walk on the ice. I don't like this man."

"No, we must stay," I said. "I must watch what he's doing to my friends." Then, "I could find out something from him about my parents."

Duncan frowned. "I don't think it's a good idea." We'd never spoken of how my parents died, but probably all the *qallunaat* on the ship knew.

Duncan wrapped my hand in his. Grease Beard brought over the paste and a bucket of water. He draped rags over the dining table and gave Marie an old shirt to put on over her dress and sweater. She twined her yellow hair into a tight bun over her head.

While Tooth Girl looked on with a gaping mouth, Marie sat happily for her treatment. She squeezed her eyes shut as Grease Beard rubbed the plaster on her cheeks and small tapered chin and around her smiling lips. After working on her, Grease Beard plastered Tooth Girl.

Putting their faces on display in a museum seemed like stealing their spirits.

While they sat like white carvings and waited for the plaster to dry, I asked Grease Beard, "Did you know my parents?"

"Yes indeed. I was on that voyage. That was the summer Lieutenant Peary brought back the meteorite—the big iron one that he named Ahnighito, after Marie." He nodded in Marie's direction. She could only wave.

"So you knew my mother and father?" I said.

"Yes," Grease Beard said sadly. "I'm so sorry they died." I winced.

"Officer Sutter," Duncan said, "remember we're in a room full of children. And this talk is not pleasant for Billy Bah." I touched his arm to let him know it was all right.

"Were you with them at the museum?" I asked. "When they became ill?"

"No. They were taken to a hospital. I only saw them a few times after we anchored in New York. Now and then the museum called on me to mount specimens of birds and the like, or paint a mural. But I wasn't there when—"

Duncan said, "Don't say any more! Can't you see this is hard for Billy Bah?"

"I would never talk about *that*. Do you think I'm heartless?"

"What are you talking about?" I demanded.

He was washing his large hands in the basin. He stopped and looked into my eyes. "You know all there is to know. They took ill and died."

"Were you there when they were buried?"

"No, I wasn't." He looked away, washing again. "No need to ask more, Billy Bah."

I let Duncan pull me away. We passed through the saloon, where Marie and Tooth Girl still waited, looking like little ghosts.

Both men were hiding something. One way or another, I'd find out what it was.

* * *

That evening, speaking in whispers behind the curtain of his bunk, I asked Duncan what he knew about my mother and father. He said he was from Maine, very far from the museum, but he had read about them in newspapers.

"I read that Minik, the orphan Eskimo boy, was adopted by a family."

"My parents? When and where they were buried—do you know about it?"

"Nothing." Duncan stroked my hair. "I wish your life had been easier. I wish your parents were still alive. You're so beautiful—try not to be sad." I pulled my *kapatak* over us and we relaxed into the softness of the furs.

Later, he told me about his home in Maine, the ice and the snow there, at times like here, the bright stars at night, and going around the town in sleds drawn by horses. "I wish I could bring you there, Billy Bah. You'd feel almost at home when the snow is on the ground. My ma and pa and little sister would treat you like family. We could live in our own small cabin surrounded by evergreens."

With a sigh, I said, "There are interesting places there, many wonders. But when I was in America, I was always lonely for my family. I felt lost."

"Perhaps you'll change your mind."

"I won't." But I was tempted more than I let on. We talked of the things I'd liked about America: grass and trees, squirrels, colorful birds, and Marie's kindly grandmother.

We did not talk of the illnesses that could kill my people. Nor did we speak of my husband.

That night, dreaming, I saw Peary's preserved owl with the glass eyes perched in his caboose in Itta. A short time later, I awoke to howling. I put on clothes, left Duncan sleeping, and slipped out from the forecastle. Cin had escaped from her pen. Head thrown back, ears raised, she joined the howls of the dogs on shore.

"You're lonely for your dog family." I patted her head.

I looked to the north. How far had Angulluk gotten on the ice? I longed for him to return. Having feelings for Duncan hadn't stopped me from missing my husband.

I tied Cin so she'd stay in her pen of boxes. Soon the crew would be up, fetching coal and taking care of the ship, cleaning rifles, and leaving for a hunt. They'd see to Cin. I went back to Duncan's bunk.

In the morning, Cin was out on the ice being chased by Marie and Charlie the cook. I climbed over the side and ran to grab Cin. Charlie took her to her pen.

"That dog escaped last night. She chewed a hole in a canvas bag. And she chewed a hole in one of the sails in that bag, too," Charlie grumbled.

While I held Cin, Charlie put on a collar and hooked her to a heavy chain.

This isn't the way to treat a dog!

Marie yelled, "Stop! Don't!" Then one sailor held Cin and another pried her jaws open.

"Enough!" I yelled.

Duncan emerged from the darkness. "It's all right, Billy Bah." He held me back. I kicked him in the leg but couldn't break free.

"Stop!" Marie yelled.

Cin thrashed about and made stifled yelps as Charlie filed down her front teeth.

"I'm not hurting the dog," Charlie replied. "Anyway, it's over."

To my relief, Cin appeared as energetic as ever. She jumped up on Marie. Then she gave me a gentle, playful bite on the wrist with her squared-off fangs. She'd already forgotten what had been done to her.

I looked out into the darkness, over the ice.

CHAPTER FIFTEEN

• • • • • • • •

Every night, Duncan and I talked, and still he would not tell me what he was hiding. We spoke of Grease Beard, as well as Peary, and I began to understand that an insatiable curiosity motivated the *qallunaat*. They wanted to know everything about my people, and just as I collected my own experiences in my secret box of treasures, they slipped their memories into books, cameras, and museums. Did they realize how much pain and fright they caused us?

Even Duncan was surprised, he said, by some of the things the *qallunaat* had done to my people. I told him of the time when I was around six, when Peary invited his workers in Itta to his house for tea and biscuits.

We had gathered in the room where Peary's men slept in narrow beds. The room had a monstrous black stove with an arm that bent through a hole in the ceiling. Red blankets hung on the walls for warmth, like the furs in our igloos. On this day, Peary put up a white sheet on one wall and set up a camera facing it. Mauripaulak spoke for Peary: "Who wants to go first? Lieutenant Peary is going to take your pictures."

"I will!" I knew about cameras. I'd seen Peary taking photographs of his wife.

"Then take off your furs," Mauripaulak said. "Take off everything. Lieutenant Peary doesn't want any clothes in the photographs today."

Before I realized what was happening, Mitti Peary grabbed me and pulled off my *kapatak*.

"Stop!" my father said.

"We won't hurt her," Mauripaulak said.

Mitti Peary left me in only my fur panties.

People broke into loud talk, dumbfounded. Ignoring my father's shouts, Mitti Peary positioned me in front of the sheet, and Peary took two photographs: one from the front and one from the side.

"You can put your clothes back on in a minute, Eqari-usaq," she said in English. "First, I need to measure you." She took out what I later came to know as a tape, to measure my height and around my waist and head. Mauripaulak recorded the numbers in a notebook. Finally the Pearys were done with me and I could dress.

"Next?" Mauripaulak invited. "Lieutenant Peary has gifts for you all. Needles, buttons, wood."

That got everyone's attention. And so the trap was set, especially since the room was warm, which made it easy for Peary to get us to take off our clothes. There were even those like the shameless boy entertainer Angulluk, who seemed to enjoy it. Naked and fat, he swung his arms back and forth, happily posing, as if he did this every day.

One of Peary's men made tea. My sister, Nuljalik, let herself be photographed without protest. My brother, Inunteq, shot Peary an angry look when Mauripaulak urged him forward. I did not watch when his or my parents' pictures were made.

The afternoon passed, and my family returned to our igloo, holding two needles and a small piece of wood. But after that day, it was hard to look at Peary or Mitti Peary and not feel them measuring me.

* * *

Years later in America, I liked to go into the room that Mitti Peary called her study. No one scolded me for being there, for pulling the leather-bound books off the shelves. Some books had beautiful, colorful maps—"Your land's at the top of the world," Mitti Peary had explained.

One morning, I found a book with photographs of naked people in it. I recognized the boy Angulluk, his tummy round like a woman's, viewed from both the front and from the side. *These naked adults and children are my people!* My stomach tightened. I flipped through the pages to see if I could find myself. When I didn't see any more pictures, I closed the book fast, as if I'd been burned.

Kneeling on the carpet, I searched the shelf for the book I liked best and placed it gently on the floor. I looked at the photographs: a walrus, roaring; Peary's ship, the *Hope,* surrounded by ice floes; Mitti Peary in a long striped dress, holding a parasol, towering over a man in furs, my father's friend Ikwa.

I drew in a deep breath. There was the picture I'd come to find. The photograph showed my mother frowning, her mouth open, in the act of talking. I knew that expression. She was cross, as if the sun were in her eyes. She wore her hair in a messy topknot, and over her shoulder, just barely visible in the picture, a baby peered out of her hood. That baby was me! I thought of my mother, entertaining me with her songs and her string games, and broke into a sob. When would I ever see her again?

Suddenly, I noticed Mitti Peary standing over me. "You've found the book I wrote," she said softly.

I looked up, tears running down my face, and showed her the picture. "It's Anaana! Take me home! I want my mother."

"Shhh," she said. "Billy Bah, I know you miss your mother. She misses you. I'm sure there isn't an hour in the day when she does not think of you. I didn't realize living here would be so difficult for you." She bent down and placed her arms around my shoulders. Then she went to a cabinet, pulled out a photograph, and handed it to me. My mother! "This is yours."

"Thank you," I said, filled with surprise and gratitude.

I kept the photograph in my special box and looked at

it every morning when I woke up, at night before I went to sleep, and whenever I was feeling lonely; the white man's magic was sometimes comforting.

* * *

"Your *kapatak* looks beautiful on you," I said.

Marie stroked a foxtail hanging from a sleeve. "I *love* it!"

In the forward saloon, Mitti Peary and I held up an oil lamp to take a better look. Marie's *kapatak* was truly a thing of beauty. No other garment would ever compare to it, I thought, still wishing I'd been its maker. Most coats with hoods were black seal fur. Marie's was black, too, but Ally had fitted a handsome triangle of white fox pelts over the chest. White fox tails trimmed the hood and sleeves. Her black sealskin *kamiit* also fit her perfectly.

"You did an excellent job, Ally," Mitti Peary said. "You, too, Billy Bah!"

Ally beamed as Sammy, in her arms, tugged at the foxtails on Marie's hood.

Mitti Peary appeared very handsome in her new coat, too, and I was proud of the way she could move, because I'd cut the pelts exactly right. Even so, relations between us were growing more strained every day that Angulluk did not come back. Though he'd been foolish enough to go off on a dangerous journey, I faulted her for putting him up to it.

"I can't wait until Dad sees me wearing my new coat!" Marie said. *She'll be lucky if her father is still alive.* I sighed. Was Angulluk still alive?

"In honor of these fine coats, I'm giving you seamstresses the rest of the day off," Mitti Peary announced.

Not long after, we walked out to the deck. As if he knew I was looking for him, Duncan appeared in his wool coat and hat. How I wished I had extra furs to make him a coat, but the sailors already had winter clothes, though they were barely able to keep out the cold.

Mitti Peary paraded about on the ice, and I glimpsed the strong, brave woman I'd known from my childhood. She even broke into a run and chased Marie. She'd hardly left the ship lately. "Billy Bah," she said, "I'm so grateful to you for making me this coat. How easy it is to move in it! But I'm tired out now. Keep an eye on Marie, will you? She wants to take Cin for a run."

"Yes," I said, out of habit, then wished I hadn't. I'd hoped to spend the day with Duncan. Maybe I still could.

It was time to see what was happening in the village. Marie and Cin dashed ahead, while Duncan and I struggled to keep pace. Soon, Cin was tumbling and running with her brothers and sisters. The dogs raced about the igloos, barking, while Marie, Tooth Girl, Runny Nose, and their friends ran among them. Navarana shuffled out of her igloo to watch and laughed.

I held her look for a few moments. Ignoring Duncan, who was by my side, she took my mittened hand and grasped it tightly. In a heavy whisper, her eyebrows together, she said, "You belong in the village, *panik*."

"I will come back when Angulluk returns from his journey," I said. To myself I added, *Or when the sewing is finished, if he does not return.* For a journey on foot, my husband had been gone a long time, but not nearly long enough for me to assume that he'd been lost.

"I need to talk to Navarana alone," I told Duncan. "Watch Marie." He nodded. Then I followed Navarana into her rock igloo, filled with the familiar smell of seal broth, and let her feed me. One of these days, I thought, I'd be like this old woman, who could only eat soup that was mostly water with bits of soft organs floating in it.

"Your voice sounds faint," I said. "How are you feeling?"

She waved away the question with her gnarled hand. "Fine, but tired. This winter will be my last."

I felt my heart stop for a moment, my mouth go dry, tasting fear. "Never say such a thing!"

Her reply was sharp. "I only say the truth. I'm losing strength. My time is coming."

"That can't be—" I said.

Navarana ran her fingertips across my fingertips, then kissed me with her nose. She was sitting up straight, as always, but her breathing was hard. I touched her cheek, her fine chin and jaw, brushing my hand against her dry, wrinkled skin. We sat together in silence, as I had no more words to offer. With a heavy heart, I said good-bye, pressed my face against hers, then crawled out of the igloo.

Marie played tag on the ice with the children of the village, Duncan racing along with them. Before joining the group, I looked around at the women scraping skins near the igloos and the men dragging the bloody carcasses of seals onto the beach. I missed being part of their lives.

Duncan took my hand, and we watched Marie play. In her beautiful *kapatak* with the hood pulled up over her hair, Marie resembled her playmates. Her shouts even sounded like theirs. I waved to her. "Time to return!"

She dashed off in a different direction, Cin at her heels. We went on like this for a minute or two, until finally I caught up with her and held her to me, warm and snug.

Marie, catching her breath, said, "Let me show you something." Her eyes were full of mischief.

Unlike the footprints Marie used to make with her boots, which had a square heel, the footprints made with *kamiit* were oval. With her finger, she drew five little circles around an oval.

"What does it look like?" she asked.

"A *nanoq* paw print!"

Marie laughed. "Exactly!" Beside us, Cin barked.

All the way back to the ship, Marie made paw prints, changing fingers so they wouldn't freeze. She created a long winding trail of them leading up to the ship and, on deck, made lots of prints along the ship's middle, near the galley, where the aroma of Charlie's corn bread wafted out.

Laughing, Duncan and I admired her work.

Marie said, "I'm going to fool the sailors!"

Duncan went inside the ship to fetch Charlie the cook. Soon, Charlie was inspecting the prints. "By the holy St. Denis, 'tis a bear! These prints are fresh!"

I laughed so hard, tears came to my eyes. "Quiet!" Marie warned, though she, too, was giggling. The crew-members, a few at a time, and even Mitti Peary came out of the cabins. Soon nearly everyone on the ship was there, talking, pointing at the prints, then arguing about who would have to go after the bear.

Duncan slapped his thighs and hooted with laughter. "It was only a joke played by little Miss Peary."

The captain was angry! Mitti Peary took Marie firmly by the hand. Before she led her away, Marie looked back at me and Duncan with a sly smile.

CHAPTER SIXTEEN

• • • • • • • •

The following morning a snowstorm blew down from the north, the first large storm of the winter. By myself, I paced back and forth on deck, under the tarpaulin, crying as I pictured Angulluk lost under an avalanche of snow.

For days hail beat down, keeping Ally and Sammy, Mikihoq and Tooth Girl on shore. The cold seeped through the boards of the *Windward*. I'd once been in awe of the ship and the ingenuity of the men who built it; now I wondered why the crew hadn't abandoned it for the winter to live in cozy igloos. During breaks in the storm, Captain Bartlett had his crew busy shoveling to keep the deck clear. Duncan had built Cin a house, a shelter that was covered on the top as well as the sides, and lined with as many blankets as could be spared.

One night in the forecastle as I pulled the curtain closed to rest until Duncan came, I heard two sailors talking about me. "Did you ever see that Eskimo girl running on the ice with the dog and Marie? She's like another child. Then, in the next minute, she's in a bunk with a crewman. Those Eskimo girls start young. Who knows how many partners she's had. I bet anyone who takes her gets a sore rash and a bad itch."

"If I was Duncan, I'd stay away from her."

"He said if she wasn't already married, he'd take her home to Maine."

The first voice said, "Sutter bid for her, too. He said he wanted her strictly as his artist's model. He's a liar."

I tried to push the conversation from my mind. The gossip went on, getting worse. But I strained to hear.

"Sutter's spent time with Eskimos before. He was on a voyage that took some of them to New York. He left the ship before the Eskimos were taken to live in the museum. He said that thousands of people came to the docks to get a look at them. People were more interested in seeing the Eskimo children than Peary's big meteorite."

"Too bad they took sick and died."

"That boy, Minik, saw what they did with them. It was in the papers."

Then another, louder voice, one of drunken singing, drowned out the other voices.

What did Minik see? I hugged my knees and huddled under my *kapatak*, listening to my heart beating. After Duncan came to the bunk, I waited until the men settled down and we heard snoring. Then I asked him what they'd meant. "They talked about Minik seeing something, and 'the papers.'"

"Newspapers. Some story that was printed. But most

of these men don't know how to read. It's gossip. Sailors are ignorant men. They will believe anything they hear and *repeat it*. Idiots!"

"Duncan, now you're telling *me* lies."

He buried his head on my shoulder. After a long silence, he said, "Well, newspapers don't always tell the truth."

Though I barely remembered what "newspapers" were, I tried to let the idea sink in that their stories could be wrong.

I drew a breath deeply. "The truth about what?"

"I don't know." Duncan held me tighter. "Let's not talk about it anymore."

Duncan fell asleep. I sat up and reached under Duncan's bunk and brought out my wooden chest. In the dim lamplight, I touched my treasures: the little seal and other animals my father had carved for me, feathers, pieces of smooth silk. Acorns and buttons. The empty cardboard box of animal crackers. The photographs of my mother and me. The comb from Mitti Peary. Then I felt a long shape—a large whale's tooth? *I didn't put it in here.* Who did?

Duncan rolled over. By the way his breathing changed, he was awake. He stretched his arm out for me. "Billy Bah?" he whispered.

"I'm here." I kept my voice low.

"What are you doing?" He sat up.

"Somebody put something in my chest."

"I did. I gave you a lot of things. Needles. Coins. A cross that was my mother's."

"And ivory."

"Yes," he said. "A whale tooth. Though it's a different kind of whale than in the Arctic. When you can look at it in the light, you'll see that I carved a ship on it."

He laid his head on my shoulder. He was much gentler with me than Angulluk was.

"Why did you give me these things?" I asked.

"Soon I'll have to let you go, won't I, Billy Bah? I don't want to. I wish I could take you to America. But there's Angulluk." He sighed. "And Christmas is coming. And who knows what will happen to us all? This ship could sink in the next storm."

"Don't say that!" I replied uneasily. "Never say a thought like that out loud."

I thanked him for the gifts and put the box away. On deck, Cin began to howl and the men around us stirred from sleep. "Someone shut that dog up!" a sailor grumbled.

"I'll go out." I put on my furs.

"Do you think she's hungry?" Duncan asked.

"She hears the dogs howling on shore and she's lonely. She wants her own kind." *Like me.*

* * *

Opening the box again made me think of America when I'd packed up my things to finally return home.

One day, Mitti Peary brought me into her study, where a tall man with dark hair and a slim mustache sat at her desk. He was her brother, Emil Diebitsch. "Billy Bah, there's a ship that will soon be leaving for Greenland to bring Lieutenant Peary supplies. Mr. Diebitsch will accompany you on the voyage. You and he will leave for New York in the morning." She paused. "You'll have to ride on a train again. I'm sorry. I know how trains frighten you."

What joy and shock I felt at her sudden announcement! I said, "Aren't you and Marie coming?"

"Not this time," Mitti Peary said.

Why did Mitti Peary sometimes live with her husband and sometimes not? And I still didn't understand why they traveled to my land. But all that mattered was going home! In another few minutes, I was packing ribbons, acorns, feathers, and all my other keepsakes.

The next morning, I clung to Mitti Peary one last time, rubbed noses with Marie, and hugged Mayde and old Mitti Diebitsch.

This time, when the roaring monster came rattling toward me, belching its black smoke, I hid my eyes but did not scream or cry. In the same way, I braved the sea voyage on a new ship, the *Falcon*. The *Hope* had gone down in a storm.

From the railing, I watched and waited. One sun-filled day, Itta's red cliffs finally came into sight. I cried for joy to see the ruddy cliffs dotted with millions of auks and other birds; the glacier that reached like a pebbly ribbon down to the beach; my village on the bluff with its tents and rock houses and piles of debris; an escaped dog trotting along the crest.

Soon the ship anchored and hunters in kayaks came out to greet us. My father and my brother called to me from their kayaks. I threw my arms in the air. My father and my brother paddled back to land. People gathered on the beach, and even from a distance, I could recognize their shapes—my mother, my sister with a baby! I saw Peary in his blue uniform and cap, Mauripaulak and a few of Peary's other men.

As we neared the shore, I jumped from the rowboat and ran toward my father. He lifted me, hugged me, stroked my hair, then set me down. We rubbed noses. "Ataata!"

"My little seal!" he said.

I rushed toward my mother. "Anaana!" I said, happy tears in my eyes. My mother wrapped me in her arms. It was everything that I wanted: her warmth, her tenderness, the way she babbled sounds in my ear as if I were a baby again. She smelled of salty sealskin. Anaana seemed smaller to me now (or was I taller?), her skin dirtier than I'd remembered. Her smile was wide, her delight unmistakable.

"Look at you, dressed like a *qallunaaq*. I'll find clothes for you."

"I want to walk in *kamiit*. I will never wear these boots

133

again!" I unlaced them and threw them across the sand. Barefoot, hand in hand with my mother, I climbed the familiar path from the beach to the village, surrounded by a sea of my own people, listening to the fast, happy words of my own language.

Once I arrived at my parents' igloo, I dressed in some of my sister's worn-out clothes, which were too big for me. I stuffed grasses into the toes of the *kamiit* to make them fit. I was, again, the girl I was meant to be, in the place where I was meant to live, among my true family.

Good luck followed, and that very day a hunter caught a narwhal. After our great feast, it came time for me to speak to the villagers, to answer everyone's many questions about the white man's land. They gathered around me in a circle. I said, "In America, there are so many ships that they crowd a bay. The sky is nearly covered by houses. The people live like cliff birds, high above the ground. Smoke fills the air from the peoples' cooking fires. They look out of windows made of glass that is clear as fresh ice. In winter, the sun shines all day. You would not believe how many people there are in America, too many!"

I began to describe the strange beasts that pulled people in carriages and the monsterlike trains racing through tunnels. One of the older hunters interrupted me. "Are you sure this is what you saw, child?"

No one accused me of telling lies, though some adults felt I was too young to understand what I had seen. From my chest, I took out my precious treasures, one by one, to be passed around: pieces of silk, acorns, ribbons, bird feathers, the box of animal crackers. Eyes narrowed, hands grabbed, bodies leaned forward, mouths opened wide. My precious things were touched and smelled, rubbed and bitten. I tried to keep the children from going off with my treasures. "I want to go to America!" one boy said as he held my red feather.

People gave me quizzical looks when I talked about a gigantic gray animal with floppy ears and a long trunk I'd seen at a zoo.

I felt equally relieved and disappointed when my father took over as storyteller and presenter. He held up two rifles that Peary had just given him in payment for my service to his family. These items the hunters respected and understood.

I collected my treasures and returned them to their chest. From now on, I'd keep them to myself.

CHAPTER SEVENTEEN

• • • • • • • •

At last, the blue and green streaks of the Ancestors replaced the storm's raging snow and winds, but there was
still no sign of Angulluk. I kept looking across the ice
from the ship, hoping, waiting. Marie and I worked under
the canvas roof, sorting the cans and tins of food spread
on the deck. Duncan, Captain Bartlett, and Charlie the
cook emptied still more crates, and Mitti Peary made
notes. "Five . . . six . . . no, seven cans of peaches!" Marie
counted. "Let's ask Charlie if we can eat them tonight."

"We'll save those for Christmas," Mitti Peary said.

"But, Mother, that's over a month away."

"Count yourself lucky that we'll have any food at all."
Mitti Peary looked up from her writing and asked the captain, "*Do* we have enough food to last through the winter?"

"Barely. If we ration these cans and have the Eskimos
hunt for us."

Marie whispered to me, "There's chocolate and nuts
hidden somewhere in these boxes. Help me find them."

I nodded, though of course I didn't care about either
chocolate or nuts. All I could think about, aside from Angulluk, was getting away from the ship, and especially the

sailors and their gossip. Today, I'd return to the village. During the storm, I'd finished sewing both Marie's and her mother's *kamiit* and mittens. I only regretted that I'd leave Duncan.

Suddenly, Marie gave a shout. "People are coming. Maybe it's Dad!"

Two dark forms moved across the ice toward the ship. Snowdrifts had shifted in the wind over the night and we could now see nearly as far as the beach.

Why only two people? My heart raced. I put down cans, ran to the ship's rail, and climbed down. Plunging onto the snow and ice, I ran out.

A man in furs strode toward me. "Eqariusaq!"

My eyes welled up with tears. "Angulluk." I rarely called him by his true name.

He lowered the sack slung over his shoulders. We rubbed noses. His nose looked too red, as if stung by frost-bite. He was exhausted.

He saw the tears, lifted me into his arms, and set me down again. His voice was raspy but cheerful. "You're heavy, you fat seal!"

"And you're a smelly walrus!"

Duncan came up. He waved to me and forced a smile. I nodded to him, and he turned away.

"Where is Piugaattoq?" I asked my husband.

"In the village. With Ally. They're celebrating—we killed a *nanoq*."

"A *nanoq*! How? Where? Tell me!"

"Well!" Angulluk cleared his throat. "It was a big male. An enormous bear, magnificent! Piugaattoq took the honor. His bullet pierced the bear first, in its side. Five of us also took aim and hit it. Qaorlutoq got in close, dodged the claws, and thrust his harpoon into the neck. Then I fired a shot to the head and killed it."

A great nanoq, *what a prize!* I was eager to hear more, but when we climbed aboard the *Windward,* a whole crowd pushed near, hurling questions at Angulluk and Bag of Bones like seabirds fighting over fish. Then Mitti Peary pressed in. "Did you find him?" she asked. "The lieutenant?"

Angulluk coughed. "I walked far without water. I need to drink."

"Please let my husband go inside," I said.

We tumbled into the saloon. I took Angulluk's arm so we wouldn't be separated.

I helped him off with his furs, and we sat together on the floor. The bottoms of his scuffed, dirty boots were badly worn. I wished I'd had enough skins to make him a new pair. Charlie brought drinking water and pots of hot tea. Bag of Bones, whose English was improving, ended up talking the most.

"Mitti Peary," Bag of Bones began. "We didn't find the lieutenant. We didn't get to the fort, or anywhere close."

"Then where have you been all this time?"

"Only a few days away from the beach. Travel to the interior is impossible, Mitti Peary. We sheltered ourselves during the storm. And we had a *nanoq* to track. We worked hard to get that bear."

Angulluk shot Bag of Bones a warning glance.

"I see," she said stiffly. "I gave you all valuable guns and you didn't even try to find Lieutenant Peary."

"It's winter," I said angrily. "It's our way to follow animals. It's not our way to walk long distances in blinding snow and storms." *Her love for her husband is a dangerous thing,* I realized. *Because of it, she can justify anything.*

Angulluk, with a cup of tea in his hands, looked at Bag of Bones and frowned. Marie, red-faced, slipped onto Mitti Peary's lap. She began to cry. "I want my dad!" Mitti Peary took her away, and my husband put down his empty mug. "I'm ready to go back to the village. Find your belongings and put on your *kapatak,* woman. *Qaa, qaa!*" He spoke as any hunter would, in the same tone that he used on his dogs.

* * *

The pungent smoke of three faraway cooking fires met us as we approached the shore. The orange flames stood out in the darkness, rising above the igloos. The feast for the *nanoq* had already begun!

On the beach, a pack of dogs fought for entrails, bones, and bloody scraps. Angulluk pointed at one of our puppies. "How large he's grown!"

"It's true," I said. How could I have spent so much time on the ship that I hardly recognized our own pack?

139

I'd barely given the dogs a thought. Tooth Girl's family had been feeding them.

We made our way toward the towering fires of crackling blubber and dried mosses. In the center of the village between the houses rose a high scaffold of stones, where the hunters had hung great slabs of *nanoq* meat on a rack. Holding knives, people crowded around steaming pots. Some sat, others stood, eating chunks of meat. The flames of the fires climbed high over their heads. How strange, yet familiar and exciting, it all felt after many nights of sitting with a knife and fork at a table.

I followed Angulluk into one of the crowded shelters. In the darkness, I could only see faces of those closest to the spitting flames. It was hard to recognize anyone. Soot from the fire blackened their cheeks and mouths. The aroma of blood mixed with the smoke. Angulluk took a knife and speared a chunk of meat from the pot. We passed the juicy, hot meat back and forth, chewing lustily.

How proud I was of Angulluk; how glad I was to see him.

I hadn't even said good-bye to Duncan, but my sadness passed in the closeness of all the people.

A short, hooded figure slipped in beside me. Fat and oil dribbled down his cheeks.

"I helped to kill the *nanoq*," Bag of Bones said.

"So I've heard. You're making something of yourself."

I let him tell the story again. "I threw my harpoon. Once, twice! Growling, the bear towered on hind legs, glaring at me." He imitated the bear. "Piugaattoq shot the bear in the chest. Then Angulluk finished it."

Angulluk gestured. "Piugaattoq's eating the liver. He earned it."

Piugaattoq sat with Ally; Sammy was in his mother's hood. Blood and soot smeared his face. By now he was a fat toddler, his hair long as the fur of a baby musk ox.

A dipper of water was going around. Angulluk drank and handed it to me; then I passed it on to Piugaattoq. Ally squeezed blood from a piece of meat into the empty dipper for Sammy.

We ate and ate until we were completely full. *This is the way life is supposed to be,* I thought. *Feasting, sharing fresh meat, not canned mush.* And the *nanoq* fur would make a coat and new pair of trousers for Piugaattoq. There would be leftover for my husband's clothes.

Angulluk pressed in close. He never left my side. He picked up one of the last pieces of meat from the pot. "Take it."

"It's yours," I said. But he put it into my mouth.

When the meat was gone, we passed around the dipper and drank the hearty broth.

"Come," Angulluk said. "We'll bring the empty pot out to the dogs."

"First I want to put my things in the tent." We left the bonfire and walked past the row of rock igloos. Whale oil smoke filtered out of them; they were warm and cozy. But ours was dark and cold.

I set down my bag. "You've been gone for a long time."
I had remembered my anger toward him. "Fat One! You
said you wouldn't leave me on the ship for more than a
few nights."

"I wanted to come back, but the snow was very deep.
I'm here now!"

He put the pot down and we rubbed noses. I took his
hand and pushed open the flap of our igloo. "Come inside,
Angulluk," I said.

"I have to tend to the dogs. You light the lamps and I'll
be right back."

I yanked his arm and pulled him into the tent. "The
dogs don't need to lick that pot right now."

"I need to tie them—"

"They can wait," I said. "I want you. Now!"

He smiled and grabbed me. Still wearing our furs, we
rolled into the tent. As he began to tug at my *kapatak,* I
felt the cold. "Let's light the lamps," I said. But Angulluk
kept on pulling off my furs.

"Even the ship would be warmer than this tent," I said.

"But you don't want to be on that ship. You're glad to
be with me, Eqariusaq. Aren't you?"

I was. A surprising thought came to me: *I'll stay in the
village with Angulluk from now on. I won't return to the ship. Not
for a long time, maybe not ever again.*

That was what I wanted to believe.

CHAPTER EIGHTEEN

• • • • • • • •

For an entire week, the moon shone bright and silvery in a clear sky, as if to welcome Angulluk. Our lives fell into a comfortable rhythm, though we lived in deep winter's shadow, when death often comes, when people as well as animals can freeze. I liked seeing the village and the frozen sound by moonlight, and smelling the burning seal fat in our lamps, the soft lights they cast; the white man's lanterns had been too bright. At night, Angulluk and I enjoyed each other's company in the warm, fur-lined darkness and I pushed away thoughts of Duncan.

I'd told Angulluk that I suspected something terrible had been done to my parents in America. "Maybe they'd had to take off their clothes, pose for photographs. The sailors said that Minik *saw* something. What could have upset him?"

"I don't know." Angulluk agreed with Duncan that the sailors were stupid men who told lies. "After everything that has happened, how can you not hate Peary?"

I didn't completely understand it myself. "He wasn't responsible for my parents' deaths. He wasn't there." I could never truly hate Peary, who was so friendly, or Mitti

Peary. Though she'd sent Angulluk on a mission in which he could have died, she'd acted out of desperation. Neither she nor her husband seemed to do bad things on purpose. Or did they?

"You're far too forgiving of the *qallunaat*," Angulluk said.

"You may be right."

After that conversation, I noticed he insulted me less. He didn't talk of trades. We spent all our time alone together or with his friends, sledding the snow-beaten trail to the valley to check our fox traps and searching for the elusive herd of musk oxen. Then one day, Duncan and two other crewmen, rifles on their shoulders and sacks on their backs, appeared in the village. The sailors wanted to hunt, and they chose Angulluk, of all people, to be their guide!

I didn't volunteer to go. It was too awkward to see Duncan and my husband together. Before the men set off, Duncan and I talked in low voices.

"The captain is sending us for musk oxen," he said.

"I didn't know you knew how to hunt."

"I'm a poor shot." He shrugged. "But food is running low and our skills as sailors are worthless now. And the captain will give me what I need to—"

He looked at me hard. The silence revolved between us like swirling snow. "Billy Bah, would you be willing to—" he started, then broke off. "We have to go now."

Did he want me to divorce Angulluk?

I watched as the men set out. If only the Fat One's brothers could see him, at the reins of the dogsled, proudly leading the *qallunaat* across the snow fields in search of a great prize. The group came back empty-handed that night. The Fat One, puffed up, tried for musk oxen for the next eight days. Most times Duncan went with him.

I used any excuse to stay behind. Navarana's family needed me, I said, which was true. The old grandmother lay in bed with a fever, and in the meantime, Mikihoq could hardly keep up with her chores.

One afternoon, just as I was gutting a seal on the ice with Mikihoq, I heard the barking of an approaching dog team. Angulluk, Bag of Bones, Duncan, and the other men trekked toward the village, while Angulluk drove a sled full of musk ox fur and meat.

"We killed two!" he said. "Men from the village took in two others."

Bag of Bones told us, "Angulluk killed both musk oxen with just a few bullets. I helped to bring down one of them."

My husband grinned at me. "Come, woman! We'll feast in the village tonight!"

I jumped for joy. "*Kiiha!* Someone has worked hard to bring home tasty meat."

Duncan gave me an angry look when he saw me rub noses with my husband. He and the other *qallunaat* followed the crowd at a distance as we moved toward the village. Angulluk steered the heavy sled, which overturned as the path inclined, and then there was a dogfight. Angulluk shouted and swung the long dog whip, while Bag of Bones and I kicked the dogs to keep them from eating the meat. One bit Bag of Bones and he fell back, blood streaming from his nose. He struggled to get up. Villagers ran down to help us.

In the meantime, another group of hunters arrived with their own full sled. There was such a crowd, and I was so busy pulling back the dogs, cursing at them, then lifting slabs of the heavy meat, that I hardly noticed Duncan and the crewmen standing by themselves, Duncan turned away from the others.

With the dogs under control, Duncan stepped forward. "Come to me soon, Billy Bah," he said quietly, "for a day, or a few nights?"

I stood back, but looked into his eyes. "I can't come to the ship alone," I managed to say in a low voice. "I belong to Angulluk." Then, "I'm sorry. Good-bye."

Duncan knitted his brows. Angulluk scowled at him, then at me.

Duncan and Angulluk started over the ice to take meat to the ship, crossing from one world to another. Of course the sailors wanted meat, but now I saw that Duncan had become a hunter and chosen Angulluk to be his teacher in an attempt to see more of me. Duncan had a plan; he was ready to do something—and if he did, I feared the two men would fight.

As the day went on, after I helped cut the meat and

smelled it cooking, my heart turned toward Angulluk. He'd provided well for the village, and I couldn't wait to share in his happiness. Feasting was one of life's greatest pleasures, and no *qallunaaq* could ever truly understand what it was to us.

Angulluk returned as the feast was starting. It didn't take long to finish off the musk oxen. We picked the ribs clean and boiled the tongues. Then we crushed the bones and boiled down the fat, opened the skulls, and boiled the hooves into soup. I took broth to old Navarana, lying ill in her igloo.

She sent me away before I could visit for long. "Go to your husband. The proud hunter is waiting for you."

With full stomachs, we felt strong enough to face the storm that began that evening. Wind and snow blew fiercely for three days. Angulluk and I were glad to stay in the igloo. In the darkness, I spoke his name. Perhaps it was finally time for me to stop calling him the Fat One.

"You are a good enough hunter to feed not only a village but a ship full of *qallunaat* as well," I said. "Are you going to provide for us from now on? Or will we still live on birds' eggs when we return home?"

"Be quiet!" he snapped. But we rubbed noses.

When the sky cleared, Bag of Bones crawled into our entrance. "I drove my sled to the ship. Mitti Peary wants you two to come, and Akitsinnguaq, too. Today is Christmas."

It was a cold, dry day with only the barest sliver of

moon and no stars. As we trudged through the snow, our Ancestors showed themselves in the milky streaks that filled the sky above us. Ahead, the wide horizon glowed green and purple. Magic hung over the earth.

Good smells of roasting meat met us as we climbed onto the ship. So they still had some of their musk oxen. We pushed our way into the forward saloon full of crew-members. Marie, with gold ribbons in her hair, wearing a dress with red bows on her chest, danced around a little Christmas tree. The tree glowed brightly with candles and was draped with strings of popped corn. At first glimpse, the tree was a mystery. Where had it come from? Marie explained that her mother and Grease Beard had created it with wire, wax, straw from packing crates, and ground coffee for bark.

Cin was inside with us, too. Duncan was stroking the dog's belly. He rose. "Billy Bah! Merry Christmas!"

His smile was forced.

Tooth Girl clutched my hand and, a little frightened, backed away from the tree. She and Bag of Bones stared, in awe. Even Angulluk kept his distance, though he couldn't stop gazing at it.

"I'm so glad to see you!" Marie threw her arms around me.

Mitti Peary greeted us with handshakes. After we'd taken off our *kapatait,* we sat on the floor and Marie gave us our stockings. I tipped mine upside down. Dried dates, roasted peanuts, red-and-white striped candies, an orange, and chocolates fell into my lap. Such rare gifts! We all received the same things.

These presents would be the talk of the village, and we'd parcel them out and try to save most of them for stormy days. Tooth Girl licked a piece of candy. Bag of Bones, more experienced in the goods of the *qallunaat,* peeled his orange.

"Don't you love Christmas, Billy Bah?" Marie asked.

"Yes," I said. "You made stockings for us! My Marie!" We rubbed noses.

"Charlie's about to serve us all a grand meal. Musk ox steaks, and canned peaches and corn bread, and raisin loaves that Mother and I made. We're using up most of Charlie's stores, but it's Christmas! After we eat, we'll sing and have games."

Duncan came over and boldly took a seat on the floor between my husband and me. The three of us watched Marie dance about the tree. Duncan caught my eye, then glanced back to Marie. Angulluk, staring at Duncan, looked like he was about to stab a seal. I felt sorry that I was the cause of his anger.

In my mind a single thought echoed: *I am divided.* While surrounded by my husband and friends, I felt alone, unsure. Without warning, tears began to stream down my face.

I realized I loved both men.

CHAPTER NINETEEN

• • • • • • • •

Snow filled the sky and blanketed the land with heavy drifts on the day Navarana's family called me to her igloo. The old woman wanted to see me alone. I found her on her sleeping platform, wrapped in furs, and so weak after days of fever that she could hardly stir. Yet her dark eyes shone from her wrinkled face, and her voice was clear and bold, her mind lucid as a pool of fresh water.

"Panik, I will not live to see the sun again," she said.

"Death will not take you away for a long time yet, Aana."

"I will die before tomorrow. I am weak, and we have entered the long, hungry passage of winter. It is folly to feed my old and useless body."

"No, Aana," I said. But she'd made up her mind.

"*Ta! ta!* Listen, Eqariusaq, while I have strength. It is in my heart to tell you the vision in front of me. It is your future." She let me lift her head with furs. "I see you as a mature woman, wisc, insightful, and steady. People admire you. You've endured many trials in your youth and enjoyed some good times, too. Your restlessness has left you. The many hindrances to your happiness have gone away."

"Thank you, Aana." I was grateful for the blessing. I took her bony hand, cold to the touch. Did I dare ask her what else lay in store?

"Will I ever feel life in my womb, Aana?"

"The vision does not show me. You and many women friends are sewing furs. You all talk and laugh as you work."

"Are you seeing me here, with the villagers?" I asked. "Or at my birthplace, Itta?"

She frowned. "Neither. You are on a ship. There is blue water behind you, and ice floes. It is a sunny day. The sailors are doing their chores. You're independent of the *qallunaat,* even as they are all around you. The spirits say you can find contentment among them, so long as you remember who you are. If you are content within, any place can be home. They say: 'The world is your home.' That's surprising. I did not know such a thing was possible!"

She coughed, and her voice was quieter. "Your happiness will grow. Your understanding of people will grow. With understanding will come freedom, the freedom to accept all that life has to offer. Wait a little longer; trust that when the season is right, when you are no longer feeling pulled or divided, you'll find yourself even stronger than you are now. Making decisions will come easily for you, and you will learn to speak from your heart."

"I will remember, Aana." It was so much to take in, though I felt hope that the best part of my life lay ahead.

I looked into her ancient face. I needed to ask one

more question. "Do you know where my mother and father are?"

She closed her eyes and gripped my hand. "They are coming toward us now, two figures in black seal furs. He has a mustache and small beard. She is short. They're talking . . . arguing over who will be the one to speak to us. Ha!"

I smiled, closed my eyes, and I, too, could see my beloved parents.

"Eqariusaq, your father has a message," she declared. "He says that their spirits will soon be reborn."

She paused to listen. "You must not grieve for them. They've found their way and have everything they need."

"*Ai!*" I said. "Yes, I can hear them, too!"

"*Our time is approaching,*" they declared. "*As we have always been together, we journey together now. We will never be separated. All is well.*"

Happiness washed over me. "Thank you for calling them to us." Then I addressed my parents. "*Anaana! Ataata! Thank you for coming. May we meet again soon.*"

"*Farewell,*" they said together. Then they were gone.

Navarana gave a long sigh. "Once death releases me from this body, I hope to live again in my own igloo. Perhaps I will be ready in good time so Mikihoq can welcome me back into the world. She is with child."

"I hope that will be," I said, though my happiness was tempered with sorrow. For soon, old Navarana herself would be gone. Even when reborn, the crotchety old woman would no longer be there to stir the big pot of soup, or to mutter and scold.

She coughed and looked at me once more with her shadowed eyes. "Call the others in. It's time for the family to sing for me."

"Yes, Aana." I took her hands. "Thank you. Farewell."

Her death was so near that we'd begin the songs of lament. Before I left her side, I studied the deep lines running across her forehead, her high cheeks, and her mouth, now peacefully set. I wanted to remember her face, framed by her long white hair.

Soon the family gathered in the igloo. Mikihoq, her husband, Qihuk, their children, and I raised the lamenting songs. I believed Navarana could get well, if she willed it. But this was her final privilege. We could not stop her.

She died during the night. When the morning stars rose, we bundled her in furs and took her to a corner of the village, under the shelter of an outcrop.

I was sad to see Navarana covered with stones, and yet grateful, too, that she had a kind and hasty death, and even a serene expression. Unlike my parents, she was given a proper burial. By her sides lay her two lamps, her sewing things with her *ulu,* her cooking pot, and her wonderful steel-bladed axe. She'd lived a long life and a full one. She'd been luckier than most. *This is the way death should be,* I thought.

In the coming weeks, I missed her keenly. I hadn't fully appreciated her. If only I'd paid as much attention to her counsel earlier as at the end. Now no one was left to talk at me, to admonish and advise from the perspective of many long years. I would have to make my own decisions; I would have to discover what the spirits advised on my own.

* * *

Snowstorms hid the next risen moon and kept the hunters from going out, even to the nearby ice. Working by lamp flames, repairing clothes, I thought about Duncan. There was no talk of going to the ship, or anywhere else.

Another dark moon cycle followed. Our caches of meat grew sparse, and snow drifted so high that we couldn't find all the provisions. Bag of Bones and the other children dug in the snow near the igloos for seal bones and scraps; we boiled them for soup. Some people ate fat from their lanterns. We all became sad and listless from hunger. Angulluk and I turned to each other at night for warmth, but not for pleasure.

The bad weather went on and on, and the villagers killed a few of their precious dogs for food. But at last, a full moon shone and hunters trekked out through the pathless, snow-covered land and brought back seals. Our courage returned with the food and the sweet light of the moon. The village came alive again with children's screams and laughter.

And then one day, a weak white sun shone forth. Pure, sunlit colors came into focus. What joy! Angulluk untied the dogs, and they fought over the seal entrails. Their coats showed reddish or deep brown, new colors that came with the sun. The puppies had grown to adults, almost as large as the rest.

As the sky opened, I looked out to the horizon at the golden rays. It was the moment I'd been waiting for. "*Ai!*" I said, rising to my feet. "At last!"

People poured down to the beach. Angulluk and I ran along with them. Soon children chased back and forth on the ice and dogs scampered everywhere, barking. I raised my arms and slid happily.

Sammy, dressed in sealskins, his thick hair now shoulder length, ran after Tooth Girl and Runny Nose onto the frozen bay.

"Come back, Sammy!" Ally called. He raced into a wet patch, slipped, and drenched himself.

Mikihoq, her pregnancy beginning to show, ran down the hill and grabbed him. If only Navarana could have joined us!

Would I live to see as many sun-returns as she had? It was the *young* mothers who often died in childbirth, or just after. For the first time, I saw that there might be some advantage to staying childless.

Now, as my father had taught me to do on the first day of sunlight, I took off one mitten, held my hand in the air, and smiled with half my face. My actions felt like a partly remembered dream, and I yearned for my father to tell me the missing parts. *"Ataata,"* I told him, *"I give the salute, to help the world be reborn, and so that I will also be reborn."*

The sun drew out of sight, but far into the night, the song drums sounded. In the darkness, we gathered and feasted on seal meat. We emptied the oil in our lamps and replaced it with new seal blubber, to show our eagerness for the change in seasons and to quicken the transformation. The heavy snows were melting in small streams, and hunters talked of driving sleds into the distance.

By the next moon, I'd twisted enough sinew to make new lines for the dogs, and Angulluk had readied the harnesses. He and I and Bag of Bones took a short trip to the valley to empty snares and traps and bait them again with stinking meat. After skinning the game, we drove back on the sled with carcasses and pelts of three rabbits and two foxes. With more furs, I could sew new spring clothes for Angulluk and me.

Whenever the sky cleared, I walked to the beach to watch the sun rise, a little earlier every day. I imagined Duncan as a lean figure bouncing as he walked over the ice from the *Windward.* "I hope he visits me," I said aloud.

If Angulluk never traded me to a *qallunaaq* again, it would be good for our future. Still, longing rose in my chest.

I missed Marie, too, and considered walking out to the ship. But I had work to do.

As if knowing I was thinking of her, Marie came to

my igloo that day, along with Mitti Peary and Cin, who'd grown larger than her brothers and sisters; she'd had more to eat.

I left off my work for a while and went out with them. As Cin romped with her former pack and we ran alongside, I said, "Marie, Cin belongs with her kin. You should give her back."

Mitti Peary looked at Marie. "That's what I've been saying."

"But I love her!"

"Does she still howl at night?" I asked.

"Yes," Mitti Peary said.

Marie crossed her arms and set her mouth. How pale her skin looked in the new sunlight.

"Billy Bah, the other hunters have said no. Now I'm going to talk to your husband," Mitti Peary said. "The weather would make it easier now to search for Lieutenant Peary. Could you help me persuade Angulluk?"

I looked away, angry. "I cannot tell Angulluk to go after Peary," I said. "We have suffered enough doing that. Besides, he's thinking only of hunting now. The village needs food."

The sunlight showed the frown lines around her eyes and mouth; she looked older than she had before winter. After a while, she took Marie's hand and they went off in search of Angulluk.

Later, in the igloo, Angulluk told me he'd given in to her. "I'm building up a supply of cartridges."

"But how do you expect to get to the fort? There are still huge snowdrifts blocking off the way north."

"The sea ice. It's still hard."

"It could crack open and you could drown," I warned.

"Perhaps. But right now, the conditions could be perfect. There's sunlight and the ice is solid and deep."

We argued about it for a long time.

"You won't find anyone to go with you," I said.

"Qaorlutoq will come, if I ask him. And Mitti Peary has persuaded Duncan to go."

I caught my breath. "Duncan! Why?"

"She's promising him a new rifle," the Fat One answered.

"What a feeble group," I said. "You, the orphan boy, and a sailor. Not one of you knows Musk Ox Land well. Or enough about traveling on sea ice."

"We *can* get there," Angulluk replied. "Duncan will have a compass and a stove that gives out far more heat than our lamps."

How could either man want to go on a dangerous trip, much less with each other? Despite Angulluk's outward calm now, I'd seen the way he'd acted around Duncan on Christmas Day. Our hunters did not fight when there was a disagreement over a woman; instead, one would generally leave the community and join another. But accidents happen when emotions run high and people aren't thinking clearly; and neither man could be in his right mind now if they were planning to go off on such a journey.

There was nothing more to do than go to sleep and hope that he would have a change of heart. Fortunately, the next day, word came that the herd of musk oxen had been spotted in the valley. So our men made plans to hunt. Angulluk wouldn't have time to go to the ship to tell Duncan and Mitti Peary that her mission needed to be postponed.

Angulluk said to me, "No need for you to come, Eqariusaq. I've arranged for a woman to mend and dry my clothes, and to cook for me."

I felt a pang; some man from the village was loaning Angulluk his wife. In return, Angulluk was probably promising use of his rifle another time, with the expectation of large game shared by the village.

"I see," I said. I wanted to know who the woman was, but according to custom, I held back. I'd find out from other women anyway.

The sun was high enough to blaze brilliantly the day they drove out. It was the first warm weather, the finest yet of the spring season. With the search for Peary postponed, the hunt, and the new sun, I should have been content. But as I thought of Angulluk, a sob rose. Why should it bother me that another woman was taking my place? The brief exchange would mean little to him.

I looked out to the *Windward*, so clear and bold against the horizon now, with the yellow stripe standing out on its hull; it seemed to beckon. In a few moons, the ice would melt and set the ship free. Duncan would sail away, perhaps never to come back. The urge to see him came over me, though I was uneasy about visiting him without my husband making the trade.

As I walked out to the ship, a mass of small black eider ducks flew overhead. The first of the season! I waded on through heavy wet snow. When I climbed onto the deck, crewmen were washing clothes in buckets. Duncan rushed over and grabbed my hand.

"Your search for Peary will have to wait. My husband left on a hunt. I've come to visit."

"Let's go to the fo'c'sle." He left his clothes in the bucket. Sailors watched as we embraced.

How had I not noticed before the extraordinary color of his eyes, green flecked with brown? The winter's darkness had hidden them.

I looked around to make sure Mitti Peary and Marie weren't nearby. Then I went inside the sailors' quarters.

Duncan and I spent a stolen, secret hour. We'd had many playful nights, but this was like gulping water after a great thirst.

Heavy feet came toward the bunk. "Duncan! Come out!" It was Captain Bartlett.

Duncan held me tighter.

"I know the Eskimo girl is on board," the captain said, "and that your laundry is freezing in a bucket."

"I'll be on deck in a shake or two, sir."

A wave of fear passed through me. What would happen to us?

"Billy Bah," the captain continued, "Mrs. Peary wants to see you. You'll find her in her cabin."

Captain Bartlett marched off and the door slammed.

* * *

"Thank you for coming to talk to me, Billy Bah." I stood near Mitti Peary's doorway and she did not invite me to sit down. Pacing about the cabin, she said, "The day is a fine one and yet Angulluk is not here. I expected him."

Without apology, I told her about the hunt.

She looked down from her great height. "When he shows up, let him know he is to set out with a search party. Immediately."

"No. The air is warming and it's too late to start a journey over ice. Wait until some of the deep snow melts. Then someone can go by sled on land."

"All winter, Angulluk and the others have been making excuses. First it was too dark to travel, then too cold, too snowy, too ice-locked. And now it's too warm."

It was no wonder they'd all turned Mitti Peary down. Angulluk should have, too. I raised my voice. "The fort is *very far away*. You're risking Angulluk's life."

"I won't give up on finding Lieutenant Peary," she said. "Have your husband come to me." Then, her tone warmer, she added, "Marie is playing with the dog on deck. I know she'd like to see you."

I left her sitting on her berth with her head in her hands.

In Cin's pen near the pilothouse, Marie, supervised by Charlie, was pouring milk from a can into a bowl. Such a waste of valuable food!

Marie climbed out of the pen and took my hand. A pale afternoon sun hung in the sky. "Mother won't let me go out on the ice anymore. She's afraid it will crack. Can you take Cin for a run?"

"All right." I stroked Cin's head. I was glad to see no one had sawed off her teeth in a while. I took off her leash and soon we were running on the wet ice. Cin rolled in the shallow pools surrounding the *Windward,* then shook herself.

I took her back to Marie when the low sun told me it was time to leave. I did not say good-bye to Duncan. It was what I wanted.

Marie gave me an extra-hard hug. "Visit me soon, Billy Bah."

As I walked, I looked back at the sun setting beyond the dripping *Windward.* I glowed with happiness. It felt so good to have come to Duncan on my own, and I wished I could be with him always; I pictured us in a cabin in Maine, surrounded by snow-covered evergreen trees.

But I still loved Angulluk. He'd be angry if he knew what I'd just done. Looking about me at the sound, I felt helpless. The ice was shrinking toward land. If Angulluk, Duncan, and Bag of Bones *did* attempt to find Peary, they would be in great danger.

In the next few days, I made Angulluk a pair of rabbit-fur mittens. He'd be surprised and slide his hands into them with pleasure, and I hoped the gift would bring us together. I knew that I preferred Duncan's company. He spoke gently and never bossed me. Still, maybe I could be content with Angulluk, as I had been until he'd started trading me to Peary's crew. But what if he found out I'd gone to Duncan?

One morning, a boy came with the news I'd been waiting for. "Angulluk is driving his sled in!"

I put on my furs and ran down to the beach with Tooth Girl just behind me. Angulluk and his hunters came slowly nearer, their sleds laden with the skins and bloody meat of musk oxen. Angulluk shouted, urging the dogs on. His group had separated from the other villagers; there were no women with them.

Bag of Bones carried shaggy skins on his shoulders. The sled he dragged was empty, broken, and his dogs walked loose beside him. But he wore a big grin.

I ran up as Angulluk called out the traditional "We have arrived!"

We rubbed noses. "You are a great hunter! I made something for you, something for a great hunter to wear." He smiled at me.

Bag of Bones set down his burden and cracked his whip to keep the dogs away.

The dogs snarled and snapped. The men whipped

them and pulled and staked them far from the meat. By the time the dogs were tied together, nearly all the people had gathered.

The four hunters stood together. "As you see, we killed five large musk oxen," Angulluk began.

There was much cheering. Enough food for everyone for some days.

Every hunter had a chance to speak.

Bag of Bones, arms flailing, described each shot and each harpoon thrown. *Kiiha!* How he'd changed! He was becoming brave, even distinguished. I looked forward to hearing the stories again at the feast. Food was more delicious when it was brought in triumph.

CHAPTER TWENTY

• • • • • • • •

Like emotions, spring weather can change unexpectedly. Only days after the feast, the melting snow froze, and the harbor ice was as hard as boulders. Angulluk's new mittens served him well.

One cold morning, he announced, "I think I can go after Peary and find him." He raised his chin. "The ice is solid."

Blood pounded in my head. "Do not risk it."

Of course he marched off to the ship. Was he trying to prove his bravery to Duncan? The thought that Angulluk and Duncan could both die on a journey was more than I could bear. Qaorlutoq, too, was becoming dear to me. I wanted to protect him, like a mother.

Navarana's vision of the woman—wise and free—came to me. Women often trekked with their husbands on hunting trips. Why couldn't they also help search? I had as sharp an eye as anyone. And if the Fat One was just playing a trick on Mitti Peary, I wanted to know.

The morning they were to leave, as Angulluk picked up his wrapped rifle, I crouched between him and the entranceway. "I don't like waiting for you. This time I'm coming with you."

"You're staying here, stupid woman."

"If a boy in old dog furs can go, so can I."

His eyes flashed. "No."

"I will not stay behind."

In the lamplight, he smiled. To my surprise, he said, "Dress yourself, Eqariusaq. Get more seal meat. We have to finish packing! *Qaa, qaa!*"

Angulluk and I crawled out to see Bag of Bones and Duncan coming to meet us.

Duncan wore the blue wool cap I knew so well, an old fur coat, heavy wool trousers and socks, and *qallunaaq* boots. When he saw me in all my furs, a large bag over my shoulder, astonishment lit his freckled face. "You're coming?"

"Yes." Not that I looked forward to such a dangerous journey. Or being with both men.

On the beach, Angulluk went over the trek as we tied snowshoes to our feet. We'd walk north on the ice of Payer Harbor, keeping close to shore. It would take most of the day to get to the place the *qallunaat* called Cape Sabine. Then we'd go inland and find a sheltered camp for the first night. Traveling on foot, carrying our food in shoulder sacks, would be difficult. I wished we could have gone by sled, but a sled wouldn't be much use if the snow in the interior was deep and uneven. And Angulluk didn't want to risk shattering our one sled on rough sea ice.

A weak yellow sun shone in a cloudy sky as we set out. The air was sharp, and with each sliding step, I drew the cold into my chest. I blinked as the wind stung my eyes.

Still, it was exhilarating to be out on the sound, seeing the horizon changing as we trekked.

We passed the *Windward,* a dark form on the glowing snow and ice. I saw two tiny lights.

All morning, we marched without stopping. Angulluk and Duncan took the lead, and Bag of Bones and I trailed behind. We came to where water had once foamed and roared, then froze solid in shapes of waves. We needed to head farther out on the harbor to find smoother ice. My heart beat fast as we turned away from shore. If the ice cracked, no one could help us.

We rested once we made it over the roughest stretch. I sat on a mound of ice, opened my bag, and sliced off a piece of seal meat. How good it felt to be off my feet. Chewing the tasty fat, I took in the wide, frozen ocean. By the position of the sun, I knew it was early afternoon and we'd have at least another hour of daylight.

Far ahead loomed tall cliffs. It must be Cape Sabine. Somewhere near there, Angulluk said, a trail through steep hills led inland to the fort where we hoped to find Peary.

I turned toward the tracks we'd left. Lights on the *Windward* had vanished far behind us. Then I saw a long, jagged gap in the ice. I gasped. How suddenly it had opened! Black water lay between us and the land.

I jumped to my feet. "Angulluk! Look!"

"*Ai!*" His hunter's eyes had already seen it. "Move fast! Now!"

Duncan, Bag of Bones, and I talked at once. "Can we get around it to shore? Are we trying for Cape Sabine?"

Angulluk set out north, and we hurried toward the cape. He said, "As soon as we get far enough, we'll cross to land. Then back to the village."

Suddenly, the ice under my feet lurched. An explosion burst in my ears. The ice was opening very close, and the solid mass under us was moving outward in the bay. We kept up our pace in our snowshoes, but the crack opened faster than we could trek.

After an agony of pushing forward, the water was stretching ahead of us. "Which way?" Bag of Bones asked.

"Ahead!" Angulluk commanded. "We have to find a way to the fort now."

We pressed on, though the sun was low on the rim of the land. We'd have to walk in near darkness with only stars for light.

Finally, we drew near the cliffs of the cape. Duncan said, "How do we get there?"

Angulluk sent Bag of Bones running ahead and peered after him into the faint light.

Bag of Bones yelled, "I see a way!"

In the black channel, where Bag of Bones pointed, Angulluk made out a dim shape and guided us toward it. A block of ice as wide as an igloo appeared to float close to the other side. But the channel between us and the block looked too wide to leap across.

"Take off your snowshoe frames. Get ready to run." Angulluk and Duncan heaved the frames and our bags and packs onto the block. Next they slung across their rifles.

Bag of Bones threw his bag and missed. It sank in the water. "Two days of food."

No one scolded him.

"You first, Qaorlutoq," Angulluk ordered. "Get a good start."

Bag of Bones measured his distance. He ran and leapt out over the dark water with a great shout. He sprawled on the slippery block, and held. We let out our breaths.

"You now," Angulluk said to Duncan.

Duncan hesitated. "What about Billy Bah?"

"I'll come with Angulluk. I can make it," I said, though I wasn't sure.

Duncan ran, jumped, and barely reached the block, falling forward on his chest.

I was next. Angulluk stood at the edge, showing me where to take off. The channel seemed to grow even wider.

I ran toward the blackness. I leapt. A shock of icy water closed over my head and poured under my jacket, stinging my body. I fought to rise and breathe.

Duncan reached for me. "Grab on, Billy Bah!" I gripped his hands with my mittens. The weight of water soaking my clothes pulled me down. He couldn't lift me far enough. Bag of Bones grasped my arm. But I slipped back into the channel.

Then I felt myself pulled up and dragged onto the ice block. I was on my knees, coughing up seawater. I looked up to see Angulluk. Quickly, he helped me to my feet on the rocking ice island. When I was steady, he took my hand and we jumped across the second chasm.

"Can you talk, Eqariusaq?"

"Pain. My throat." My whole body burned, especially my fingers and toes.

With Angulluk holding one arm and Bag of Bones the other, I stumbled toward shore. It was hard to move in the soaked skins and furs. As we plunged ahead, Bag of Bones gasped out that Angulluk had sprung across the water and swiftly wrapped his arms around me before I sank farther, ordering Duncan to grab him, and Bag of Bones to pull Duncan. Then all three had heaved me onto the ice.

Angulluk traded mittens with me. I clapped my hands and strained to bend my fingers. They began to sting again, a good sign. But my toes remained frighteningly lifeless.

Darkness fell. The wind screamed to a high pitch like ghostly wailing. We reached the beach and came to a hollow sheltered by a snowdrift. "Duncan, keep Eqariusaq moving," Angulluk said. "Qaorlutoq and I will build an igloo."

After stamping my feet, I wanted to lie down, but Duncan held me up and walked me in tiny steps.

Finally, I couldn't stand any longer. Angulluk rolled out a skin, and I sank down in the half shelter of the rising snow house. The men built the walls around and over me. With a skin, Bag of Bones made something of a door. Duncan lit his cooking stove with matches and sharp-smelling kerosene from a can.

Angulluk helped me take off my drenched *kapatak* and *kamiit,* drew his furs onto me, and wrapped himself in a thick wool blanket of Duncan's. Soon jets of pain shot through my limbs. I bit my lip. Duncan melted snow in a pot to warm my hands and feet and then gave me tea. I was shaking too hard to hold it, so he tipped the cup to my mouth.

My husband and I huddled together. We ate the rest of the seal meat in my bag and Duncan's biscuits and canned meat. We drank several cups of tea. Then, exhausted, we fell asleep.

Soon after, the spirits sent us a storm. It began with a thick, wet snow. Winds gusted from the north. Our igloo collapsed and the men struggled to rebuild it. I felt the presence of my parents very near. *Perhaps we will die,* I thought. The idea didn't frighten me.

In the thick darkness, we lay huddled together. How long could we last before our bodies would go to sleep, never to awaken? At least we had seal meat, the stove, and tea.

After what I guessed was three days, the storm ended. I peered out to see crisp stars in a dark sky. Angulluk dressed, then beat ice out of my frozen *kapatak*. What choice did I have but to wear frozen clothes? They hung heavily and sent a chill through me. They cracked as I walked. After a while my body heat began to soften the furs. But my stomach rumbled.

We climbed and descended hills, waded through waist-high snowdrifts, labored over snow-covered rocks. Sometimes I couldn't tell jutting stones from shadows. Even as we trekked bent over, the frigid wind blew against our faces. I fell, picked myself up, and kept going on trembling legs. My head was dizzy and my mouth dry.

We couldn't see landmarks, only at times the harbor to the east, with its terrible black chasm of open water. Even when we were past the channel, we didn't dare walk on the ice again.

We came to a place where a drift of snow rose to our waists. The men went first, partly clearing a way, and I followed. A shrill wind blew suddenly from behind and toppled me forward. My nose and cheeks, already lashed by wind, stung in the freezing snow.

Angulluk helped me to my feet. Each of us holding on to the person ahead, we trudged behind Angulluk. The wind drove hailstones into my eyes. I stumbled and fell again.

With his strong arm around me, Angulluk half carried

me. I labored forward, my legs almost too heavy to lift. I shielded my face with my frozen mittens.

We made it out of the deep drifts. I said, "I have to rest."

"We must not stop," Angulluk said. "You know the danger, Eqariusaq."

"We *can* stop. You can build us a shelter."

"We're not stopping, woman!"

I took another step, then another, teeth chattering. Walking didn't warm me anymore. My aching fingers were too stiff to bend. Hair whipped from under my hood and froze like wood splinters. My exposed face—how it burned! We pushed on.

Angulluk stopped, listening to the boom of ice cracking in the distance. Planting my aching, heavy feet, I listened, too. Another boom. No, it couldn't be the ice. Gunshots.

"Someone's out here. Maybe people from the *Windward* looking for us," Angulluk said.

"Trying to show us the way," Duncan said.

Angulluk replied, "But the shots would be coming from the south, not the north."

"How could people from the ship get so far ahead of us?" Bag of Bones said.

Before us was nothing but the whiteness of blowing snow. Surely it must be a good thing that some man, either a hunter or sailor, was nearby. But I was so tired and hungry, and my hands, feet, and face stung so much, it was like a strange dream. Angulluk had quickly taken out his rifle, removed his mitten, and with a click, chambered a shell. He fired into the air, loaded and fired again.

We heard another shot.

"Go! Toward the shots," my husband said.

"Who is it?" Bag of Bones said.

"They might help us," Angulluk replied.

So with Angulluk holding me on one side and Duncan grasping my hand on the other, we staggered on.

CHAPTER TWENTY-ONE

● ● ● ● ● ● ● ●

Colors flashed in the wind and blowing snow. Was this vision real? There were moving figures, barks, shouts, more gunshots. A sharp burning in every step, I moved forward with Angulluk pulling my numb hand. Just ahead, a form appeared, wearing the muddied *kapatak* of a *nanoq* and waving a red kerchief. Peary.

I caught my breath. His eyes were the same, blue and full, with more wrinkles than before around them. His face, except his ruddy pointed nose and thin, chapped lips, was all icy whiskers. Even in the wind I picked up the musky scent of his furs.

"Billy Bah!" he said in his deep voice. He put his large mittens on my arms. "You're covered with ice!"

Unable to speak, I met his eyes. I could hardly believe our good fortune.

We'd come to a camp with a rough but fair-size igloo, a sled packed with provisions, and six tethered dogs. My old friend Mauripaulak, Matt Henson, fed them slabs of meat. I knew him at once from his *kapatak*, with its white fox shoulders and red fur body and hood: I'd sewn it for him. "Billy Bah! Angulluk!" He looked at me with alarm.

Angulluk said, "Eqariusaq fell through ice. We need to warm her."

In the entrance to the igloo, out of the wind, Angulluk squatted before me and slid off my furs and boots. I raised my arms, but though my teeth chattered and my upper body shook violently, neither my legs nor feet would move.

Working fast, Angulluk rubbed snow on my feet until they were pierced with needles of pain. Good; feeling had come back. He rubbed snow on my hands and face until sharp sensation came to them as well. Then he pulled me into the igloo.

Angulluk wrapped me in a woolen blanket and set me before the flames of Peary's kerosene stove. He heated water, filled a large bowl, and put my feet in to soak. Then he patted my feet dry and, despite the intense pain, rubbed them. Angulluk then boiled strips of seal meat and gave me the broth to sip. As warmth spread and strength rose inside me, my shaking gradually slowed. All this time, he eyed me tenderly.

Soon, Peary and Mauripaulak crawled in. From his bag, Mauripaulak brought out a warm flannel shirt and trousers for me, and a wool hat, so I was dressed like a *qallunaaq* man. I bent down and looked at my blue toes. My left foot was more tender and red than my right, the bottom broken open and oozing blood. Mauripaulak dabbed the wound with a cloth. Angulluk treated it with seal fat.

"You may lose your toes," Mauripaulak said.

I jerked upright. "No! They will heal."

"Perhaps," Mauripaulak said. He dipped the cloth into the bowl of water and wrung it out. "You'll know in a few days—if they turn black."

I tested my big toe by tapping it with my finger. The pain was a sign of life.

Peary said, "Matt Henson did a good job of amputating my toes, and here I am walking again. He could do the same for you."

"Do not say such thoughts aloud."

Mauripaulak wrapped my foot and gave me wool socks, much longer than my feet, to put on. I hugged myself in the blanket, while searing pains started in my toes and moved up to my thighs. Angulluk and Bag of Bones talked at times in our tongue, though mostly the men spoke English.

"How extraordinary that you should all be here," Peary said.

"We started from the ship to find you," Bag of Bones said. "We came to a crack in the ice. We started to go back but—"

"What!" Peary interrupted. "The *Windward* is in Payer Harbor?"

Bag of Bones nodded. "Mitti Peary asked us to look for you and—"

"*Mrs.* Peary is here?" Peary's expression turned from one of shock to a bright, broad smile.

"Mrs. Peary and Marie," Duncan put in.

"The missus, Marie, and the baby?" Peary asked.

"No baby," Angulluk said. "Unless you mean Sammy, Ally's baby."

"No, I mean Mrs. Peary's baby girl. Francine."

Bag of Bones looked puzzled. "We don't know of any other baby."

"We have letters for you from Mitti Peary." Angulluk retrieved the papers from a sack. Silently, Peary read quickly through the pages, written in Mitti Peary's beautiful curving loops. He paused here and there, then dropped his head; he coughed, and for a moment it seemed he might choke. "The baby died of an illness," he said. Then, "My poor Jo." Then he came to another page, splattered with ink and filled with Marie's larger handwriting, and his face softened.

Peary folded the sheets and held them to his lips, then put them in his bag.

So Marie had had a little sister, who'd been born and died since Mitti Peary's last trip to our land. How sad that Peary had never met his second daughter.

After some quiet, Bag of Bones gave details of my accident. Then Mauripaulak told us that we were about midway between the ship and Fort Conger. Peary and Mauripaulak, while tracking musk oxen, had been caught in a storm and separated from two young hunters who worked for Peary and had wintered with him at the fort.

"The fort is large and comfortable," Peary said to Angulluk, "and I know a fairly flat route to get there. Tomorrow we could take Billy Bah on the sled. It will be a good place for her to recuperate."

"*Nga!*" I said. I'd grown sleepy with the broth but now was wide awake. I remembered something I hadn't thought about before. We'd be cooped up in that ghostly place where the spirits of the doomed *qallunaaq* party roamed. "Take me back to the village."

"How is it along the coast?" Peary asked Angulluk. "Is the snow smooth enough for sled travel?"

"It was hard even to walk. You couldn't drive a sled there."

The men speculated whether drifts were too high inland to go to Payer Harbor that way. "Between here and the harbor," Peary said, "are hills to cross. Snow remains on the higher elevations. We may need to wait before we can go to the ship."

Before we had started out, I thought we'd give up and turn around well before getting to the interior. Or we'd make it all the way to the fort, locate Peary, and return with him to the *Windward*. I hadn't considered that we'd find Peary, then be stranded with him. In time, the snow and ice would melt and we'd get back to Payer Harbor. But how long would that take, and would we have enough food? And would my throbbing feet fully heal?

Angulluk and I should have never come on this journey, I thought. *Mitti Peary was wrong to send us, and we were wrong to agree.*

CHAPTER TWENTY-TWO

· · · · · · · ·

The next morning, while Mauripaulak changed the wrappings on my feet, Angulluk and Peary harnessed Peary's sled and headed south to explore the area toward Payer Harbor. After two days, we heard their dogs coming back. It was as feared: snow was too deep to try crossing the hills. We would have to go north to Fort Conger. There was nothing I could do but let myself be covered by a skin, lie on Peary's sled, and be pulled by his dogs while Angulluk, Duncan, Bag of Bones, and the others, even Peary with his crippled feet, walked. I felt the terrible cold and every rough bump underneath me. The trek lasted two days and nights, the men building snow igloos for sleeping. I hardly reacted to anyone around me. It was too much effort to talk. Angulluk gave me his last piece of seal meat. On the third day, we set out without anything to eat besides what Peary and Mauripaulak handed us: small white pills. Peary said, "These will give us some strength. They're dried milk." That night we slept cold and hungry.

Finally, on the fourth day, Peary pointed ahead, saying, "There it is!" As the sled drew near, I sat up. I'd expected a large, gloomy building like ones I'd seen in

America. Instead, the camp was mostly snow-covered stacks of wood and two smaller buildings, square and built of wide planks. As Peary proudly explained, the fort had been bigger but was too hard to heat, so he divided it into two one-room cabins. Twenty-five men had lived at this outpost, so after Peary and his party came, there were plenty of extra beds inside, even after he broke up a number of them.

Peary helped me to stand on my swollen feet and was about to lead me into one of the houses when I said, "Where are the bodies of the dead men? If they're buried here, I will not enter. Angulluk can build us an igloo."

"Men did not die here. Nearby, at Cape Sabine," Peary replied. "A group called the Greely party. They were running out of supplies and left. Some built a boat and tried to sail south, but they drowned. Some died in a shelter at the beach. Greely and a few of his party were rescued when finally a ship found them."

I hobbled into the surprisingly warm cabin and glanced about for bearded faces of white men lurking in the shadows. I imagined them seated around the plank table, reaching to the shelves for plates and mugs, knives and spoons, sleeping under the blue and red wool blankets that covered the beds.

But soon I forgot about spirits and turned to the stone fireplace and its roaring fire. Two of Peary's hunters came in and greeted me. They had reached the camp a day before us.

"Stop!" I said as one hunter, Aapilaq, laid a new plank on the fire. I was looking at the flames with horror. They were burning cut-up pieces of wood: wood that was brought by ship, I reminded them, on long voyages. We sat at the table, and I argued about this wastefulness. The wood they burned was enough for a whole village of hunters to fashion into many sled runners and harpoon shafts, useful for generations to come.

Mauripaulak, who fully understood our language, joined us. He said, "It's all right, Billy Bah. With the logs outside, we have more wood than we need. As you can see. If we can get some of it to your people, we will."

Peary and Duncan stamped snow from their boots. Angulluk and Bag of Bones removed theirs. Angulluk hung my *kapatak* and *kamiit* on hooks by the fireplace, where they began to thaw and drip, giving off a musky odor. At last, days after I fell in the water, my furs could dry.

All the men were caring for me now, and Angulluk and Duncan vied for my attention. With a mug of tea warm in my hands, and my mouth full of Peary's too-salty canned meat, I could almost forget the constant throbbing in my feet. I took off my socks to inspect them and found that my right foot had turned red and blotchy, hard to the touch, and my left foot bluish gray. Blisters had risen. Though my toes were dark purple, they hadn't turned black, and I could move them.

The cabin soon filled with a bitter aroma I remembered from America. Peary was turning the handle on a small box and grinding brown beans for coffee. He tapped the ground beans in a pot and poured in boiling water. "Not bad for coffee that has been here twenty years," Peary said, taking a sip from a mug. "One of these days, if I see Adolphus Greely, I'm going to thank him for it."

"It's lost its flavor," Mauripaulak said. "We need to use more beans."

"We have a huge supply," Peary said, wiping his reddish mustache. His handkerchief was embroidered by Mitti Peary with a letter I knew to be ℘, the only letter I could read.

Angulluk took a sip of coffee and made a face.

"Do you want a taste, Billy Bah?" Duncan asked.

"No, thank you." The idea of drinking things left over from white explorers who had died still made me shiver.

Peary went to a trunk and, raising a small cloud of dust, took out bundles of papers. "Here are letters," he said, "and charts, and a calendar from 1881 to 1882." He took out candles and set them on the shelves, then began putting objects on the table: a gold pocket watch, a smoking pipe, a photograph in a frame of a lady with long ringlets, and a box with carved figures for the game called chess. Peary told us he planned to take as many of the Greely party's possessions back to America as he could, to return them to the survivors or their widows.

"You should bury all these things," I warned him.

Peary laughed. "They won't bite us. And I'm so grateful to these men for their beds and blankets, pots and pans. I haven't lived in such comfort for a long time. I've greatly enjoyed the peacefulness and solitude of the place. Sometimes when the men go out hunting, I stay and read a book by the fire. I'm almost sorry the winter is coming to an end."

How selfish! "Mitti Peary didn't need to be worried about you," I said. "And Angulluk and I, Qaorlutoq and Duncan would have been better off if we hadn't set out to find you. Surely you would have come and found us yourself."

"Yes. But it's good all the same that you came looking for me. We *might* have needed rescuing," Peary said. "I'm delighted that Mrs. Peary sent you. Otherwise, I wouldn't know she was here." He paused. "I could never do my work in your land if it wasn't for her belief in me."

He was *thanking* her for nearly sending me to my death! Then he added that it was Lieutenant Greely's wife, Henrietta, who'd arranged for one search party after another to sail here looking for her husband. One ship was tragically lost, others found no one and sailed back, but she persevered until a rescue ship succeeded in finding the survivors. "As it was, six men lived, and all would have starved or frozen to death if help hadn't come soon. This woman, like my own wife, would have done anything for her husband."

I thought of all I did for Angulluk, and all that he did for Mitti Peary, who in turn served her husband; in a way, he was driving us forward like dogs harnessed together. Was he worth our risks? Peary hadn't even asked how Ally and Sammy fared.

"Let me show you something, Billy Bah," Peary said. He helped me to my feet and guided me to his bed on the far side of the room. He'd carved letters in the planks of the wall. "I did it with my pocketknife, just after Matt Henson amputated my toes," he said. "To inspire me and buck me up. It's an old language called Latin that I learned as a boy." He read out loud: *"Inveniam viam aut faciam.* It means 'Find a way or make one.' One day I will make it to the North Pole. You'll all see!"

"Yes, I'm sure you will." Did he hear the edge to my voice?

He looked at me intently with his clear blue eyes. "There's a reason I'm showing you this quotation, Billy Bah. You must not let your injury stop you. I speak to you as if you were my own daughter. What decisions can you make to take you into the future?"

Peary like a father to me! "I had a good father. Please leave me be." I pulled away.

Later, as the men slept, I thought about Peary's words. What power did I have to do anything, to make any kind of choice, especially with my injuries? It was hard to think about the days and seasons ahead. I wanted to walk easily again, to go back to the village, and when I could, to return to my own people in Itta—to see my sister, to talk to the spirits of my parents at their burial house. Perhaps there, upon my return, I'd start my life over. But I knew that life in Itta, as anywhere, could be difficult; people gossiped, and they might not welcome me. Navarana had said it didn't matter where I lived if I discovered a contentment within, a different kind of "home."

How could I find it? Did it even exist?

CHAPTER TWENTY-THREE
● ● ● ● ● ● ● ●

Every day at Fort Conger, I inspected my feet, helping my husband or Mauripaulak wash them and smooth on seal oil. The red swellings turned blotchier; the purple spots lightened to browns and yellows. As blisters dried, new ones rose. The largest, on my left sole, was big as a seal's eyeball. I didn't walk at all for five tedious days. Without skins to prepare or sew, I grew restless and bored. Duncan slept in Peary's cabin, and Angulluk kept him from visiting me.

A half moon had passed since the accident. Then one afternoon, when Angulluk and Bag of Bones and the two men from Itta were out hunting, I wanted no more of the smoky room; I needed air. There was no one to stop me. So I got up, reached for my *kapatak*, painfully slid on my *kamiit,* and took burning, shaking steps out the door.

Smoke poured from a chimney of Peary's cabin, and through its small, paned window came an orange glow. I heard sharp voices carried on bursts of wind. I was able to stand on a pile of planks and look through the window. Peary, Mauripaulak, and Duncan sat around the table by the fire. They talked fast, frowning. Then I heard my name. I strained but couldn't understand more. Duncan, facing the window, crossed his arms and flung words across the table at Peary. Mauripaulak was hunched over, weighted down by some worry. He poured a drink from a green bottle, the glass sparkling in the lamplight.

I made my way to the front and slowly opened the door. The room was separated from the entry by blankets nailed to the ceiling. I slipped inside. The voices and clinks of mugs kept on. Pegs for traps were on the wall. I gripped one, and finding a hole in the blanket, I peered through. The men's faces shone out of the shadows, and their teeth flashed. Peary lifted a mug, full to spilling, but ignored it as he looked across the table to Duncan.

"There's no use asking me, seaman," Peary said. "I won't do it. Never again."

Mauripaulak frowned. "You look at her, Duncan, and you're not seeing anyone else. You're not taking in the whole situation. You'd regret it."

They must be talking about *me*! I drew in a ragged breath, heavy with dread.

"Matt," Duncan said, turning to Mauripaulak. "I'd give her a home and take care of her. It has nothing to do with the lieutenant."

"You're wrong." Peary gulped from his mug and set it back down. "After what took place at the museum, the world's eyes have been on me whenever anyone talks of Eskimos."

I gripped the peg even harder. *What took place? My parents?* Had Peary lied? Were they murdered?

Mauripaulak sighed. "What's best for the Eskimos is to stay where they live. Plain and simple." He ran his hand through his curly black hair. "I have seen some things in my time. Nothing so bad as *that*."

I pushed away the blankets and walked into the room, my feet burning with every step. "What are you talking about?"

For a moment the men didn't move. Mauripaulak drew another chair to the table. "Billy Bah. Please sit down," he said, and stood to help me to the chair. Close to the hot fire, I began to sweat but kept my furs on because I didn't want these men to stare at my body. Duncan, who had stood, sat in the chair beside me. I let him take my hand in his large one, steadying me.

"Someone tell me. What did you mean about the museum?" I said.

I looked at each one's eyes. They were not cold or angry, just sad.

Mauripaulak finally broke the silence. "Well, Billy Bah—"

"Don't meddle with it," Duncan warned, his voice low.

Letting go of Duncan's hand, I faced him. "I need to know."

"It happened—" Mauripaulak started.

Duncan slammed his hand on the table. "Don't!"

Peary cleared his throat. "It's better coming from me." He took a drink. "After the Eskimos died in New York, the museum made them into an exhibit."

"What?" I said. "I don't understand."

Duncan put his arm around me.

Mauripaulak took a breath. The *qallunaat* at the museum, he said, boiled the bones, then put shapes on them with wax to make figures meant to imitate who they were.

I shivered at the picture that formed in my mind. Figures for curious people to stare at. Statues with my parents' bones inside, shown like Peary's lifeless birds with glass eyes!

I shook and cried. Duncan drew me close. "I didn't want to tell you. I knew it would make you sad."

Then, as if to soften the horror in my face, Peary said, "The display wasn't up long. People got angry, so the museum took it down."

"After Minik saw it," I said, piecing together what I'd heard from the sailors.

"Yes," Mauripaulak answered. "The people at the museum tried to fool Minik. When his father died, they wrapped up a log in furs and pretended to give a funeral. But later the boy saw the exhibit."

I had a bad feeling in my stomach. "Lieutenant Peary, what did they do with the figures?"

"The museum must have buried them." Peary turned his eyes away. He was lying.

"Lieutenant Peary took no part in any of those things

at the museum," Mauripaulak said. "Neither did I. Nor anyone you know." When my parents were being kept at the museum, he said, Peary was home in Washington, DC, then traveling from place to place, seeking funds for future voyages. As for him, he went to see my mother and father and the others, first in the museum and later in the hospital. He did his best, also, to cheer up Minik. But Mauripaulak didn't know anyone was planning such an exhibit, hadn't seen it coming, and had no power to change what the museum did.

"There are some bad people in America," Duncan said, "but most of us are good, decent folks. Not like those heartless people at the museum. Remember that." He tried to take my hand, but I pulled away, rocking back and forth. Later, in private, I would pray that my parents' spirits be released, to go into babies when the time was right.

Not everyone could be buried properly. Some fell through the sea ice, not to be seen again. Some were crushed under avalanches of rocks or snow. Rarely, old sick people went to drift off on ice floes alone, when they felt it was time to die. The spirits of all these people somehow transported themselves to where they needed to go. My parents had already found their way to the rock graves in Itta.

But that the *qallunaat* could be so senseless and cruel!

Peary eyed me. "Your year went well. I hoped your parents would have that, too. It ended badly." There was a line of sweat across his brow. He wiped it. "I will never allow any Eskimos to come to America again."

I turned to Duncan. "Were you making plans to take me to America?"

"Not unless you want it. Let's talk about it another time," he said gently.

"You tried to deceive me!" I said. How could he have discussed the idea with the men and not with me first? What other things should I have known and did not? "You weren't honest. Just like the others, you betrayed me. You're as bad as they are. Worse!"

I pulled away, and before I knew it my arm swept across the table, knocking over mugs. The green bottle fell and broke into pieces. Sharp-smelling, yellow liquor poured out. I lunged, slipped on the liquid, and fell face forward on the floor. The piercing pain in my feet swept over my whole body. I began to sob.

Duncan turned me over gently and picked me up. "Let me go!" I yelled. I kicked and punched him as I cried. He held me, and I finally gave in, stretching up to circle his neck and letting myself be carried back to the cabin.

* * *

I lay in my bed, bound in blankets as tightly as if I were in a grave of stones, and tried to push away the image of my parents—wax figures. In an exhibit. If only Peary hadn't invited them to go to America. If only they hadn't desperately wanted to go. If only I'd kept my stories to myself.

I thought of a time about four years earlier, when I'd been married for just two moons. That day, Angulluk and my father had helped Peary to move a gigantic boulder into his ship from a small island far to the south of Itta. It was a stone known by hunters of long ago to have fallen from the sky as a shooting star. We didn't know why Peary wanted the stone but had agreed to help him. Above the *Hope's* deck, the sky stone now hung from a crane on three chains like a giant water pot above a seal-oil lamp. Mauripaulak draped a red, white, and blue flag over it. A few summer snowflakes started to fall, whirling in a chilly wind.

Ally and my mother and adopted sister, Aviaq, standing near the bridge of timbers that connected the *Hope* to the island, watched as hunters and white men surrounded the sky stone. Peary held Marie high in the air for the crowd to see. Mitti Peary broke a bottle over the stone. Marie said, "I christen thee Ahnighito!" and the white men cheered. Their actions made no sense. The snow was falling more steadily now, and the winds were picking up speed. We waited for Peary to take us back to Itta, which he promised to do before going on the much longer journey to America.

By the time our family crowded into the ship's saloon with the rest of Peary's workers, the winds were howling. The sailing had to be postponed because a gale had risen from the sea. Aviaq clung to my mother and sobbed.

My people knew that the storm was a bad omen. The sky stone wanted to remain on the island. During the past few summers, it had broken Peary's chains, ropes, and winches, stubbornly defying all who tried to move it. The spirits were punishing Peary.

The next day, however, the weather cleared, and our sail to Itta was a smooth one. My mood remained low. Peary had offered to take several of our people to America when he returned with the sky stone. They'd come back to Itta with many riches the following summer. Against all reason and my protests, my parents had volunteered to go.

"You'll hate spending your days cooped up inside a white man's house. The crowds and the fast-moving, screeching trains will terrify you!" I said.

They wouldn't listen. Two days later, alone with my *anaana* as she packed her *ulu* and her sewing things, I pleaded, "Stay here! You'll be miserable there. And I'll be miserable without you."

"I want to see America," Anaana said. "Your father and I are eager to go. I'd like to see birds as colorful as the feathers you collected. I'd like to see trees."

I cried bitter tears. "Please understand. America is a terrible place. I'm tempted to go because I don't want to be separated from you. But I could not bear the white man's cities again. The sky is swallowed up by houses. The noises are unbearably loud. The air is full of bad smells. It's hot. Did you not understand anything I was telling you?"

There was no answer.

I took another approach. "Don't you want to stay, to care for Aviaq?"

"She's coming with us," Anaana said.

This was a blow!

"I've only had you for a short time, Anaana! Now you're leaving." Exactly two years earlier, I'd returned from America. This summer, within days of marrying me off, my parents had adopted Aviaq, almost as if to replace me. "I still don't see why."

"It's a fine and rare opportunity. Peary wants the *qallunaat* to know more about us. And a few of us—the lucky ones—can learn more about them."

"If you're going to the white man's land, you're unlucky." I tried one final argument. "Think of that stone and where it came from. Think of that storm. Aren't you afraid you'll go down in a shipwreck?"

"Of course I'm frightened, but your father and I have decided." I could see the desire in her dark eyes. "You are grown up. You and Angulluk can take care of yourselves."

"But who will take care of *you* in America?"

My mother looked at me, puzzled. "Don't you think your father can hunt seals and walrus in America? Feed and clothe us as always?"

"No, you'll depend on the *qallunaat* for every meal. You don't understand! Stay here."

Parents are not always wiser than their children.

CHAPTER TWENTY-FOUR

● ● ● ● ● ● ● ●

A full moon of days passed at the fort, and my blisters went away. One foot was still reddish, and the other bluish gray. Both hurt when left bare.

Inside, I felt dead. "Talk to me," Duncan said, squeezing my hand. I was too weary to make conversation or return the slightest affection.

Later, when I told Angulluk about my parents, he said, "It's just a story, like other stories. When we were children we thought the *qallunaat* would eat us. Remember?"

"It's true!" Rage erupted from inside me. It came out like a hoarse scream.

He watched me, puzzled. "Eqariusaq! I don't know how you could believe such lies."

"I wish it were a lie." I balled up my hands and cried myself to sleep.

* * *

The men were eager to go back to Payer Harbor.

Peary drove the sled I rode on, and Mauripaulak the other, which was weighed down with food and everything from wood to kerosene. The sleds moved slowly over the soft snow. Peary and I were sometimes forced to walk on our injured feet while the dogs pulled the sleds over rough terrain.

One of the first nights, barking woke us in our snow igloo; in the morning we saw prints in the snow like dogs' prints. But they spread larger. Peary said, "Wolves. A few times on Ellesmere I've seen them in groups. Enormous, and snow-white."

I'd not seen wolves since I was a child, on a hunt far away from Itta with my parents. As we continued our journey, I sat up and looked for them. When we stopped at a musk ox carcass, I noticed white hair and large prints around the chewed-over bones.

At last we came to the final stretch of steep, icy hills. The men untied the dogs and let them run loose. I took a few painful steps, then kept going. The men took turns hauling the sleds. Ten days after leaving the fort, we rounded a ridge, and the cliffs above the village came into sight. Just as the sun went down, we stood on an icy mound gazing at the distant, dark masts of the *Windward* and its tiny lights, twinkling like two stars. Fortunately, the ice in Payer Harbor still seemed firm in most places.

There was no moon, so we built igloos and made one last camp to avoid the dangers of falling through the ice. The next morning, I came out of the igloo to find that Peary had gone ahead. "He left well before sunrise," Mauripaulak said. "To arrive at the ship on his own."

"Peary likes to be first," I said.

Mauripaulak laughed. "You're right! Today, May sixth, is his birthday. Peary said he could smell the birthday cake Marie made for him."

"Marie probably *did* make a cake for him." I thought fondly of Marie mixing the cake, sliding the pan into the oven of Charlie's big iron stove, a sweet aroma wafting into the galley. But for this worthless sweet food, she'd use up the last of Charlie's sugar, canned milk, and flour. Eventually, we villagers might have to provide for those on the ship—and put our own survival at risk.

Other thoughts had come to me on the journey. I loved Duncan, and yearned for him. But he'd lied to me; he'd known about my parents all along. He was as much of a *qallunaat* as the Pearys. During the past few weeks at the fort, when we'd stayed in different cabins, our forced separation had been a relief. I had nothing left of myself to give, not even a smile.

Now, after packing up under a warm, orange sun, the rest of our party set out. As we neared Payer Harbor and the many islands of the sound, we divided into two groups. Mauripaulak, Duncan, and the two hunters took the sleds out on the ice toward the ship, while Angulluk, Bag of Bones, and I trekked toward the village.

Our people came out of their igloos and called to us. I managed a smile. How happy Angulluk was, and how the dogs barked to see him. Ally and Piugaattoq greeted us, lit the lamps to warm our igloo, and spread soothing seal oil on our raw faces. Tooth Girl and her family brought a steaming broth. Soon hunters came with more food. I didn't want their company, but I was pleased when Angulluk invited Bag of Bones to come inside our igloo to feast with us and to spend our first night home. The three of us slept deeply.

* * *

"The *qallunaat* were generous," Angulluk said when he returned from the ship. "Captain Bartlett paid me thirty-six bullets. He gave Bag of Bones an axe."

"Look at this," I said, unwrapping a foot to show the peeling skin. "Touch it. Still cold. I don't know if I'll ever be able to walk again like I used to. Do you think those payments make up for that trip?"

"You chose to go," he said.

"You led us all onto the ice and risked our lives."

No answer.

I asked, "Did you tell them on the ship about my falling into the water? What did they say?"

"The captain said, 'The gap you crossed means the ice will break up soon, and the ship will at last come free.' Mitti Peary said, 'I can't wait for us to sail!'"

I gently touched where the largest of my blisters had been. "They didn't care. She didn't thank me for going? I hate her. I hate all the *qallunaat*."

"Marie asked for you," Angulluk said. "She was unhappy to hear you'd fallen."

"I hate her, too." I was lying.

"She wanted to come and see you. Her mother said it wouldn't be safe."

Not safe for Marie to walk on the ice, but of course safe for me.

"Promise me you will not work for the Pearys again."

Angulluk glanced down at my blisters. "Be reasonable, Eqariusaq. Mitti and Lieutenant Peary offer goods we need. Without guns and ammunition, we could die."

"Plenty of us live without rifles. What makes you think the *qallunaat* will always be here to trade for more bullets?"

Again, no reply. He leaned toward me and rubbed noses, rubbed faces, before I pushed him away. I could see the compassion in his eyes. And I knew that his rifle had helped save not only us but other villagers from hunger and death.

"If you can't promise me, then I'm leaving you."

"Don't talk like that." He put his arms around me, gently, carefully, but I was so sore, I flinched. He drew away but patted me softly.

"If the *Windward* is still seaworthy, Peary will take us back to Itta," he said. "Life will be better."

"My feet may never be better. And all for that second rifle of yours and thirty-six bullets." *I hate you, almost as much as I hate Mitti Peary.*

"Be thankful you're strong. We did our best. You're very lucky that you didn't lose any of your toes."

"I can't walk without pain." Even inside warm seal fur, my feet were cold or had no feeling at all. I also still felt a chill and burning on my nose, cheeks, and ears and in the corners of my eyes. The furs and food in my igloo and the sight of the villagers comforted me, but something inside me had given up.

Angulluk watched my face. Then he said, "I can't imagine you, of all people, Eqariusaq, feeling sorry for yourself. After all that has happened in your life, why are you now so full of despair?"

I gave a long sigh. A good question. "I hate the Pearys. All the *qallunaat*. And you, too, for sticking up for them. If you'd talked to Peary about the museum, you'd know the truth about—"

"Eqariusaq! Are you still thinking about that?"

His words cut like sharpened bone. "Yes. It happened, and I can't understand why you don't believe me."

"The white people aren't so bad. We went off to rescue Peary and *he* rescued us. At the fort, Peary and Mauripaulak took good care of you. They gave us their food. Today, Peary invited the village to the ship to celebrate his return. I told him we'd come."

"I won't go."

"You will. Ally will go out. The whole village will." He added, "Getting along with Peary is important. His ship can take us back to Itta."

I let this last painful realization sink in. "For once, you may be right."

The more skillful we could be in our dealings with the *qallunaat*, the better off our lives would be. I'd known that.

Avoiding them wasn't the answer. So, later that day, I walked with Angulluk from the village out to the ship, determined not to limp, and studying the ice for breaks.

It was easy to spy Peary on the ship. What had his reunion with Mitti Peary and Marie been like? He had not seen them for nearly four summers. Now, senior crewmen formed a row and saluted him. In just two days, Peary had transformed himself. He was smiling, and his beard was shaved off, which made him look younger, the man I'd known in my childhood.

As Angulluk and I climbed on board, Peary was talking with the captain, wrapped in the white *nanoq* coat Ally had made him. Even with his limp now, and his red, raw face, he was striking, his sharp gray-blue eyes scanning the ship's lines. Peary gestured to the captain, who turned to the sailors. "You've all carried out your duties well, and we made it through a hard winter! Tomorrow, have the men start stem-to-stern scouring. When the snow melts to the waterline, we'll add details, scraping barnacles and scum." Peary pointed aloft. "And we'll fly the Stars and Stripes today and every day the sun shines! The ice will break soon, and the *Windward* shall sail out with colors flying— for home!" The crewmen raised a cheer.

Peary exclaimed, "Billy Bah!" and gave me a fierce hug before I could stop him. He acted as if we hadn't been in the same fort all those days. He shook Bag of Bones's hand. "Angulluk." He grasped his shoulders.

The captain and crew beamed, lit by his spirit. How could I hate him? In courage and will, he was the most impressive *qallunaat* to travel to our land.

"Come into the forward saloon," Peary said. "Join the celebration!"

He swung around and called, *"Hainang!"* to Ally, Sammy, and Piugaattoq.

Ally climbed aboard first, lifting Sammy on deck, and Peary swept her up, put her down, stroked her hair, and bent and kissed Sammy on the nose. He slapped Piugaattoq on the back.

Ally held Sammy out. Peary swung him around and around.

"I am happy," Ally said. "Sammy, this is your father. Pearyaksoah."

Sammy looked up at him with wide blue eyes, as if remembering him.

"Look how big you are, Sammy!" Peary said, ruffling the toddler's shaggy hair. "You've grown to be a little man."

"He can run now, and talk. And he even knows how to say some English words."

Peary said, "So! He's smart, as well as strong. Handsome, too."

Ally continued to boast, her whole body swelling with pride. For once, I was glad. I couldn't begrudge her this moment of happiness. *Peary will never leave his wife, I* thought. *One day he'll return to America. Ally must know this and still she loves him.*

"Go out of the cold," Peary said tenderly, giving Sammy to her. "I'll be there in a few minutes."

A strange wail filled the air. Then, loud singing.

Cin howled. Sammy cried and hid his face in Ally's furs.

Peary said, "Sounds like Matt Henson got the gramophone working."

I'd never seen the forward saloon so crowded, or heard it so loud. The gramophone sounds, which I'd all but forgotten, rose with the talking and singing. People from the village and the crew alike sat on benches, at tables, and on the floor, drinking tea, eating biscuits. Everyone except a few of our older people had come to see Peary. Mikihoq, round with a child, sat with her family.

Marie danced in a red dress that was now too short. I caught sight of Duncan near the galley door, drinking from a mug. My breath quickened. Marie pulled me toward Mitti Peary, who was pouring tea. I noticed how carefully she filled a cup for Ally, as if she wanted Ally to like her. It must have been hard for Mitti Peary, I thought, to meet Ally's baby when her own baby had died. The *qallunaat* certainly knew how to mask their feelings!

"Tea?" Marie asked me.

"Later," I said to Marie. With Angulluk following, I pushed through the crowd to Duncan.

Duncan grabbed my hand. He led me and Angulluk

into the privacy of the galley. The three of us were alone. We looked at each other.

Duncan said to Angulluk, "I want to trade for Billy Bah, for good, for the rest of my life. I want to marry her. Give her to me. In exchange, I'll give you everything I own. My rifle and bullets, clothes, tools, wood. And more."

So that was why Duncan was going on the hunts and the search party! He'd been acquiring goods from Mitti Peary and the captain so that he could use them for a permanent trade. For *me*.

In shock, I felt my heart stop for an instant. "Duncan, don't say this," I said. "We didn't agree. You're just like my husband. Making plans for me."

Angulluk scowled. "You can't have her."

Duncan said, "Trade her to me for a month."

"No trades!" Angulluk was jealous.

Duncan turned his gaze into my eyes. "Billy Bah, I'm asking you now. Divorce him. Come and live with me on the ship."

I looked back into Duncan's kind green eyes. He desired me more than I realized. Ever since the accident, I'd been pushing him away; this was the first time in many days that I was truly seeing him. Something in me wanted to go to him. But if Duncan thought I would go to America again, he was wrong. He should have known better.

"She's mine." Angulluk was firm.

"Say something, Billy Bah," Duncan pleaded. "Won't you say anything?"

I couldn't seem to open my mouth.

Then Duncan said, "She came to me on her own without being traded."

"You're lying," my husband countered.

"No, he's not. I did go to him. Once." Then I added, "But that was a long time ago. It doesn't matter now."

Angulluk's eyes flashed. He wasn't hearing me; he was only thinking of his own pride. I thought the men might break into a fight.

Instead, Duncan turned to me. "We can't be private now. I don't care. Billy Bah. Eqariusaq. Will you be my wife?"

Angulluk put his hands on my shoulders and moved me behind him. He set his feet squarely and faced Duncan. I couldn't see his expression.

Looking around him at Duncan, I asked, "Do you mean, go with you to America?"

"Yes. In time, when you're ready."

"No, Duncan." At that moment, I truly made up my mind. "I can never go there again. I'm sorry." The words came out and I realized how deeply I meant them.

"Fine." Duncan shoved past us and slipped into the crowd.

* * *

Alone with Angulluk in the galley, with the loud sounds of the party in the next room, I took a deep breath. I was afraid he'd be angry. Instead, he looked smug.

He'd stood up for me and this was a good thing. "Angulluk," I said, "have you decided *never* to trade me to the *qallunaat* again?"

"We'll see."

"Tell me. This isn't something to tease about. Look what happened."

He stopped smiling. "I won't trade you to Duncan. As for the other *qallunaat,* no, probably not. At least not for a while."

He made a mistake. So he wasn't going to give up his quest for white man's goods, even though he already had two rifles and could trade his skills as a hunter for cartridges. He wasn't going to treat me as I deserved.

"If you're not sure," I said, "I'll leave you."

"You can't manage without me."

"You're mistaken." We both knew it was true. In the past few seasons, I'd shown how valuable my sewing was to the *qallunaat,* as well as to our people. And I'd also become more skillful in bringing in food. "I don't need you."

He kicked me in the stomach. I fell backward, rose to my feet, and charged, hitting him. Just then, the galley door swung open.

"Billy Bah! I've been looking for you!" a deep voice called.

It was Mauripaulak. "What's the matter? You two argue like dogs. Come on, join the party."

I nodded, still dazed. I was relieved to see that Duncan

had left the saloon. Mauripaulak waved us to a small table. On it sat a shiny machine in a wood case that Peary called a gramophone. It opened up to a spreading horn. Mauripaulak turned a handle, then set a little arm on a spinning disc to make the sound. Bag of Bones stood beside Mauripaulak and frowned. If I hadn't seen one of these *qallunaaq* machines before, I would have wondered, too.

"It doesn't have bad power," I reminded Angulluk. "It can't harm your spirit." He nodded.

The gramophone sang out the *qallunaat's* nonsensical words: *"You'll look sweet upon the seat . . ."*

Marie came up to us. The machine had stopped and she turned the handle and moved the switch to start it again. When it ran down, she asked Angulluk to do it. He grasped the handle, testing it at first, then wound smoothly.

Mauripaulak took my hands and spun me around in a dance. Afterward he danced with Marie. The song on the gramophone ended and Marie showed Tooth Girl how to turn the handle. But Tooth Girl turned it so fast, Marie had to hold her hand.

Peary entered the saloon, and Marie dashed through the crowd to her father. The strange music came to a halt. Sailors got up from a table to make room for Peary, Mitti Peary, and me. Captain Bartlett took a seat with us. Grease Beard also joined the table. He lit his pipe.

Marie climbed onto Peary's lap. She pressed her face against her father's and played with his long mustache. I'd never seen her so happy. She kissed him on the cheeks again and again.

On the far side of the room, the gramophone started up. Bag of Bones was working it carefully. The same song played once more.

Ally, Sammy, and Piugaattoq crowded in on the floor near our feet. More villagers pushed close.

Peary wet a biscuit in the tea, took a bite, and began to tell about his travels. Mostly, he spoke to Mitti Peary, who gazed at him lovingly. From time to time, she shook her head in disbelief.

He talked about his two attempts to reach the North Pole since he'd last seen his wife. "After the first time, I lost my toes. Both times I'd been stopped by blizzards and had to turn back." For these trips, he'd chosen the northern tip of Ellesmere Land as his starting point for venturing out on the sea ice. So he'd claimed Fort Conger as a good wintering spot. He related how my group had found him but said little about my fall through the ice and my frostbite.

The gramophone kept playing. Captain Bartlett described how he'd waited for Peary longer than was safe before sailing for Payer Harbor, then found a big iceberg blocking the way out.

Mitti Peary sighed. "It's been a long winter here, too, Bert. Especially without you."

"We've survived by using many of the supplies that were meant for your expedition," Captain Bartlett put in.

"We used all the new guns and ammunition trading with the Eskimos," Mitti Peary said. "I had them hunt for us and sent them out twice to look for you. The first time they spent their time tracking a polar bear."

She could only think of herself!

"You did all the right things, my love," Peary said, squeezing her gloved hand. "All is well. We're safe, and the ship seems to be in fine shape."

"So far, I'm not aware of any major damage," Captain Bartlett added. "I see no reason why we can't set sail this summer." He put down his pipe. "Are you planning to come home with us, Lieutenant Peary?"

The air grew still as we waited for Peary to answer. The gramophone played the same song over and over.

Peary looked at Mitti Peary when he spoke. "We'll see how the ship is when the ice melts. We'll see if I have enough oil to last me another year. I'll decide after that."

Mitti Peary turned pale. Peary gave a tiny smile. He stroked her cheek, but she didn't respond.

"You're coming home with us when the ship breaks free, aren't you, Daddy?" Marie said.

"We'll see," he said.

The realization that he might stay swept over her like the roar of an iceberg turning over. "Dad, you must sail with us! You've been gone for *years*. We've come all this way for you!"

When he didn't answer, Marie got down off his lap. "Mother. Make Dad know he has to come home."

"No one is leaving anywhere for quite a while. Let's not talk about it now." Mitti Peary's voice was low.

Ally saw her chance to get Peary's attention. With Marie no longer on Peary's lap, she lifted Sammy to him.

Mitti Peary sniffed. "We've gotten to know each other, Ally and I," she said with an edge. "She made Marie's *kapatak*."

Sammy grabbed Peary's mustache. "Look how he remembers his father," Ally said.

I was shocked that she said this—in front of everyone. Was she testing Peary?

Mitti Peary glared at Ally. Marie looked stunned, as if she might burst into tears. Then Peary offered Ally a sad smile and passed Sammy back to her. I could tell he wanted to hold Sammy, but not in front of Mitti Peary.

Ally studied Peary. She was hurt but held her chin up. "Sammy will be a great hunter, and a great leader like his father."

Mitti Peary looked away. "Marie, darling," she said. "Tell Matt we must have a rest with the music. Tell him it's time we put away the gramophone."

For one moment, Peary looked like I'd never seen him before—uncertain. Perhaps he lived between two worlds as I did. He had a *qallunaaq* wife and Ally, whom I believed he loved very much.

But a moment later, Peary's face relaxed. "Come with me, Captain. Let's measure the condition of the ice."

How calmly he left the room! I could learn something

from Peary. He was selfish and often used my people for his own ambitions, but he could take command of himself. He knew how to make the whole world his home. Was that the strength and freedom old Navarana had wished for me?

It was time to be myself. Hold strong.

CHAPTER TWENTY-FIVE

● ● ● ● ● ● ● ●

The next morning, in our igloo, Angulluk gave my arm a hard yank. "Eqariusaq! You went off with Duncan without my permission!"

"Fat One! That was a long time ago. Well before our journey." Then, playfully, "Go ahead, show me you're my husband, make me yours again." And he did show me, happily. But then he squeezed my wrist so tightly I cried. "Let go! You're hurting me."

He'd changed our unspoken rule: we did not fight during lovemaking.

I saw in his eyes calculation, mixed with triumph. Finally, he released his grip and I pulled away.

Now I know I want to find another husband, I thought, but I could not say it. Later, when dressed and outside, I'd say the words.

As I heated broth over the oil lamp in my cooking pot, Angulluk and I looked at each other silently, more in sadness than in anger. To make things better between us, I almost wanted to accompany him hunting that morning, to watch for seals at the blowholes, as my mother had often done for my father. But he left by himself.

Outside I heard Mitti Peary's shrill voice, mixing with her husband's deeper tones. If it had been Peary alone, I might have gone to meet him. Staring at the fire, I wrapped my arms around my chest, tried to make myself invisible, and waited for Mitti Peary to pass by and bring her wants elsewhere.

Peary loved conversation and visiting. I could hear him asking how our people fared, congratulating them for surviving the winter so well.

At long last, the talking moved on. Blissful silence. I crawled out the entrance tunnel and walked through the village. It was a sunny day, one of the first of late winter, so it was natural that all the villagers had dispersed, to set traps, hunt seals, or explore the soggy, awakening landscape. Few of us, it seemed, had any skins for sewing; it was still too early in the season to have enough to make our new summer clothes. But I knew I must do something.

I decided to practice using my feet again by hiking to the valley, the only land free of snowdrifts, and perhaps to the hills beyond. I'd follow the well-trodden paths, and not only would I get away from the Fat One for the day and prevent myself from getting riled up, I'd check on our three traps from the previous season. The foxes had their thickest fur at this time of the year. Wouldn't I enjoy having a beautiful fox fur *kapatak* for next winter? The plan for the day formed, like a seed, growing.

First my gaze, as always, went to the beach and the

rippling salty gray ice beyond it, where the *Windward* rose like a great pile of giant bones. Duncan would be mopping the deck right now, repairing the rigging, or washing the sails—sails that would carry the ship, and my Duncan, from me forever. Or was it possible that the ship, broken in ways that could not be seen, would never cross the ocean again?

Part of me hoped that Duncan would be forced to stay for as long as possible.

Not far from shore, the Fat One moved gracefully on the ice. Despite all that had happened today, I found myself wondering if his boots, ones I'd lovingly sewn and decorated with cuffs of young seal fur, were keeping out water.

Don't turn around and notice me, I thought. He didn't, or pretended not to.

The beach was empty except for three hunters patching kayaks. I approached them and asked, "Have you seen Peary?"

"He and his wife went up into the hills," one man said.

From the icy sun-filled landscape that stretched out around the *Windward,* there came a familiar small green figure, yanked forward by Cin on a leash. Cin carried something in her mouth: a white man's shoe.

"Billy Bah!" Marie said, rushing toward me. Her eyes were red; she'd been crying. "I've run away from my parents! I've come to live with you."

"What? Tell me what's happening."

215

Marie kicked at one of the brown-gray patches of melting snow that still lay on the shore. I untied Cin, who was thrashing about in need of exercise, and I threw the shoe across the ice for her to fetch.

"Billy Bah," Marie said crossly, "you ought to keep Cin on her lead. Otherwise she'll run off and—"

"I'd catch her and teach her to behave."

"You *wouldn't* hit her, Billy Bah!"

"Only if she disobeyed me."

I whistled. Cin ran toward me, shoe in mouth, and brushed against my leg. I stroked her head.

Marie looked at me, surprised. "You can make dogs obey, just like Dad."

I tossed the shoe, farther this time, and Cin retrieved it. "Tell me why you're running away from your parents."

"Mother says I'm going to America with her when the ice melts. I won't go! I want to stay with Dad."

"Your place is with your mother," I said.

"I'm staying here."

"You can't. Peary goes out onto the ice for many days at a time. Who would take care of you?"

"You, Billy Bah! I can live with you and Angulluk." Smiling a little, she looked to me for an answer.

"No." Then, more gently, "I wish you could stay. I'll miss you when you go."

The truth is, I would have enjoyed raising Marie as my own child, dressing her and feeding her, teaching her to sew. But, of course, I couldn't.

"It's better you remain with your own people, Marie."

"No one can force me."

Her parents certainly would. What should I do with her right now? The best thing would be to bring her back to the ship. But then I'd need to face Duncan.

As if I were a hunter, surrounded by dangers on all sides, I needed to consider my next move.

Marie threw the shoe to Cin a few more times, until it disappeared into a hole in the ice, another casualty of the frozen sound. When I whistled, Cin bounded forward on wet legs and paws, arriving at my feet, her thick, wet tail wagging.

"I'm taking you back to the *Windward,* Marie." I'd walk her to the ship, then turn around without boarding.

"I won't go!"

I took her arm, and her body went rigid. She even made fists. She was serious about running away. Something had happened between her and her parents.

"Where are your mother and father today?"

"Off by themselves for a long walk," Marie said bitterly. "Arguing about Ally."

"I see." I rubbed Cin under her throat and on her neck.

Marie turned to me and said, "I hate my father. Ally, too."

"Marie," I said softly. "This is just the way things are in our land. Women have babies all the time with men who are not their husbands. All the hunters share their wives."

She went back to kicking wet sand on the beach. Then

she ran toward the village, Cin taking the lead. I felt a sharp pain in my feet as I rushed after her. "Where are you going?"

"To find Akitsinnguaq. Her family will take me in."

Marie to live with Tooth Girl? The idea was absurd.

Tooth Girl's igloo was empty, so I suggested that Marie come with me to the valley to build a new fox trap. When I reminded her that this was the place where she'd followed rabbit tracks with Tooth Girl, she wanted to come. It was also the place where I'd most likely find Marie's parents.

We stopped at my igloo, picked up strips of seal meat and a bag of water, and set off, with Cin sniffing the ground. In the hill's shadows, we came to the valley. The sun had melted the snow in the middle, and gray boulders dotted the ground.

Those boulders are moving. "Look, Marie!" I said. "Musk oxen." The hunters were missing a great opportunity. "Ha!" I laughed. "Not a single man in sight!" Here was the largest herd I'd ever seen, pawing the ground for willows, just a short walk from the village.

In the distance, white wolves moved against a nearly white background. Cin growled, and her pointy ears pricked up. "It's all right, Cin," I said, gripping her leash. One wolf stopped and turned to look at us, then trotted off toward the musk oxen.

I took Marie's hand. "There are wolves nearby, but

they won't bother us. We'll let them make their kill and keep our distance."

Giant white rabbits skittered away, disappearing behind lichen-covered boulders and into the warm brown and red patches of awakening vegetation. I'd discovered a colony of rabbits, fifty animals or more. If only I had materials for traps; I noted my surroundings for the future.

"Musk oxen, wolves, rabbits! I've never in my life seen so many animals all together at one time," I marveled.

Prey and predators seemed remarkably out in the open in this valley, not hidden from each other in shadowy pockets. The hunting in Musk Ox Land was excellent beyond belief.

There might be a future here, I thought. Perhaps it would be a good thing to stay on this shore a while longer before returning to Itta. If I could tuck away caches of food before winter, I could prosper without Angulluk. I'd just need to find another hunter or family to give me shelter.

Marie picked some yellow wildflowers. When all the snows melted, there would be many more flowers, perhaps spreading across the whole valley. There were also beautiful stretches like that near Itta.

Beneath the shadow of the cliffs, the snow took on a greenish tinge. As we began to go uphill, I realized how hard it would be to climb with my injured feet. Better to return to the valley.

Beyond a small hill, among the mosses and rocks, Marie noticed scattered clumps of white fur, and a bushy white tail partly hidden under snow. "Fox droppings. Wolf droppings, too," I said. "And here, wolf prints. A wolf got this fox."

The perfect place to build my fox trap.

I explained to Marie that a fox trap was like a tiny rock igloo, and we gathered stones, picking ones of equal size and stacking them in rows. We collected more stones, and before long we'd built the first wall. Cin rolled up in a ball, sleeping.

The sun felt good on my face as I chewed a salty strip of seal meat. We took turns drinking from the water skin.

"I know how to build a rock igloo like the ones in the village," she said. "With some help, I could make my own. Right next to yours and Angulluk's."

I sighed. It was touching how Marie kept to her dream.

I hugged my knees, closed my eyes, and took in the sunlight while Marie worked on building a second wall of the fox trap.

Cin jumped to her feet and bolted away as urgent shouts came from above. Peary, in his blue jacket on top of the nearest hill, waved his arms frantically. *A warning!*

A gray-and-white dog zigzagged toward us, its muzzle covered in blood. Its mouth foamed.

The dog doubled up and gnawed its side. It was *pillarotoq*. Rabid. A shiver went up my spine.

Cin circled it, barking louder. The dog, snarling frantically, came still closer.

We shouldn't run, I thought. Not that there was a place we could run to. "Marie! Stay very still." She crouched in back of me.

The dog moved in so close that I could hear its uneven breath. I picked up a rock and threw it, but missed. The next rock hit the side of its foaming mouth. The dog eyed me. Before I could grab another rock, it lunged. Cin leapt. The crazed dog jerked and twisted to throw Cin off.

I found another rock, aimed at the dog's yellow eyes, and threw with all my might. The dog fell, blood ran from its mouth, and it thrashed about.

Peary bounded down the hill. He stopped and aimed his rifle. A loud shot echoed. He'd put a bullet right through its head.

Marie ran to Peary. "Daddy!" He moved us away from the dog.

Marie buried her head in his chest.

"Billy Bah! Thank you," Peary said. "You saved Marie."

"You and I."

Soon Mitti Peary caught up and Marie ran into her arms. She cried harder than I'd ever seen. Then she turned to her father and hit and kicked him.

When Peary told me of my parents' deaths, all that night I kicked and screamed—at Angulluk. I understood what it was like to have your whole life change between one moment and the next.

I pulled her away. "Marie! Stop."

We were both shaking. I squeezed her tightly and finally she stood quietly, still crying but not as hard, her head down. Then she went to her mother, who embraced her.

Peary offered me a look of gratitude and seemed about to burst into tears. He could face any kind of danger, but he couldn't handle Marie.

As a child I'd been in awe of him, as if he were more than human. Now I saw him for what he was: a man who'd been kicked by his child and had nearly lost her. Even if he was a great leader, I felt I was his equal.

CHAPTER TWENTY-SIX

● ● ● ● ● ● ● ●

The next day, I woke with my feet sore from the hike, my whole body feeling heavy, and I was angry. Why wasn't I happy to be back?

Alone in the igloo, I took out my box of treasures. As I held a comb, I remembered how I yelled as a child when Mitti Peary pulled it through my hair. I never used it but liked the comb's brown and reddish colors, the way light shone through it. Sparkly or shiny things, like glass beads and bottles, attracted me and everyone in our village. I used to think such things were magical.

An empty box of animal crackers I had prized now only reminded me of the animals I saw in cages in a zoo with Mitti Peary and Marie. We'd come to a pen where a fox paced back and forth, stopping to chew on its leg, which was raw. At home, if an animal was very sick and in pain or acted crazed, we killed it. Foxes should be turned into food and their furs made into clothes, or else left to live in burrows and raise their young. That day I had thought: *The fox and I are captives in the white man's land!* I'd held back tears. To comfort me, Mitti Peary reached into her bag and said, "I have treats. Animal crackers." I took the brightly colored box and studied the pictures on it. The biscuits inside it were shaped like animals, too. How delightful! But this special gift didn't make up for the terrors of that day.

The acorn that I lifted out next brought back a happier memory. I had been curious about the trees that grew to be so big. I started looking at them closely, and seeing how they were different. I came to love them. The tree this acorn came from was an oak. As the weather turned cold, its leaves changed to bright yellow. One day, I climbed out onto a high branch. Right over my head, I heard scrambling. A gray animal with a furry tail scurried down the trunk headfirst. How funny it was! I'd heard them called squirrels. It stopped and held an acorn to its mouth, its tail twitching. Feeling as free as the squirrel, I climbed down, branch to branch, and dropped to the grass, where I picked up acorns and put them in the pocket of my pinafore.

Next I held up the red feather. Mitti Peary sometimes took me to a park that was full of chirping birds. One day, I climbed a path with the sun warm on my back and a cool wind against my face. Water from rain still dripped from the trees. I saw the feather on the ground ahead and ran to it, so happy to be outside and moving—as in summer at home when I'd scale bird cliffs in search of eggs.

The park's path wound upward, and I climbed to the top. The view opened. I'd come to a cliff where the land ended and the sky began. Blackbirds swirled in a great cloud above. Looking at the feather now, I still remembered how my heart leaped.

I took out a pink ribbon that summoned a picture of Marie; a scrap of black satin was a reminder of her grandmother, swishing about in her shining dresses; a cup with a rim of blue flowers: Mitti Peary, her white-and-blue china dishes holding pears, peaches, and red candy. Yet the cup itself, cracked and chipped, didn't look beautiful anymore. It didn't hold such magic. Why had I hidden these keepsakes from my family and friends? Did I really think villagers seeing them would beg to go to America—to die there?

Holding them, I knew that pieces of cloth and ribbon and a broken teacup, or things like them, would not lure my parents to another land. More likely, it was Peary's huge ship and its speed that impressed them. If my keepsakes had power, it was over me, and only because they helped sights and sounds spring back clearly. Perhaps I'd kept these objects all these years because *I'd* yearned for America. *I'd* been the one most in danger of wanting to sail back there.

I'd allowed the land of the *qallunaat* to absorb some of my spirit.

Now I knew that I'd always stay in my own part of the world. Nothing, no one, even Duncan, could tempt me to leave the people and land closest to me.

What should I do now with my precious keepsakes?

Were they all *useless*? I separated out the photograph of my mother, Duncan's gifts, and the *nanoq* and seal figures that my father had carved, put them in a bag with my needles for sewing, and tucked the other objects back in the box. For an instant I imagined a hole in the ice and me dropping the whole box into the sea below.

I drew on furs and went outside. With the box tucked under my arm, I looked toward the beach from the village rise and a new picture formed. Taking slow steps on my healing feet, I walked to the place set apart on the far side of the village where Navarana was buried in her grave house.

"*Aana,*" I greeted her.

"*Hainang,*" Navarana said in return. Her gruff voice sounded cheerful.

In my mind's eye, I could see the spirit of the old woman stirring a pot of soup. We talked for a while and I told her of my trek, my fall in the stinging water and frostbite, coming upon Peary at last . . . and the long tedious days inside the fort. "*I no longer want to be like the* qallunaat," I said.

"*Good! You've been cured of that sickness, at last! Ha!*"

"*I hate the* qallunaat."

"*No good. You cannot harbor strong feelings about the* qallunaat *if you want to take command of your life. Just as a hunter cannot manage a sled team if his dogs are fighting. Do not let your dogs be out of control for long or you will lose your sled, never moving forward. And don't allow any person,* qallunaaq *or other, to*

226

cut across your path and cast you off. You have a right to your path as they have a right to theirs."

"I will remember, Aana," I said. I didn't completely understand, though pieces were starting to grow clear. I should not weaken my own strength. If I didn't consider myself an equal to the *qallunaat,* and my husband, too, I'd still find myself under others' feet in all my dealings. I should master myself. Then maybe I'd find that strength and calm she'd told me about long ago.

I looked out at the village and bay from the hill, then turned back to her.

"Tell me of the vision you saw earlier. You pictured me with a group of women on Peary's ship. You said I'd find contentment among them."

"You must discover the future on your own, Panik. What will come, will come, based on all the steps you take on your journey today and tomorrow."

I sighed, though I knew spirits left you to solve your own problems.

I bid Navarana's spirit farewell and told her I'd visit her again before it was time for her to enter into the world through a birth. Then I began to gather stones.

It was understood among my people that whenever someone created piles or chambers out of stones, for whatever purpose, storing meat, marking places on a landscape, or covering the remains of a dead person, no one else would disturb the stones. Even Peary's meaningless piles were safe.

I covered my box of treasures, stone by stone, lovingly protecting it. There! Giving the box a place of honor here felt satisfying and good. Then I turned my back on my cairn and the graves surrounding it and headed back toward the village.

* * *

The spring rains came in torrents, and the Fat One and I stayed inside our igloo, listening to the howling wind, pounding rain, and the thundering roar of sea ice breaking into floes. As I waited for the storm to end, I prepared myself to leave him, though I couldn't yet imagine where I would live, if not in our igloo or on the ship. Eventually, I'd return to Itta and my sister, but how? When?

On the third day of the storm, all our other food gone, Angulluk went from one meat rack to another and returned with a hunk of dried seal. I watched him lean against the wall as we ate, his face wet, his dark eyes desperate. Instead of talking, we listened to the rain as it steadily fell on the roof. *How much longer can I stand this?* I thought. There had been times when we'd welcomed the isolation that a storm would bring. Now we were both weary of each other, but at least I wasn't so angry.

Did all fiery angers eventually turn to sadness? Would sadness eventually turn to understanding and relief?

I thought of Duncan.

I needed to see him again, if only for a few encouraging

words to take me to the next step of my new life, without him.

A new thought came to me. Maybe it was fortunate that I did not have a child, or else it would be even harder to leave Angulluk.

I jumped as a series of earsplitting cracks rang out louder than gunshots. The ice of the sound was breaking apart.

Angulluk smiled. "The rain has stopped."

"At last."

We dressed and ventured outdoors, joining the other villagers, and took in the new landscape with murmurs of surprise. The winter snow melted and water flowed from the hills and cliffs, past the village's rock dams, and flooded the beach. A newly created river cut into the sea ice.

Angulluk and I headed to the beach to scan the harbor. A cloud of sea mist lifted, revealing a horrifying scene. Out in the harbor, as blocks of ice revolved alongside it in the currents, the *Windward* listed to one side, ready to capsize.

Ancestors, don't let the ship sink, I prayed.

I held my breath and let Angulluk speak. "Look at that!" He turned back to the village to spread the news. Other people were crowding a hill.

Ropes pulling the masts dropped, the ship rose suddenly, then rolled on the opposite side. I cried out as it rocked again, then settled upright.

Duncan, be safe. Marie, be safe.

Bag of Bones and Angulluk carried a kayak to the water. I wanted to go with them, but kayaks were only for hunters.

"We'll see what they are doing," Angulluk said. Then he added, as if to show he didn't care about the *qallunaat*, "With the ice breaking up, it's a good time for hunting."

Angulluk, Bag of Bones, and two other hunters readied their harpoons, paddled across the flooded beach, and entered the river that rushed into the harbor.

Gulls circled overhead, and their shrill cries encouraged me. Musk Ox Land did not have large bird colonies like Itta, though this shore, too, was coming alive. I searched for bird eggs on the cliffs, looking out to the blue water and ice of the harbor all morning to see the kayaks approach the *Windward*. Soon there would be news.

Meanwhile, high above the harbor, I came upon an empty gull's nest, paw prints, and droppings: a fox had gotten the eggs. So foxes climbed these cliffs. Yet no villager had thought to put a fox trap here. Mine would be the first! I collected stones, climbing with them to the spot, one by one, but was too tired to finish the walls.

In the afternoon, I stopped at the rise above the beach to see the hunters drag in a great narwhal the length of a kayak. What a prize! With lines over their shoulders, they heaved the whale to higher ground.

I ran down toward Angulluk, and as in old times, we rubbed noses and faces. He grinned and laughed. *Ai*, his eyes squinted happily! I could tell he had spotted and was first to spear the whale.

Ordinarily, I'd have been eager to hear about the sea hunt before anything else. But I asked, "Did you get to the ship?"

Angulluk's smile vanished. "Shut up, woman! Let me speak."

I lowered my head but gave him a fierce look.

When villagers gathered, Angulluk, whipping his arm, recounted how, after his clean strike in the head, each hunter's harpoon pierced the narwhal. It was a mother whale with a calf. Mauripaulak took a boat, harnessed the calf, and brought it to the ship to entertain Marie. On a long line, it swam back and forth alongside the *Windward*.

When my husband finished, I asked, "Marie?"

"She's fine," Bag of Bones said. "No one was hurt."

"The captain called down. He said he can free the ship soon," Angulluk added, sounding satisfied. "Any day, the *qallunaat* will sail away."

"Even Peary?" I asked.

"I don't know."

"Will the captain take us to Itta?"

"We'll find out. No more talk of the *qallunaat*," my husband said. Looking at the bloody whale at his feet, he grinned. "Eqariusaq, get ready for a feast!"

* * *

231

In the following days, I could see sailors standing on sections of ice around the *Windward,* cutting the ship free by sawing ice into blocks. One morning, hunters returned with a baby narwhal—Marie's narwhal, probably. Its meat was the most tender and delicious I'd ever tasted. We'd crossed the invisible line between spring and early summer, dark and light, hunger and plentitude.

Soon, too, we had stewed rabbit after I snared several in the valley. I finished the fox trap I'd started on the cliffs, and in its rocky shelter hung a chunk of rotting rabbit meat for bait. If I could build more fox and rabbit traps, I'd have enough furs to sew new and beautiful clothes for myself.

A few days after the young narwhal was caught, Bag of Bones stood proudly outside my igloo, wearing *qallunaaq* trousers and a frayed sailor shirt.

I scolded him. "Why are you dressed like that?"

"Mauripaulak gave me these clothes." He lifted his chin.

Somehow, seeing Bag of Bones looking like a *qallunaaq* bothered me, but his hair, now washed and trimmed to shoulder length, was a big improvement. The white man's practice of washing wasn't all bad.

"I'm going to make your clothes from now on."

"Would you, Eqariusaq?" His dark eyes shone.

"Yes," I replied, surprised at my offer. It was the equivalent of saying I'd adopted him. We rubbed noses. Though we'd probably continue to live apart, there was a stated bond between us. In effect, I had a son.

I grew quiet while he talked, full of gossip.

The crewmen now spent their days sawing the ice around the ship to help it break up faster, he said. Cin was cooped up on deck and barked a great deal. Marie cried when she saw that her narwhal calf had escaped. "She doesn't know we ate it," he said with a grin.

"The *qallunaat* have no sense," I said. "No one can keep a whale on a rope."

"I said as much," he agreed. "Mauripaulak did it only to please Marie."

"Did you see Duncan?"

"He's all right." Bag of Bones dug into his pocket and gave me a small mirror. "It's from him."

I took it and looked at myself. The last time I'd used a mirror was on the *Windward,* after Mitti Peary bathed me. Just before I'd been traded to Duncan. Now I could see myself the way he did: a woman with a pretty face. Was the mirror a good-bye gift?

That night, a storm blew upon us from the north, and high winds drove rain against the igloos. The next day, excited cries passed through the village. I met Tooth Girl and her mother, Mikihoq, and Ally and Sammy on the path to the shore. I hoped what we found wouldn't be bad.

The sunlight was too strong to see over the water. I cupped my hands and squinted. Winds and currents had cleared most of the ice from the harbor. But where was the *Windward*?

I put my hand over my mouth. Duncan was gone. Marie, her mother, Peary. All of them, gone!

Ally came to me, shock in her face. "Could they have left us for America so suddenly? I thought they'd take us to Itta! I was sure Pearyaksoah would make another trek toward that place he calls the North Pole."

"So was I."

We stood together feeling our losses, our broken hearts. Sammy dug in the sand.

Mikihoq joined us and folded her arms across her pregnant belly, satisfied. "*Aait!* The *qallunaat* have gone back to their land!"

"There are other possibilities." I dared not say that the ship sank in the storm. A shiver ran up my spine.

Ally read my thoughts. Forgetting herself, she said, "Could a ship sink to the bottom, without any of it showing?"

"Eventually, parts of it would surface," I said.

I remembered my father once going on a hunting trip and returning with a plank large enough to make runners for a sled. In the area of the beach where he'd found the wood, he said, hunters had for many years been collecting odd pieces: a propeller, a rudder, a broken chain, the weathered and ghostly woman's face that had been a figurehead.

"Our hunters could make good use of all that wood," said Mikihoq.

Ally's lips curled. Otherwise she gave no expression to the pain she must have been feeling. I realized something: Ally's unfailing high spirits required great effort. All along, I'd thought of her as a little stupid. But she was smarter than I'd realized—and brave.

I nearly shouted at Mikihoq. "Don't say another word."

I wanted to stagger away from them, find a hiding place, and creep into it, alone. Instead, I stood on the beach and reached out to take Ally's hand.

CHAPTER TWENTY-SEVEN

● ● ● ● ● ● ● ●

Ally and I scavenged the beach, then the cliffs, for gulls, eggs, rabbits, foxes, or anything else that our restless hands could turn into food. Sammy trailed behind, singing a nonsense song and brandishing a long-handled bird net. Then Ally strapped him into the folds of her carrying hood as the trail grew steeper. The other villagers had gone to the valley to hunt musk oxen. Piugaattoq and Angulluk had joined them, without asking either Ally or me to accompany them; clearly, they'd arranged for other women to help them with their chores and share their tents.

I wanted to ask her: "Are you happy with Piugaattoq? Could you be content if you never saw Peary again?"

Instead, I told her, "I built a fox trap near the top of the cliff."

She looked at me with a strange seriousness. "How clever of you, Eqariusaq."

"Musk Ox Land has more rabbits and foxes than Itta. Have you noticed?"

"No, but that's what Navarana said."

We climbed. The sun was hot on our backs, and Sammy fell asleep, even though the winds roared. When we

reached the trap, I found it empty aside from fox droppings and a snatch of white fur on the chamber's floor.
The boulder I'd placed above the door of the trap had not
fallen on top of the fox, as it should have when the fox
tugged on the dangling meat.

"It got away! My trap was no good," I said.

Sammy called from his place on Ally's back.

Ally took him from his carrier, held him, and reflected.
"The boulder wasn't positioned right, and it should have
been larger." She told me what she remembered about
building traps.

Ally searched the cliff and found a larger boulder.
Since she was holding Sammy, she had me carry it. "Now
all we need is bait," I said. Then I began, "If I should join
another igloo, I can help bring in food—"

Ally nodded. "You're leaving Angulluk?"

"I think so."

"Eqariusaq, you can live with me and Piugaattoq until
you find another husband."

"We'll see. Thank you." Her generosity surprised me.

"You are clever, strong, and attractive! Many hunters
will want you."

"I'm not ready to think about a new husband—not
yet." We continued up the trail. I told her my plans of laying another trap on the cliffs and several more traps in the
valley.

Above me, I heard a croaking sound. Ally pointed her
nose to it. "For you," she whispered.

It was a gull with a broken wing. I swung and caught it in my net. Then I quickly broke its neck. A few minutes later, I'd baited the fox trap.

"We make good hunting partners," I said.

Even on a day when my heart was breaking, I'd been productive. I was making a good friend in Ally; I should have done so years earlier. Our choices, or our fate, joined us together like two runners on a sled.

As we moved back down the trail, my hunting bag empty but my step lighter, Ally gasped.

"What is it?" I asked. Then I followed her gaze, past the cliffs, to the blue ocean. Billowing into view came the white sails of the *Windward*.

I felt my tears begin: shock, anger, joy, all at once.

Ally laughed, then she cried, too. "Such a relief! But I don't understand."

"Captain Bartlett was probably testing the ship. Like the way our hunters try out their dogsleds at the start of a new season."

"*Ai!*" Ally said. "You are smart!"

* * *

Only a narrow gulf of water separated the *Windward* from the land and yet it seemed as wide as the ocean, impossibly far away. I wished that the *qallunaat* would come to shore, to tell us their news; I wished to see Duncan. But the winds were strong for small craft, and wisely, our hunters stayed on land. Two days passed, and in that time the

Windward made another short voyage into the sound, to return within the hour.

Bag of Bones paddled out to the *Windward* on the next calm morning, the same morning my husband and Piugaattoq returned from their hunt. On the beach, butchering the seals with Ally, keeping an eye on Sammy digging in the sand, I waited for Bag of Bones.

When he came back, he said, "The sailors have been testing the ship."

"So I thought. What else?"

"They'll sail for America soon. They didn't say when."

"Did Peary talk about bringing our people back to Itta?" I asked.

"I forgot to ask."

Giving Bag of Bones a sharp look, I set down the hide, whisked away some flies, and wiped my hands on my *kamiit*. My foolish boy could not be relied upon to perform a simple task, even though its outcome was so important to both of us.

"Did Pearyaksoah have a message for me?" Ally asked, her dark eyes hopeful.

"No," he said. Then, turning to me, "Duncan says he will visit you soon."

To say good-bye, I thought.

I looked out at the blue water, at the *Windward* and the ice floes beyond it, and between two of these I thought I saw a dark speck. A few moments later, Tooth Girl ran toward us.

"Come, look!" she said. "It's *another* ship!"

From a bluff above the shore, we saw that a second vessel, the same style as the *Windward,* was sailing into the harbor. It came toward us, larger and larger. Finally, it moored alongside the *Windward.*

It didn't take long for kayaks to be dragged to the shore. Five hunters, including Angulluk, went to investigate. Even Bag of Bones, who should have been exhausted from his previous journey, stroked out to the two ships.

Nearly the whole day passed before Angulluk and the others came to meet us on the shore.

My husband said, "Today I've seen more *qallunaat* goods than I believed possible. Guns, planks of wood, steel needles, knives. Salted meat and fish packed in oil and other food of all kinds."

"Who came? Why are they here?"

Bag of Bones waved his arms. "The ship is called the *Erik.* People in America sent it to find the *Windward.*"

Angulluk saved his most important words for last. "Peary wants to talk to you."

"What about?"

Angulluk wouldn't answer. I could tell he knew Peary's intentions, though, and was making plans.

* * *

The next day, Bag of Bones called me to the beach again. The *Erik* had lowered two boats. Duncan, Peary, Captain Bartlett, and Mauripaulak disembarked from one. I

hugged Duncan, and we stood apart from the others. I
didn't care who might be watching, but no one paid attention. Everyone surrounded Peary and the strangers.

I looked for the flecks of brown in Duncan's green
eyes. He had more freckles on his face. His ears looked
larger since he'd cut his orange curls.

"I've missed you, Billy Bah!" He took my hand.

"I've missed you, too."

"After the ice broke up, I wanted to come ashore. But
we had too much to do."

He didn't have to explain; I'd hurt him when I wouldn't
agree to marry him. "I knew you wouldn't come."

"I've missed you so much. Even if I can't have you, even
if we only have a short time together, I want to be near
you now."

As he spoke, Duncan seemed sad but steadier. "I'll be
going to America soon, and how I wish you'd come. But
it's best that you stay. It was selfish of me to try to make
you go."

"You're not selfish."

Peary called, "Billy Bah! I want to talk to you and your
husband."

"What about?"

"Let's meet in your igloo," he said.

I sent word with a hunter to find Angulluk as quickly
as possible. A large group of people was gathering with
the *qallunaat* on shore. Peary introduced the strangers.
One was the captain of the new ship.

My eyes lingered on Duncan a moment; then I walked the path with Peary. Angulluk caught up, and we crawled into the rock igloo. I offered seal meat, but Peary refused it.

"The ships will sail for America in a few days," he said. "I'll be staying to winter, and then will go north."

"Will Marie and Mitti Peary sail to America?" I asked.

Peary's eyes looked sad. "Yes. Only Matt Henson and a few others will be staying." Then he said to me, "Mrs. Peary let me know how important you were to her this winter. She says you spent time with Marie and helped her in a hundred ways. You did an excellent job sewing her *kapatak*. I'll need seamstresses to get ready for the expedition. I'd like you, Billy Bah, to choose the women and take charge of their work."

Stunned, I looked at Angulluk. He was grinning.

"Ally will be one of the seamstresses," Peary said. "She has already agreed. But she doesn't want to be in charge. She says you would do a better job of organizing the women and all that must be done. I agree."

Silently, I accepted the compliment. Boastful Ally had generously put me above herself. She'd surprised me again.

"We'll go with Peary to Itta," Angulluk said. "Soon after, Peary has agreed to take me and some hunters to the walrus rocks on the *Windward*. Think how many walrus the deck will hold. I could feed my dogs for a year!"

"We're sailing to Itta soon?"

Peary said, "With anyone who wants to go. We'll anchor at Itta for a few weeks—enough time to ready the ships and to hunt for walrus. After that, Billy Bah, I'd like you and the seamstresses to sail back here to Ellesmere Land. Of course, their families can come with them."

Angulluk jerked upright and slammed his fist against his thigh. "Eqariusaq and I will stay in Itta."

"I need Billy Bah here on Ellesmere Land," Peary said. "My new camp is here." He explained that from this point on, he'd leave on his great journeys across the sea ice from Ellesmere Land, not Itta. He'd continue his search for the place he called the North Pole.

I was listening with fierce attention.

Did I want to work for Peary? Was I willing to return to Musk Ox Land?

"Hunting is good here," Peary went on. "This is the better side of the sound in winter. The best furs for our coats."

"Yes, and no," I argued.

"Itta is our home," Angulluk said. "Eqariusaq and the women can sew in Itta."

"But then we won't have the furs!"

"Billy Bah and I will live in Itta." Angulluk was firm.

"Then it wouldn't make sense for Billy Bah to sew for us," Peary said, just as firmly.

Angulluk folded his arms. No doubt he was thinking

about guns and wood. He, of all people, was passing up *qallunaat* bounty. "After the hunt, Eqariusaq and I will stay in Itta. You can't have her!"

Should I join Peary's party without Angulluk? Leave him? Now I must truly decide. For good.

Hands clenched, I looked from one face to the other.

Peary leaned forward. "I'm giving you the chance to work with a group of women, not only to help me but to show your skills—ones that will be appreciated beyond your land," he said. "If you join me, you will be known throughout history as the most important seamstress of your people."

I wasn't impressed. I had no interest in Peary boasting of me to his friends in America. But I did like to sew. It was something I was good at, something that was all my own. Peary would pay me well. I might have to eat his canned food at times, but I would never go hungry. Peary offered me a new life, and the best part of it was freedom.

Freedom! Something in me shifted and I understood. I didn't need Peary's appreciation or approval. I didn't have to obey Angulluk. I was free to take the offer or say no, and turn it down and try for a new life in Itta. Even if I made a mistake, I could change direction and wait for a different opportunity.

As a child, I had no choice but to go where my parents or the Peary family led me. For most of my life, I'd wanted to find a place where I belonged, but expected others to tell me where to go.

Now I felt strong, neither above nor below anyone else, in a place where fear could not touch me. From this place of certainty, I could live in two worlds, because there was in fact no separation. The world was my home.

How odd that I could find my freedom, my true self, undivided, on a white man's ship. Navarana's vision.

"Peary," I said, "in Itta, I will decide if I will return to Musk Ox Land with you."

"Good! I'm glad you're considering my offer."

I felt myself beginning to smile.

Angulluk threw up his hands in anger. Then he let out a big sigh.

CHAPTER TWENTY-EIGHT

● ● ● ● ● ● ● ●

At icy dawn the next day, through a sudden generous urge that surprised me as much as it did him, I gave Angulluk one more chance to keep me as a wife. We were on board the *Windward,* sailing from Musk Ox Land. The tide was full, and I could hear only the barest whistle of wind coming over the sea. We stood at the bow as the rising sun shone white through a layer of mist.

For the first time, I regretted all the years Angulluk and I had called each other ugly and stupid when neither of us meant it. I took a breath, then said, "Angulluk, my husband. We've lived through another winter, the cold and dark, and more than one blizzard. It's time for us to enjoy the sunlight and good hunting in Itta. *Together.* But you must promise me that you will never trade me to a white man again."

"Shut up, woman! I will do as I please."

"But—" I hesitated. "Listen. You knew from the first that you shouldn't have traded me to an outsider."

Angulluk stood upright with a new harpoon tipped with a carved walrus tusk. He'd made the harpoon's long,

246

heavy shaft from wood he'd received the first time he traded me to Duncan.

How could I talk to him without insulting him?

"This time, when you said no to Peary, you passed up an opportunity for *qallunaat* bounty. I'm proud of you for that. But I need to know, so we can start over, as if we'd just married: will you promise never to trade me to a white man again?"

"*Tassa!*" he barked. "Eqariusaq, stop your lying games. I know you love Duncan."

"True, but it is your fault for sending me to him in the first place. Besides, he'll soon go back to his own land."

Angulluk winced as if he had salt water in his eyes. He was holding back tears.

He was a stupid fool for not agreeing to my simple request.

"Listen," I said. "I mean it. No trades with *qallunaat*. Promise me now. Or I will leave you. Make up your mind."

"Go." There was no mistaking the firmness in his voice.

He would let me go so easily?

After a moment, I straightened and put my hand on his shoulder. "Then we are family no more." As was the custom, I said the words three times. Then, "After the voyage, we will separate."

He turned, leaving me at the rail. He walked toward the center of the ship and the pen of snarling, barking dogs. "*Tassa!*" he yelled toward the pack. "*Tassa!*"

I walked along the deck from one side of the ship to the other, past sailors and hunters, past kayaks and huge stacks of furs, tents, cooking pots, and other things. The last of the morning mist lifted and the sun shone brightly. It was a day of brisk, clear weather. The ship sailed past shimmering blocks of ice.

I still loved Angulluk, and he still loved me. Against all reason, my husband had given up on our marriage just when he'd become a good enough hunter to walk away from the white man's demands.

Go ahead, you fool! I thought. *Return to Itta with a kayak full of the goods I earned for you. You lost me because you couldn't say a few simple words.*

I sighed. In Itta, he'd show everyone how good a hunter he'd become. It wasn't just his use of the white man's weapons; it was his effort. He wasn't so lazy anymore. He'd take his place in the community.

I could only go forward now. I could accept Peary's offer.

At least I'd still have Ally as a friend. Bag of Bones had chosen to stay on with Peary; he'd already said so. I'd allowed them to become close to me, and perhaps I'd grow close to the women I'd find to sew for Peary.

Most important: I could live without the fear of being traded to another white man. I could sew in exchange for goods and food. I even had my fox traps, which Tooth Girl was baiting for me while I was away. A short time before

I'd set out on the *Windward*, I'd checked my cliff trap to find a big male fox there, half white and half brown, its thick fur changing according to the season, skull crushed under the trap's fallen stone.

How to mark the change and show that I no longer belonged to any man? I took my knife from my bag. Quickly, before anyone could see, I shook my long hair from its topknot and cut it at my shoulders. I threw the hair into the ocean and watched it sliding into the ship's wake.

I stood at the rail, until Marie came on deck. "What have you done to your hair?"

I tried to smile. Perhaps she noticed my mood, because she pressed my hand in hers.

"Look!" she said, pointing upward. Duncan rode above us in the forward crow's nest, easy to recognize with his mass of red locks peeking from under his cap. Marie called out until he looked down quickly and waved to us. He raised his telescope and went back to scanning the ocean ahead.

The cold feeling in my chest grew lighter.

* * *

Two days later, to my great joy, the bird cliffs came into view.

The *Windward* and the *Erik* dropped anchor in deep waters away from the rocky shoals. I helped Angulluk load his dogs into a rowboat. He wanted to be among the first ashore. "It is over with us. I will now find a new wife."

"You will find an old, ugly, and toothless one," I teased. We knew that young women would listen to his stories and some would look at him with big eyes at every word. If he continued to hunt as well as he had in Musk Ox Land, people would surely stop calling him the Fat One. And as for me, when I decided to remarry, I'd have an easy time because I was so good at sewing.

I'd expected Angulluk would taunt me for cutting my hair. Oddly, he said nothing.

I would miss his cheerful nature and his company. His tales of the hunts, and sewing for him. Our coupling. But I would never be traded for bullets again.

"I'll stay on the ship tonight," I said. "Tomorrow I'll come to land."

"Agreed," he said, taking my well wishes, my parting gift. I'd leave him alone to tell stories of his hunts and boast his path into a new life. As eager as I was to set foot on Itta's beach and see my sister, I would wait.

Angulluk disappeared into the noise and chaos of hunters and barking dogs being lowered in their crowded boats over the side of the ship. After crewmen rowed the hunters away, I went to find Duncan. He was washing the deck with buckets of seawater, and already sharp, cool winds were helping to rid the ship of dog smells. He put down a bucket and we stood together.

"I want to stay in your bed tonight," I said. "One last time."

His face turned red. I smiled.

He loved me, even after I cut my hair. We would not touch for a few more hours, yet our intimacy had already begun.

The night was one of our most deeply felt times. We talked very little.

"Soon I'll return to America," Duncan said softly. "I'll miss you."

I held him to me.

The bells striking on board went by quickly. I slept wonderfully. In the morning, Duncan rowed me to shore.

The sun shone on the blue water where the biggest masses of ice had not yet broken up. Black and white auks crying *piuli, piuli* crowded the floes. My heart leapt with happiness. With my face to the breeze, I said, "The auks are welcoming me back to Itta."

A flock of the tiny black birds took flight. They soared above us. Shiny black-and-green eider ducks dove around us. It was summer. I was home!

I pointed to the high red crags, and said, "The cliffs are singing." How I loved sliding through the water in the boat with Duncan, tracing the birds' flight and hearing their calls.

"*Millions* of birds are here!" Duncan said. "The heights *are* singing."

My Duncan was smart for a *qallunaaq*. Once we got to

shore, he understood that I needed to be alone. In the next days, I was going to visit my sister, Nuljalik.

"I'll see you again before you leave for America," I said. "I'll want to say good-bye to you and Marie."

"We'll have plenty of time for that." Before the *Windward* and the *Erik* set sail together across the ocean, there would be the shorter voyages of the walrus hunt and taking Peary's expedition team, including me, to Musk Ox Land. It overwhelmed me to think about the events of the next few moons; somehow I would live through them, and our final parting.

That morning, Marie had told me, "I'll miss you, but I'll be back next summer, Billy Bah! Dad says I can visit you and Cin again when the *Windward* returns to pick him up." Peary had promised Marie that in one year, he'd return to America—temporarily or permanently, I did not know. But Cin would remain with Angulluk.

Now I walked up the beach toward the village. Peary, Mitti Peary, and Mauripaulak stood outside Peary's caboose, talking. When the time came, I'd say good-bye to Mitti Peary, but today I'd keep my attention on my own people.

How wonderful to see purple flowers growing all around the rock igloos and summer tents. Though it was a time of valuable sunlight for hunting and climbing, I'd hoped some villagers would be nearby. But the men were gone after seals. The young women, children, and elders were gathering eggs and netting birds.

In the half circle of tents, I found the ruined foundation of the skin-covered dwelling where I'd once lived with Angulluk. Angulluk had loved staying in that tent, our first. We felt free there. We'd spent some of our happiest nights with the cool breeze blowing in on us.

I walked quickly by the place where my parents had lived. When I came to Nuljalik's tent, I didn't expect to find anyone, but I still said a traditional greeting: "It is I, Eqariusaq, come back to visit you at last!"

Nuljalik was there, breast-feeding two tiny babies, each with a full head of black hair. *Two babies!*

"Eqariusaq! I heard that you were here!" We touched noses side to side. Lines under her wide-set eyes showed me that she was very tired. But her face glowed with a new mother's happiness and beauty.

"Twins! Let me see." As I took off my sealskin parka, she held them up to me. "So lovely," I managed to say, through my surprise.

"Eight days ago. A boy and a girl."

"Our *anaana* and *ataata*!" I clapped my hands together. "I am happy!"

"Eqariusaq, I've been waiting for you to come so we can name the babies," Nuljalik said.

So Nuljalik remembered the conversation we'd had a year ago. Of course, I knew that she would.

"An old woman I'd met in Musk Ox Land had a vision," I told my sister, "so I knew our parents would be reborn. Still, I did not expect this. Twins!"

"I didn't, either," she said, laughing.

Nuljalik gave me the babies, one for each arm. They were light and very warm. As they looked up at me, I felt my heavy regret lift. "I will help you raise these children." That was what I would do when I returned from completing Peary's work.

"Eqariusaq, I want you to name them," she said. "Do it now."

"Shouldn't we wait until your husband is here?"'

My sister grinned. "I talked to Uutaaq about it, and he agrees that you and I should do it together. Go ahead."

"All right." But I hesitated. Would I say the wrong words?

Warily, I looked at the two wrinkled babies. Their mouths were open. The girl child yawned, and I smiled. Their eyes were black like seals' eyes. So alert!

I closed my eyes and my mind drifted to the rock grave, and I sensed my spirit parents sitting outside of it. They seemed to gaze longingly out at the hills flecked with snow, and the ocean beyond it. They wanted to join the living again, even though they'd need to first go through a dark, cold tunnel of forgetfulness. The big white dog sat up on his tail. He, too, sensed that a change was coming.

I greeted them in my thoughts. *"Anaana and Ataata, I've come at last, my dear ones. It's time."*

"Yes, Panik," they answered.

The images of my parents looking at me, smiling, made me ache. *"I miss you,"* I whispered.

254

"And we miss you also, Daughter."

"I'm sending you forth, to go into Nuljalik's babies," I said softly. *"There you will be cared for and greatly loved. You will now let go of your memories and take with you only courage, strength, and your deep affection for your family."* Opening my eyes, I looked down at the girl child in my arms. My voice was clear. "I name you Atangana." I turned my head to the boy child. "I name you Nuktaq."

My parents' spirits floated above me, then moved down through my fingers. My hands trembled.

The room spun and grew warm. Feeling dizzy, I held the babies tighter. Nuljalik grabbed hold of my shoulders. Somewhere, the white dog barked, broke free of his harness, and bounded away from the empty rock grave.

The sound of a baby's gentle cry roused me from the spirit world. Through nearly closed eyelids, I watched as Nuljalik, smiling radiantly, took the twins from me.

"They are named!" she said.

CHAPTER TWENTY-NINE

· · · · · · · · ·

Nuljalik fed the babies from her breasts and talked to them. "Atangana. Nuktaq." She said their names over and over, until she wrapped them for sleeping. I rested, too, deeply and peacefully, and awoke to find my sister and the babies beside me on a bed of furs.

My sister stretched her arms and legs. Together we sat on the edge of the platform, as if we were young girls again, and talked as the babies slept.

She stroked my hair. "But why did you cut it?"

I smiled, not answering.

Again she touched me. "You still don't have your *own* children. How sad!"

"I've come to accept it." We talked about Bag of Bones. "I told Qaorlutoq I'd sew him clothes from now on, so he won't wear those dreadful old furs. It's hard to believe, but the little pest has become like a son to me."

My sister laughed. "He's a cheerful boy. I like him, too."

"So it seems I have a son, but I no longer have a husband," I added.

"I know," she said. "Last night, Angulluk told everyone he left you. He said, 'Eqariusaq is the laziest wife a man could ever have. And she's fat and ugly.'"

"I separated from *him*." I didn't hide my annoyance. I didn't mind exaggeration, but lies were different.

We both knew the remarks were ridiculous. "You are beautiful and talented. He's *anaq*, like dog droppings."

I was tempted to say *He's as ugly as a dead fish with its eyes popping out* but stopped myself. There was no need to keep insulting Angulluk.

I gave her a gift of a sewing needle from Peary.

We talked and gossiped for a long while about all the people we knew. Finally, I told her of my opportunity to be in charge, across the sound, of making clothes for Peary's new trek.

"I heard. Peary came to the feast last night. He offered wonderful trades of guns, wood, and needles."

"So you know about it," I said, surprised.

News spreads quickly, and my sister had seen the ship *Erik* several weeks earlier. She knew both ships would sail for America before the ice set in, leaving Peary and his crew, hunters, and women to sew for them.

"Stay," Nuljalik pleaded. "You've only just arrived. Don't leave me again."

"Would you and your family want to come with me?" I asked. "It will only be for a year. The hunting is good on that shore."

She stared at me with watery eyes. "If you go, I will miss you greatly." She added, "My life is here and *not* with Peary." She still believed that Peary was to blame for the death of our mother and father. I decided she must never know about the figures in the museum.

"Peary will pay me well. I could make both of our lives easier," I said. "You know that."

My sister sighed. "We've had a hard winter with so much snow," she said. "Some of the villagers had to kill their dogs. We were all hungry until the birds began to fly back. You'll easily find women to sew. Their men will want more of Peary's guns and trade goods."

"If they come, they'll have both the musk oxen *and* the guns."

Nuljalik's eyes grew playful. "Those men will be so eager to get on that ship, they'll run like chasing a fox. All our single men will want you for a wife. You're going to have to beat them away. Are you ready for a new husband? Can you think of anyone you'd want to live with? Hold close?"

"I don't know," I said. We laughed. I didn't want to ruin our talk and our fun by telling her about Duncan. I knew she wouldn't approve. That conversation would wait for another day.

After a while, the babies were fed, and then my sister and I shared a delicious soup she had made with duck eggs and salty seaweed. She untied a large sealskin bag, half filled with auks. "I caught almost two hundred! I've been feeding them to the family and the dogs, and making the skins into children's undershirts."

"What a bag!" I admired how well my sister had pulled the insides from the seal and finished the bag without cutting the belly. My mother had passed on her skills.

Our talk turned to the feast that evening. The gathering would mark the homecoming of those of us who'd gone off on Peary's ship. And now, with the naming of the babies, there would be even more cause for a celebration. What could I give to the boiling pot? Joyfully, I remembered auks I'd caught the year before. I'd built a tower of stones and hung them by their bills. They'd be ripe by now. Any eggs inside the auks would be black and tart.

Nuljalik stayed with her babies, and I borrowed her wonderful bag and set out to the bird cliffs. A short time later, I arrived at the path that started out wide, then narrowed as it climbed and turned up the cliffs. I greeted and talked with my sister's husband, and my niece, Konala, playing with children on a low slope, before going higher. Soon I was high enough to see the crescent shape of the village. My feet must be healing, I thought, because I was climbing pretty well.

I stopped to catch a breath. A year earlier, I'd scaled these cliffs with Angulluk. Now they didn't seem quite so high. As on that day, the sky was blue, and clear enough that I could see all the way across the sound to Musk Ox Land, now for me another home. A year ago, I hadn't yet sewed clothes for Mitti Peary. I hadn't made my way in a new land, fallen in love with Duncan, or separated from Angulluk. Now Peary himself had chosen me. But best of all, I had my freedom.

In that moment I saw the future, sailing off on the *Windward* to Musk Ox Land.

I climbed higher, past auks on their roosts, and found my rock pile where I had left some inside. When I uncovered the roof, a slightly sour smell greeted me. Perfect! Well-cured, not too strong. I put the birds in the bag.

I planned to net more the next day for my cache. A year from now, I would have a good supply.

Where was the place where Angulluk had saved me from the avalanche? I took the path higher until I saw the flat boulder jutting out, and the shelter beneath.

"Eqariusaq!" A voice came from below.

Bag of Bones climbed to meet me. He talked with half an egg in his mouth. "Look what I have." He showed me a bag of auklings he'd hunted earlier, and eggs he'd left up there a year or two before. Like me, he had his secret caches on the cliff.

"There's the *Windward*!" he said. We looked out at the sparkling ice floes and the yellow-striped ship in the harbor. Close to the farther shore, I could even see the *Erik*.

Leaving Bag of Bones and setting the bag aside, I continued climbing until I reached the very top of the cliffs. I'd never gone so high before.

How I loved those cliffs, and Itta! I'd miss this beloved place, my home of homes, and yet I looked forward to the adventures ahead.

I gazed out again at the *Windward*. It seemed as if the ship were waiting for me.

GLOSSARY OF INUKTUN
WORDS IN THE
POLAR ESKIMO DIALECT

(a spoken language)

Ai! (*a-ee*): Well, so!

Aait! (*ah-eet*): Well, I see!

Ait (*a-eet*): Well, okay, what!

aana (*a-na*): grandmother

anaana (*a-nah-na*): mother

anaq (*a-nak*): dung

ataata (*a-tah-ta*): father

hainang (*hi-nang*, short for hainaggunait): hello

ii (*ee*): Yes! or Oh!

Inuk (*e-nook*); Inuit (*ee-nu-eet*), plural: people

Itta (*e-tah*), or Etah: a Polar Eskimo village; has no particular translated meaning

kapatak (*ka-pa-tok*); kapatait (*ka-pa-teet*), plural: thick, hooded fur coat

kamiit (*ka-meet*), plural: long sealskin boots worn by women

Kiiha! (*kee-ha*): exclamation upon hearing good news

nanoq (*na-nook*): polar bear

nga (*na*): no

panik (*pa-neek*): daughter

pillarotoq (*pill-ar-o-tok*): crazed

Pivviit akornganni (*piv-veet a-korn-ga-nee*): between two places

Qaa, qaa! (*kwa, kwa*): Quickly! Hurry!

qallunaaq (*kal-lu-nak*), singular; qallunaat (*kal-lu-naat*), plural: white person (people)

qujanaq (*ku-ya-nak*): thank you

Ta! (*ta*): Listen!

Tassa! (*ta-sa*): Stop! That is enough!

Ua! (*ooh-ah*): Oh!

ulu (*ooh-lu*); **uluit** (*ooh-lu-eet*), plural: women's utility knife

Umingmak Nuna (*u-ming-mak nu-na*): Musk Ox Land, name for Ellesmere Island

CHRONOLOGY OF
REAL-LIFE EVENTS

Around 1883–1884. Eqariusaq, or Eklayashoo,* later nicknamed Billy Bah, is born in or around Itta, or Etah,* Northwest Greenland, home to several hundred Polar Eskimos. Her parents, Atangana and Nuktaq, sew and hunt for Robert E. Peary during the times he is in the Arctic for explorations. From early childhood and continuing on into her adult years, Billy Bah's life will be framed by Peary's quest to be the first explorer to reach the North Pole and to claim that honor for the United States.

September 12, 1893. Marie Ahnighito Peary, daughter of Josephine and Robert E. Peary, is born in Itta.

August 1894–summer 1895. Eqariusaq, or Billy Bah, spends a year living in Washington, DC, with Josephine and Marie Peary.

August 1897. Robert E. Peary, with Josephine and Marie, returns to the Arctic for a summer voyage when he takes the giant "Ahnighito" meteorite from Cape York, Greenland, to sell to the American Museum of Natural History in New York. On the trip back to New York, Peary brings with him a group of Inuit people from Itta, who will be interviewed and examined by the museum: Billy Bah's parents, Atangana and Nuktaq; their adopted daughter, Aviaq; and Qisuk and his son, Minik. En route to New York, an Inuit man from southern Greenland, Uisaakassak, joins the group.

February–May 1898. Billy Bah's parents, Aviaq, and Qisuk die of illnesses in New York.

Around May 1899. Peary's Inuit mistress, Aleqasina, or Allakasingwah,* also known as Ally, gives birth in or around Itta to Peary's son, Anaukaq, nicknamed Sammy.

August 1900–August 1901 (the time of this novel). Josephine Peary and Marie travel from America to Itta on Peary's ship, the *Windward,* during a time when the ship is scheduled to drop off supplies for him. When Josephine Peary discovers that her husband is not in Greenland, the ship sails west across Smith Sound to Ellesmere Land,* or, as the Polar Eskimos called it, *Umimmaat Nuna* (Musk Ox Land), now known as Ellesmere Island, in the Canadian Arctic. Seeking a way to cross the sound for better hunting, an Inuit group from Itta, including Billy Bah and her husband, Ahngoodloo,* or Angulluk, join the voyage. Near the shore of Payer Harbor, the ship becomes locked in the ice for the next eight months.

April 6, 1909. Robert E. Peary, Matthew Henson (Mauripaulak), and four Inuit men, Egingwah,* Seegloo,* Ootah,* and Ooqueah,* reach the North Pole. Billy Bah goes down in history as Peary's leading seamstress for the famed expedition.

---

*spellings used by the Peary family in the late 1800s and early 1900s.

HISTORICAL NOTES

This novel is loosely based on the life of an Inuit (Polar Eskimo) girl known to the explorer Robert E. Peary and his family as Eklayashoo (or Eqariusaq, as the Polar Eskimos might say it today).[1] More frequently, the Pearys referred to her by the nicknames Miss Bill or Billy Bah. While I was writing my nonfiction book *The Snow Baby: The Arctic Childhood of Admiral Robert E. Peary's Daring Daughter,* which includes an account of Marie Ahnighito Peary's true-life adventures on the ice-locked *Windward* in 1900 and 1901, I often wondered how events would have appeared from the Inuit point of view. In this reimagining from Billy Bah's perspective, I've taken the few facts that are known about the historical figure and woven them into a fictional story.

The real Billy Bah was revered by Robert E. Peary as his most accomplished and valued seamstress. She helped outfit his men on numerous expeditions in the late 1890s to 1909, the year Peary reached the Pole. During this famed expedition, Billy Bah sewed explorer Matthew Henson's *kapatak* (or *kapetah*), the hooded fur garment he wore in the celebrated photo that appears in every one of his biographies.

In Josephine Peary's writings, Billy Bah is first mentioned in relation to Marie Peary's birth in September 1893 in the Arctic of Northwest Greenland. About eight or nine years old at the time, Billy Bah brought gifts to baby Marie and eventually taught her words of the Polar Eskimo language. Peary's expedition members called the young girl Miss Bill. Baby Marie could not pronounce either "Eklayashoo" (Eqariusaq) or "Miss Bill." The words "Billy Bah" came out, and the nickname stuck.[2] Meanwhile, according to the same account, the Greenland natives sometimes called Marie by her middle name, Ahnighito. Marie surmised from stories she remembered as a child that the woman who made her baby clothes was her namesake. However, such a person is not mentioned in the writings of either Josephine or Robert E. Peary. Nor is Ahnighito a name that is recognized by the Polar Eskimos of today.[3]

In several published works, Josephine Peary describes the year from 1894 to 1895, when Billy Bah lived with her and toddler Marie in Washington, DC. Why this nine- or ten-year-old girl became the first of her people to leave the Arctic is unclear. Perhaps Mrs. Peary, who returned to America without her husband, brought the Inuit girl along as a helper or nursemaid. It is not known if the Peary family offered Billy Bah's parents material rewards for her. In any case, it seems that Billy Bah's parents trusted Josephine Peary and encouraged their daughter to make the journey.

Mrs. Peary and her mother and sister, with whom she lived, treated Billy Bah kindly, especially considering the standards of the day, when children often labored on farms or in factories. At the same time, the year represented a dramatic, perhaps harrowing, adjustment for the bewildered Inuit girl. After the stark wilderness of the Arctic, urban Washington, DC, with its sweltering heat, wagons, deafening trains, tall green trees, and enormous buildings came as a shock. Josephine Peary dressed Billy Bah in clothing the girl was completely unaccustomed to: a woolen dress, a pinafore, and shoes and stockings. Everything about the girl's life changed, as Mrs. Peary describes in her children's book *The Snow Baby*:

> She [Billy Bah] had never had a bath until Ahnighito's [Marie's] mother gave her one on board ship, and she could not understand why she must wash herself and brush her hair every morning. . . .
>
> First, she must learn to talk, for of course she could not speak English; then she must learn to eat, for in Snowland [Northwest Greenland] her people eat nothing but meat. . . .
>
> Billy Bah has had to learn by sad experience that she could not put her toys down anywhere in the streets of Washington and find them again hours afterward, as she could do in her own country. . . .
>
> She took great pleasure in sewing for her doll, and whenever anything was made for Ahnighito, Billy Bah

*would make the same for her doll. By the time she
returned to her home she was quite a little seamstress.*

*Her trunk was a regular Noah's Ark. A bit of
everything that was given her during her stay was always
carefully put into it, to be carried back home and
explained to her friends.*

*In July it was decided the great ship should sail to the
land of the midnight sun to bring Ahnighito's father
home, and Billy Bah would return to her family.*

*She was very happy at the thought of home, but
wished Ahnighito might go too.*

*When she reached the Snowland, there was great
rejoicing among her people, and feasts were given of fine
raw walrus, seal, and bear meat, in honor of the young
member of the tribe who had seen the sun rise and set
every day for a whole year.*

*After two hours of landing, Billy Bah was seen with
a piece of meat weighing about five pounds, enjoying her
first meal in a year.*[4]

The "Noah's Ark" where Billy Bah collected her treasures
served as inspiration for the wooden chest in my novel.

Billy Bah is briefly mentioned in the Peary family writings when Marie visits the Arctic in the summer of 1897.
This was the trip in which Robert E. Peary took a giant
thirty-four-ton meteorite from the Cape York area of
North Greenland. By then Billy Bah, around age fourteen,
was married to a man named Ahngoodloo (perhaps the

Pearys' version for the Inuit name Angulluk). Many years later, Marie recalled the time in her memoir:

> *In one of the first boat-loads to come aboard [during the stop at Itta] was Billy Bah, now a married woman, and what a reunion we had! I was happy to see her and she seemed almost as glad to see me but she had certainly forgotten all that Mother had taught her about keeping herself clean and tidy. She was just as dirty as the other Eskimos. I must have looked at her strangely, for she laughed and said:*
>
> *"If I had known that 'Mitti' [Mrs.] Peary and Ahnighito [Marie] were on board, I would have washed my face and combed my hair, the way 'Mitti' Peary taught me!"*
>
> *She went off and soon returned, looking much cleaner. We went down into the cabin together, to be away from the confusion on deck, and there Billy Bah talked English with me and asked all kinds of questions about the people and the places which she had seen in the States.*
>
> *Although married, she was as eager as ever to see my new dolls and picture books and she brought me a little sealskin bag in which were tiny ivory figures of men, women, dogs, walrus, seals and bears, which she had carved for me from walrus teeth during the long, lazy Arctic winter.[5]*

That summer when Robert, Josephine, and Marie Peary returned to America on the ship the *Hope,* with the meteorite, the ship also brought a group of five Inuit from

271

Billy Bah, the year she lived in America (1894–1895)

Billy Bah, back home in Greenland, age 16 (1900 or 1901)

Marie at the helm in her kapatak *and* kamiit *(1901)*

Marie with her parents and the crew on the Windward *(1901)*

Icebergs near Itta

The Windward *and the* Erik *(1901)*

Robert E. Peary (1909)

Peary with seamstresses on the Roosevelt *(around 1908)*

275

Itta. The group included Billy Bah's parents, Nuktaq and Atangana, who worked for Peary on several of his expeditions. An adopted daughter, Aviaq, a girl of about twelve, accompanied them. Another of Peary's hunters, Qisuk, came on board, along with Qisuk's son, Minik, who was about seven years old. Uisaakassak, a native man from southern Greenland, joined the party en route. Anthropologist Franz Boas, of the American Museum of Natural History, had asked Peary to bring back one Inuk for him to study. More than one native volunteered to come aboard the ship. Or, as some accounts suggest, Peary coerced them.

Perhaps Billy Bah's stories of the white man's land enticed her parents to make a trip of their own? Sadly, their experience ended in tragedy. The winter and spring after the Inuit group arrived in New York, all but two died of influenza, pneumonia, and perhaps other illnesses to which they had little resistance. Many historians have written about this unfortunate event, and the orphaned Inuit boy Minik, who saw his people, their skeletons layered in wax, on display at the American Museum of Natural History. Peary, who was living in Washington, DC, during the time the Inuit group died in New York, had nothing to do with this gruesome exhibit. But he neither visited nor offered to help the native people once he'd left them at the museum. Perhaps he feared that further involvement in their affairs would damage his reputation in the press—which might prevent him from raising funds for his expensive polar expeditions.

Not surprisingly, only brief mentions of this incident exist in any of the writings of Robert E. Peary. Neither Josephine nor Marie wrote of it at all—the family clearly wished to put this ugly incident behind them. It's possible that Minik, who returned to the Arctic for several years beginning in 1910, could have told Billy Bah about the events at the museum. But by this time, Minik no longer had a firm grasp of his native language. Whatever Billy Bah was told of the museum or of her parents' deaths, and how she felt about the situation, is left to the imagination.

What is known is that Robert E. Peary never again took another native person away from Greenland. And despite the tragedy, Billy Bah's relationship with the Peary family continued.

Three years after the Greenland trip involving the meteorite, seven-year-old Marie and Billy Bah, who was about sixteen, happily reunited. This is the period in which the novel is set, from 1900 to 1901, when Marie and Mrs. Peary came to the Arctic for what they anticipated would be a summer voyage on the *Windward*. The official purpose of the trip was to drop off supplies for Peary. Josephine Peary, who heard of her husband's injured feet due to frostbite, probably came along to persuade her husband to return to America.

The novel takes place during a low point in Peary's career, between two failed attempts to reach the North Pole. During this time, Josephine and Robert E. Peary's marriage, which was long, for the most part happy, and extraordinarily enduring, also hit rock bottom. On board the ice-locked ship, Josephine experienced the shock of meeting up with Peary's Inuit lover, Allakasingwah (Aleqasina), called Ally, and her baby, Anaukaq, called Sammy. Though it's a true-life incident, I filled in known facts with fictional dialogue. Again, and not surprisingly, the Peary family makes little mention of these personal and painful events, even in their private journals and letters. And in her childhood diaries, Marie fondly talks about playing with Sammy when Ally came to the *Windward* to sew Marie's hooded fur coat, but she probably did not know at the time that Sammy was her half brother.[6]

Though a number of the Inuit characters in the book are historically based, others are fictionalized; the historical record includes very few Inuit names in this place and time, so I created a few characters to round out village life. In real life, the names of Billy Bah's brother and sister were not recorded. Nuljalik's children are fictional. Marie's friend Akitsinnguaq (Tooth Girl) is based on a real person, though Magtaaq, Mikihoq, and Navarana are made up. The real Navarana, wife of Peter Freuchen, lived in Northwest Greenland several decades later.

Akitsinnguaq, in real life, was probably one of the Itta group who traveled to Ellesmere Island with the Peary family on the *Windward,* and the "village" described at Payer Harbor would have been more of a camp that was occasionally occupied by native hunters from the Greenland shore. American explorer Adolphus Greely was the first to establish a base on Ellesmere Island, in 1881; Robert E. Peary was only the second to chart the region, beginning in 1898. Whalers from Canada, and perhaps from the Scandinavian countries, ventured as far north as Smith Sound in the 1800s and 1900s, but not frequently. The area was (and is) often ice-locked, and the larger whale species prefer warmer waters.

In creating Billy Bah's spiritual life, including the naming of her parents, I've drawn upon many general sources about Inuit peoples in Greenland and Canada. Beliefs among Inuit people vary greatly over time and according to region. Marriage customs, including divorce and wife trading, also vary. Little can be known specifically about Billy Bah's people's customs and beliefs. In his writings, Robert E. Peary's cultural references are sketchy. Though he dabbled in anthropology (including the measuring and photographing of naked people), his main focus was geographical exploration.

Also, it should be noted how very difficult it is for an English speaker to learn Inuktun, which, like Chinese, contains many guttural sounds unknown in our own language. The fact that Peary never mastered Inuktun isn't surprising. And because the vast majority of people in Greenland, then as now, live along the ice-free west coast, far south of Itta and where Kalaallisut (Western Greenlandic), a different dialect of Greenlandic, is spoken, Peary could not have brought a translator with him on his voyages. He was virtually the first and only explorer of his time to live among this community, which was isolated both by geography and by language. It follows that his cultural understanding of the Polar Eskimos would be somewhat limited.

Perhaps the part of the novel where I've taken the most artistic license is with regard to Duncan. There was a crewmember on the *Windward* named Duncan, but he probably had nothing to do with Billy Bah. Likewise, though Peary's crews sometimes included artists and taxidermists, Officer Sutter is fictitious.

In real life, it is known only that Billy Bah married and divorced a number of times. Explorer Matthew Henson, in writing of the famous Peary expedition of 1909, makes a very brief but intriguing mention of Billy Bah as he describes life on the *Roosevelt*:

> There were thirty-nine *Esquimos* [sic] in the
> expedition, men, women and children. . . . They were
> mostly in families; there were several young, unmarried
> men, and the unattached, much-married and divorced
> *Miss "Bill,"* who domiciled herself aboard the ship and
> did much good work with the needle. She was my
> seamstress and the thick fur clothes worn on the trip to

the Pole were sewn by her. The Esquimos lived as happily
as in their own country and carried on their domestic
affairs with almost the same care-free irregularity as
usual. The best-natured people on earth, with no bad
habits of their own, but a ready ability to assimilate the
vices of civilization.[7]

Is it reasonable to suggest by the sketchy picture Henson paints that she had relations with at least one of Peary's all-male crew? Again, the more provocative details are understandably left out of the historical account, including the half-Inuit son Henson fathered with the teenage Achatingwah, or Akitsinnguaq, fictitiously referred to in this novel as Tooth Girl.

Akitsinnguaq and the orphan boy Koodlooktoo, or Qaorlutoq, make frequent appearances in Marie Peary's childhood diaries; aside from Billy Bah, they were her closest Inuit friends. Koodlooktoo is also mentioned in the published writings of Josephine and Robert E. Peary and of Matthew Henson. He took part in Peary's final expedition in 1909.

Aside from the notes already described, there appears to be only one other biographical reference to Billy Bah, by the Danish explorer, Peter Freuchen. Freuchen would have known Billy Bah sometime between 1906 and the mid-1920s, when he lived among the Polar Eskimos. The following incident was recorded in an unpublished manuscript by Sechmann Rosbach in 1934, and translated from Inuktitut to English by Kenn Harper and Navarana Harper [now Sørensen]:

> When she returned to Greenland, Eqariusaq had refused to tell anyone about her trip. When asked, she said only that she could not remember, or did not feel like talking about it. Once, while on a sled trip bound for one of the distant Danish colonies in a more southerly part of Greenland, Freuchen and Navarana [Freuchen's Inuit wife] had passed a few days at Cape Seddon with Eqariusaq and her husband, Miteq. Navarana had never been south of Melville Bay and was looking forward eagerly to the trip. One afternoon she and Eqariusaq took a stroll on the ice. Suddenly Eqariusaq turned to Navarana and said, "When you go to the white man's country, be careful not to absorb too much of their spirit. If you do, it will cause you many tears, for you can never rid yourself of it." When Navarana told him this, Freuchen felt that he finally understood the young woman's reticence to speak of her year in America. "Poor woman!" he wrote. "I understood then that it was a desperate, hopeless longing that stilled her voice."[8]

This intriguing account suggests that Billy Bah may have longed for at least a few aspects of the life she'd known in America. Perhaps so. Or another interpretation is that Billy Bah was haunted by sad memories. In any case, I do not believe that Billy Bah regarded herself as a victim. She may not have completely understood how the white men's involvement in her community brought about certain hardships for herself and others. Or, if she did, she was extraordinarily forgiving and generous.

Readers who are familiar with the story of the orphan boy Minik will see how very different his story is from that of Billy Bah. Minik lived in America for twelve years—long enough that he could read about himself in newspapers, discuss moral issues in Sunday school, and articulate to journalists the ills of civilization. After a brief and unhappy attempt as an adult to readjust to the native ways of Greenland, he returned to drift as a misfit in America. Billy Bah lived in America for only one year, rejoined her Polar Eskimo community while still a child, and apparently picked up life where she left off (almost).

The date of Billy Bah's death is not known except that it was prior to Marie Peary Stafford's visit to Greenland in 1932.

Itta, memorialized as Etah on modern maps, is now an abandoned village. It lies near Qaanaaq (formerly Thule), the largest town of the Polar Eskimos in Northwest Greenland.

In 1993, nearly a hundred years after Billy Bah's parents and others in their group died in New York, the American Museum of Natural History returned their remains to the people of Qaanaaq.

Endnotes

1. The Inuit people of the polar region in and around Qaanaaq, West Greenland, call themselves "Polar Eskimos"; to them, the term "Eskimo" is no longer considered derogatory.

2. Josephine Diebitsch Peary, *The Snow Baby: A True Story with True Pictures* (New York: Frederick A. Stokes Company, Publishers, 1901), pp. 37–44.

3. Navarana Sørensen, native speaker of Inuktun, and a professional translator in Qaanaaq, served as my language consultant. The dialect of the Qaanaaq polar region has never been recorded and varies slightly from other dialects of Inuktun, which in turn are very different from the official, standardized orthography of Kalaallisut, or West Greenlandic, that is used throughout Greenland. To give readers a flavor of how Billy Bah would have talked, I asked Navarana to write down some words and phrases from the Polar Eskimo dialect. But, unfortunately, for the sake of readability, only a few of the simplest words made it into the final version of the novel; the nature of Inuktun, with its long words strung together with roots and suffixes, came across as confusing and hard to pronounce, for example: *takuleqangakkit nuannaartunga* (I am happy to see you), *nuannaanngitsunga* (I am sad), *pinnaatoorruatit* (you are greedy). Navarana helped me recast names recorded by the Peary family to present them in a way that would be familiar to an Inuktun speaker. When I needed to create characters' names, Navarana suggested names commonly used by Polar Eskimos today. Interestingly enough, the modern-day names often mirror the older ones from Peary's time, perhaps on purpose; Navarana herself is named for her famous ancestor, the wife of Peter Freuchen.

4. Josephine Diebitsch Peary, ibid, pp. 37–44.

5. Marie Ahnighito Peary, *The Snow Baby's Own Story* (New York: Frederick A. Stokes Company, 1934), pp. 32–33.

6. Marie's childhood journals are housed at the Maine Women Writers Collection at the University of New England, Portland, Maine.

7. Matthew A. Henson, *A Black Explorer at the North Pole* (New York: Walker and Company, 1969), pp. 151–152 (originally published in 1912 under the title *A Negro Explorer at the North Pole*).

8. Harper, Kenn, *Give Me My Father's Body: The Life of Minik, the New York Eskimo* (South Royalton, VT: Steerforth Press, 2000), p. 190.

ACKNOWLEDGMENTS

Huge thanks to Wendy Lamb and Dana Carey. Thanks to others at Wendy Lamb Books, assistants and interns, who provided critiques: Randi Abel, Shavon Bilis, Janea Brachfeld, Caroline Meckler, and Lindsay Wong. To the book's excellent copy editor, Joy Simpkins. To Liza Pulitzer Voges.

To Donna Bergman, Sylvie Hossack, and Suzanne Williams for reading the manuscript first and asking for more, and to Peter Nelson for his generosity and his expertise in helping me smooth out the wrinkles.

To Diane Amison-Loring ("Sharp-Toothed"), Stephanie Cowell, Mary Cresse, Jane Mylum Gardner, Kathryn Mikesell Hornbein, Karen Landen, Dean Stahl, and Sanna Stanley for further help and encouragement.

To Kate Gartner for the handsome cover and book design.

To Sam Weber, for the striking cover art.

To Joe LeMonnier, for the lovely map.

To Silas Ayer and Kim Fairley for providing the images of Billy Bah.

Thanks and apologies to Navarana Sørensen: Any errors in Inuktun and the culture of the Polar Eskimos are my own!

Finally, to John Tait. It takes a lot to stay in the game of writing/publishing. He makes it possible.

ABOUT THE AUTHOR

Katherine Kirkpatrick is the author of seven previous fiction and nonfiction books, including *The Snow Baby,* a James Madison Book Award Honor Book and a *Booklist* Editors' Choice and Top 10 Biography for Youth; and *Mysterious Bones,* a Golden Kite Honor Book for Nonfiction, an NCSS-CBC Notable Social Studies Trade Book for Young People, and a *School Library Journal* Best Book of the Year. Katherine lives in Seattle with her husband and two daughters. You can visit her online at katherinekirkpatrick.com.